ONLY THE TWO OF THEM

For the first time in years, no thoughts of Jessie haunted Hawk. He was aware only of Randi, of how beautiful she was and how much he wanted to hold her close. He gave no thought to learning to dance. Instead, with utmost tenderness, he bent to her and claimed her lips in a cherishing kiss.

The kiss was gentle—for a moment.

Then the power of the attraction they could no longer deny overwhelmed them both.

A deep abiding hunger filled Hawk. He crushed Randi to him. His mouth moved hungrily over hers, and Randi responded without reserve. She met him in that passionate exchange, reveling in his nearness, glorying in the hard press of his body against hers.

Any thought that they might be discovered was forgotten. They clung together, thrilling in the excitement of their newly acknowledged need for one another.

It was only the two of them—alone in the sweet, blissful heat of the night.

Other books by Bobbi Smith:

BRAZEN
BAYOU BRIDE
HUNTER'S MOON
FOREVER AUTUMN
LONE WARRIOR
EDEN
WANTON SPLENDOR
SWEET SILKEN BONDAGE
THE HALF-BREED (SECRET FIRES)
WESTON'S LADY
HALF-BREED'S LADY
OUTLAW'S LADY
FORBIDDEN FIRES
RAPTURE'S RAGE
THE LADY & THE TEXAN
RENEGADE'S LADY
THE LADY'S HAND
LADY DECEPTION

The *Brides of Durango* series:

ELISE
TESSA
JENNY

Writing as Julie Marshall:

HAVEN

HALFBREED WARRIOR

BOBBI SMITH

LEISURE BOOKS NEW YORK CITY

*This book is dedicated to everyone at Ford
Motor Company, especially those working at the
St. Louis Assembly Plant. Thanks for keeping my
husband busy working all these years!*

A LEISURE BOOK®

August 2005

Published by

Dorchester Publishing Co., Inc.
200 Madison Avenue
New York, NY 10016

ISBN 0-8439-5396-9

The name "Leisure Books" and the stylized "L" with design are
trademarks of Dorchester Publishing Co., Inc.

Printed in the United States of America.

Visit us on the web at www.dorchesterpub.com.

HALFBREED WARRIOR

Prologue

Texas, late 1860s

Chuck Green, foreman of the Bar T, was out working in the corral when he happened to glance up. He froze. Terror ate at him. There in the distance atop the low rise that overlooked the ranch was an Apache raiding party.

"Ray!" he shouted to the boss. "Indians!"

Ray Taylor rushed out of the stable just as the renegades started to attack.

"Quick! Warn the others and get in the house!" he ordered.

The ranch hands grabbed up their weapons and raced for what safety they could find in the main house. Ray only prayed they would be able to hold the savages off.

He knew the Apache had been raiding from across the border. Neighboring ranches had suffered attacks in the past few months. He also knew how

1

devastating—and deadly—an attack could be.

Ray made sure all his men were inside, then slammed the door shut behind himself. His wife, Kate, quickly barred the door as Jessie, his nephew's wife, ran to get all the guns and ammunition that were stored in the house. Ray had no doubt they were going to need it all.

The first wave of the attack closed in as the men of the Bar T took up defensive positions at the windows. Jessie and Kate joined them. They were both good with a gun and determined to help defend their home.

No one spoke. There was little to say. They all knew just by the size of the raiding party that they were in trouble.

Though the men of the Bar T were good shots, there was no stopping the raiders. They ran off the stock and set fire to the outbuildings, then closed in on the main house.

"Ray! What are we going to do?" Kate was horrified by the devastation, overwhelmed with fear of what was to come.

"Hawk and the other men are out on the range. They may be close enough to hear what's going on," Ray said, hoping their nephew might return early from checking stock. He and his men weren't due back until later that night, but Ray realized they were his only hope.

"Uncle Ray!" Jessie cried out. "Chuck's been shot!"

The foreman collapsed and lay unmoving on the floor near her.

"Keep shootin'!" Ray ordered.

"Dear God, Ray . . . the house is on fire," Kate gasped in a strangled voice as she noticed smoke coming from upstairs.

"Stay here—I'll see if I can put it out!" Ray disappeared up the narrow steps as the renegades continued their bloodthirsty attack.

It was late that afternoon when Hawk Morgan, Ted Johnson, and Will Fletcher rode for the Bar T ranch house. All three men were ready to relax and enjoy one of the delicious home-cooked meals Kate and Jessie served up every night.

Hawk was definitely looking forward to getting back, just so he could be with Jessie—his bride of only three months. During the years when he was growing up on the Bar T with his aunt and uncle, he'd never believed that he'd be able to find the peace and happiness others did. He'd always known he was different. His mother had been Comanche, and he'd been raised in her village until he was ten years old. That was when she'd died. His father, a trader who came to see them only a few times a year, had shown up a little while later. Learning of her death, he had taken his young son to live with his sister and her husband.

His aunt Kate and uncle Ray had taken him in and raised him as their own for these last ten years.

He'd had some trouble adapting, but with their support and love he'd made the transition. He lived the white man's life now, but there were always those who refused to let him forget that he had Comanche blood in his veins. And that was why he'd never thought he'd find someone like Jessie—a beautiful girl who loved him for who he was.

Hawk spurred his horse a little faster, thinking of his lovely wife.

"You that hungry or are you wanting to see your sweetie?" Ted joked.

"What do you think?" Hawk retorted with a grin.

"It ain't the food, Ted." Will chuckled.

They rode on for a few more miles, talking easily to pass the time. It was Ted who noticed the drifting smoke in the distance.

"Look!" Ted's voice was suddenly anxious. "Is that coming from—"

"The ranch!" Hawk spurred his horse to a gallop.

Ted and Will were right behind him. Dread filled them as they raced toward the Bar T. They hoped it was only a brush fire, something that could be easily contained.

But it wasn't.

They rode over the hill to find a scene of pure horror before them. All that remained of the Bar T were smoldering embers and broken-down fences.

Terror filled Hawk. He reined in violently before what was left of the ranch house.

"Jessie!" Hawk shouted as he threw himself from

his horse. He prayed she had somehow escaped with his aunt and uncle, but he saw no sign of life.

Hawk began a grim and desperate search. Rage and frustration filled him as he tore through the still-smoking remains of the ranch house. Ted and Will worked by his side, combing the area, hoping that somehow, some way, someone had survived.

But their search was futile. They found only the charred remains of those who'd died, trapped in the burning house.

"She's not here," Hawk said, looking up from examining the last body they'd found. "Jessie's not here."

It hadn't been an easy task, but they'd been able to identify the dead by their belongings—a belt buckle, his aunt's wedding ring, the guns they'd been using. Hawk had found no trace of Jessie, though—neither her wedding ring nor the heart-shaped locket she always wore.

Hope grew within him, even as he agonized over what she might be suffering at the hands of her Apache captors.

"How can you be sure?" Will asked, looking around at the carnage.

"I'm sure."

Cold-blooded fury filled Hawk as he searched the rest of the area for any tracks left by the raiding party. His own Comanche heritage tormented him. The only solace he could find was in knowing that everything he'd learned about tracking during his time in the village would help him find Jessie.

"It looks like there were ten of them, and they rode out this way." Hawk showed Ted and Will their trail. "I'm going after them."

"Not alone, you're not," Ted asserted.

"We're going with you," Will added.

They quickly buried the dead, then started to give chase. Though it was almost dark, Hawk didn't even consider waiting for daylight. Every minute counted.

He had to find Jessie. Her life was at stake.

The miles seemed endless, but it didn't matter. All that mattered was saving her.

It was late on the second day of hard riding when Hawk spotted a small piece of torn cloth caught in a bramble bush. It looked like material from the dress Jessie had been wearing the day of the raid, and it gave him hope. He believed it possibly could have been ripped from the skirt of her dress as the horse she'd been riding had passed by.

The ground was rocky there. The trail was harder than ever to follow. The three men spread out, each trying to determine which direction the renegades had gone.

Ted saw her first, lying in the dirt among the rocks, her clothing torn from her, her body battered and abused. He had been about to call out to Hawk when he suddenly heard Hawk's cry and saw him riding recklessly toward him.

"Jessie!" Ted knew he would never forget the anguish in his friend's voice.

Hawk had doubled back to let Ted and Will know he'd found the trail again. It was then that he'd caught sight of his wife's lifeless body.

Hawk reined in and dismounted. He ran to Jessie's side and dropped to his knees to take her in his arms.

Ted backed away. There was nothing he could do. When he saw Will in the distance, he signaled him. Will rode in, wondering what had happened. He soon found out. They moved off to give Hawk the privacy and time he needed to mourn.

Hawk buried his beloved Jessie there.

Pain and grief and guilt filled him.

If only he'd found her sooner . . .

The need for revenge burned within him.

Nothing was going to stop him.

Nothing.

Hawk slowly got to his feet after placing the last stone upon Jessie's grave. He looked up at Will and Ted, the expression on his face one of pure, cold-blooded hatred.

"I'm going after them, and I'm not going to stop until they're all dead. You can come with me or we can part ways here."

Will and Ted exchanged looks, already knowing what they intended to do.

"Let's ride," they answered in unison.

Hawk nodded tightly, grateful for their friendship.

He took one last look at Jessie's grave, then mounted up. He rode away, following the raiding party's trail again.

He would not quit. He would not give up until he'd claimed his revenge.

Hawk tracked the savage killers from dawn until dusk for endless days. The three men lived off the land as they relentlessly pursued their quarry. The Apache raiders moved swiftly, riding for the Mexican border, but Hawk, Will, and Ted stayed on their trail. When they did stop, it was only long enough to rest their horses; then they were back in the saddle, tracking the Apache again.

It was late on the night of the tenth day out that the murderous raiding party settled in to sleep in a small clearing, surrounded by rocks and heavy brush. They were unaware that they were being hunted down and believed they were well shielded from sight, safe in their camp.

Hawk noticed the glow of their campfire from a good distance away. He left Will and Ted behind with the horses as he approached the Apache camp silently on foot. He wanted to scout the area before launching his attack. He knew they were outnumbered, so their attack had to be fast and deadly.

Hawk carefully moved in close to the site. He hid in the rocks to get a good look at the renegades. There were ten warriors, just as he'd thought, and he could see that they were armed with rifles. Only one warrior was keeping watch. The others had bedded down for the night.

Moving silently and swiftly back off into the darkness, Hawk returned to Will and Ted and told them what he'd found.

"This isn't going to be easy, but I don't think we'll have a better chance."

"I'm ready," Ted said, eager to take their revenge. "Will?"

Will nodded. "How do you want to do this?"

"There's only one guard. I'll go in first. As soon as I've taken care of him, we'll attack the campsite full force. We'll be able to take them by surprise, so that will help."

Will and Ted shared a tense look at the thought of being so outnumbered.

"Good luck," Ted said.

"We're going to need it," Will added.

The three men checked and loaded their weapons. They had waited days for this moment. Memories of the dead drove them. They were ready.

Hawk moved in, knife in hand, to seek out the warrior keeping guard. He approached the camp without making a sound, using to his advantage everything he'd been taught about hunting as a youth in the Comanche village.

Hawk was tense as he closed in on the guard. His knife attack was swift, deadly, and silent. He returned to join his friends.

With the element of surprise now on their side, Hawk, Will, and Ted wasted no time. They rode at top speed into the camp. They began shooting at the warriors as they awoke and reached for their guns. The sound of the battle echoed in the night.

With deadly accuracy, Hawk claimed his revenge on the Apache. Most of the warriors were killed outright in their first assault. Only three remained alive as Hawk, Ted, and Bill charged through the camp again.

The three surviving Apache fired wildly at the horsemen as they ran for cover.

Will was hit. He fell from his horse and lay unmoving on the ground.

The gun battle continued.

Hawk and Ted pursued the fleeing warriors as they tried to disappear in the night.

Hawk's aim was true.

So was Ted's.

Soon the gunfire stopped; the battle was over.

Hawk and Ted rode back and quickly dismounted beside Will. They hoped he hadn't been seriously injured, but they were too late. Will was dead.

They waited until dawn, mourning the loss of their friend. When it was light, they found a secluded spot to lay him to rest.

There was nothing more for them to do. Hawk and Ted rode back toward what was left of the Bar T.

Though Hawk had claimed his revenge, his mood was dark. Regret tore at him. If only he'd been at the ranch during the attack, he might have been able to save his family and the other ranch hands who'd died with them. Hawk knew he would bear forever the pain of not having reached Jessie in time to rescue her from her terrible fate at the hands of the raiding party.

Jessie had been his love, his life.

Now he was alone.

Chapter One

Dry Springs, Texas, 1870s

Deputy Thompson sought out Jim Watson at the stable in town. "Where's Hawk Morgan? Sheriff Spiller needs to talk to him."

"Check around back. That's where he was the last time I saw him," Jim told him.

The deputy made his way to the back of the building and found Hawk in the corral working with several horses.

"Hey, Thompson, what can I do for you?" Hawk called out.

"The sheriff wants to see you. You got time to go over to the office?"

Hawk was surprised by the request. The sheriff usually called on him only when there was some serious tracking be done, and he hadn't heard of any trouble in town lately. "Sure. I'll head over after I finish up here."

"I'll let him know you're coming." Deputy Thompson eyed one of the horses and thought he recognized the black gelding Hawk was leading docilely around the corral. "Is that Bruiser?"

"Yeah," Hawk answered, not surprised that the deputy had recognized Bruiser. The gelding's reputation was known far and wide around Dry Springs. "I bought him from Sam Roth a few days ago."

"And you got him this tame already?" Thompson had heard the stories from Roth about how stubborn the powerful gelding was and what a rough time he had had trying to break him himself. That was how the animal had gotten the name Bruiser.

"Nothing to it."

"Yeah, right." The deputy knew better. There had been a lot to it.

Deputy Thompson left, impressed anew by Hawk's talent with horses. He'd always heard Hawk was good, but he'd never known just how good until now.

It was about half an hour later when Hawk reached the sheriff's office and went in.

Sheriff Spiller looked up from his desk. He was glad to see Morgan coming through the door.

"It's about time you got here," the lawman said with a smile.

"I came as fast as I could," Hawk said. "Has there been trouble in town?"

"No, no trouble here. But there is something I

want to talk to you about." He gestured toward the chair in front of his desk. "Have a seat."

Hawk sat down.

Sheriff Spiller went on, "I got a letter from a friend of mine—Jack Stockton. He owns the Lazy S Ranch over near San Miguel."

"I've heard of it."

"Most everybody has." Spiller knew the Lazy S was very successful. "Well, Jack's got trouble. He's got some rustling going on, and he's had no luck catching the varmints so far. As good as you are at tracking, I thought you might be able to help him out."

Hawk was silent, but only for a moment. He'd been in Dry Springs for several years. He had made some friends in town, but lately he'd had the feeling that it was time for him to move on. "When would Stockton want me to start?"

"You want the job?"

"Yes."

Spiller nodded. "I'm sure Jack would want you to start as soon as you can get there."

"All right," Hawk said, his decision made. "I'll have to let Jim know I'm leaving."

"When do you want to head out?"

"How's the day after tomorrow?"

"Good. Real good. If you're going to leave Dry Springs that soon, there's no point in my writing Jack back. I'll just give you a letter to take with you. He'll understand."

"Thanks."

Hawk stood up to go. The two men shook hands. "Hawk . . ."

Hawk looked at his friend.

"Jack's seriously worried about what's been going on there or he wouldn't have contacted me. I get the feeling there may be more to this than just rustling. The job could be dangerous. Be careful—real careful," Spiller cautioned.

"I will," Hawk said, appreciating his concern.

He left the office. As he made his way back toward the stable, he looked around Dry Springs. He realized that with the exception of his few friends, there wouldn't be much he'd miss about the town.

Five Days Later
The Lazy S Ranch
Outside San Miguel, Texas

"Go, Angel!" Eighteen-year-old Randi Stockton urged her palomino on to an even faster pace.

Randi knew it was reckless to ride at such a breakneck speed, but she didn't care. She'd just caught a glimpse of the fabled phantom stallion silhouetted on a rise in the distance, and she was determined to give chase.

This wasn't the first time she'd seen the elusive horse. Legend had it that the magnificent white stallion had belonged to a fierce Comanche warrior who had been killed during a raid, and that the stallion had been running free ever since. According to the tale, only the finest of warriors would ever be able to catch him, and it seemed there was truth to the story. No one had even come close in all these years.

But just because no one else had, didn't mean Randi wasn't going to try. And while it was true that she wasn't a warrior in the pure sense of the word, she never hesitated to fight for what she wanted, and she wanted that horse.

Leaning low over Angel's neck, Randi raced on in the direction the phantom had disappeared. Angel was fast—really fast. If any horse could keep pace with the stallion, she believed it would be Angel.

Randi concentrated on her quest, hoping against hope that this would be the day she'd finally catch up to him. But suddenly Angel tensed and altered her pace.

Puzzled by the change in Angel and wondering what had startled the animal, Randi glanced around.

It was then that she caught sight of another rider pursuing her.

Terror seized Randi.

The bare-chested man who was chasing her looked like a Comanche warrior.

Fear ate at her, but she fought it down. She was armed, and Angel was fast. She just hoped she could outrun the warrior.

Randi spurred Angel on.

Any thoughts of finding the phantom stallion were gone now.

All that mattered was getting away.

She had to escape.

Hawk had been on the last leg of his trip to the Lazy S Ranch when the sight of a clear-running stream had enticed him to stop for a while and cool off. His ride that morning had been a long one, and the hot summer day was dry and dusty.

Hawk had stripped off his shirt and had just started to wash up when he'd noticed a young boy on a runaway horse in the distance. Certain the youth was in trouble, he hadn't hesitated. Hawk had mounted up on Bruiser and charged after him. He just hoped the boy didn't get thrown or hurt before he could reach him.

Randi didn't usually admit to being scared, but right then she was. She'd learned early in life how to take care of herself, and she could under most circumstances. Even armed as she was, though, she knew she was vulnerable, for Angel was becoming winded and her pursuer was gaining on her.

Randi glanced back again, only to discover the warrior had drawn even closer. Desperate, she veered off to the right. She hoped to thwart her pursuer with evasive action, but to no avail.

In that very instant, he was upon her.

As their horses raced on side by side, the warrior reached out and snared Randi about the waist.

"Help!" she cried out in fright as he dragged her out of her saddle.

Her captor ignored her cry and crushed her to him, her back pinned against the side of his hard, powerful chest.

"Angel!" Randi watched in horror as her horse, her only hope of salvation, galloped away.

Randi was desperate to break free of her captor. She fought him with all her might. His strength proved overpowering, though. She was trapped and helpless.

Hawk struggled mightily to control Bruiser and to keep a firm hold on the youth at the same time. He'd expected to be thanked for saving him from his runaway horse, not attacked, but the boy was furiously fighting him. Hawk shifted his grip on the youth, hoping to still his resistance, and it was then that a shock of pure physical awareness jolted through him.

Suddenly Hawk realized—this was no boy he'd rescued.

This was a woman!

He was stunned.

"Hold still!" he ordered harshly. He tightened his hold on her even more now to ensure she was protected. He didn't want her to fall and be hurt.

Randi was stunned, too, when she heard her captor's angry command. It surprised her that the warrior could speak English, but she wasn't about to give up her fight for her freedom. She'd heard stories of what happened to Comanche captives, and she was determined to escape him and the terrible fate he no doubt had planned for her.

She struggled even harder, but to no avail. His strength was as unyielding as iron.

The depth of her fear and panic grew even more.

"I said hold still!" Hawk snarled as he finally managed to bring Bruiser to a halt. He only wished this wildcat of a woman were as easy to control as his horse.

"No! Let me go!" she shouted.

Irritated by her frantic struggles when all he'd been trying to do was help, Hawk decided it was time to oblige her.

"Yes, ma'am," he drawled.

Yes, ma'am? Her captor's response shocked and confused Randi. No warrior would ever talk that way. . . .

And then he released her.

Stunned by her sudden freedom, Randi gasped as she awkwardly half slid, half fell to ground. In her descent she lost her hat, freeing her hair from its simple binding to tumble about her shoulders in wild disarray. It took her only a second to regain her footing, and when she did, she drew her gun and spun around, bringing her weapon to bear on this stranger who'd dared to accost her.

"Who are you and what are you doing here?" Randi demanded. She glared up at him, startled to find that her first impression had been right—this man definitely looked like a warrior. His skin was bronzed by the sun, and there was no doubt of his Comanche heritage in his high cheekbones and dark good looks. But then confusion set in.

Although she'd believed him to be a warrior, she realized now that his hair was cut shorter than that of any Comanche she'd ever seen, and he was wearing denim pants and boots and a gun belt.

"Easy, there," Hawk said quickly, surprised and more than a little impressed by her aggressive behavior. He kept his hands away from his gun, and he made no sudden moves. He didn't want to give her any reason to start shooting. "I didn't mean you any harm."

"You could have fooled me!" Randi charged angrily, trying to hide her confusion. This man was not at all what he'd seemed. "What do you want?"

Hawk stared down at the blond beauty standing so defiantly before him. How he'd ever mistaken her for a boy, he didn't know, but then, he'd never seen a female wearing men's pants before. Hawk had no idea who she was, but he already knew she was a wild one, and certainly not a woman to be taken lightly, judging from her expert handling of her sidearm.

"My name's Morgan, Hawk Morgan."

"Yeah. So?" Randi wasn't about to let her guard down just because he'd introduced himself. She kept her gun on him.

"And I was rescuing you," he finished.

"Rescuing me? From what?" Randi was outraged that he'd thought she'd needed help. "I didn't need any rescuing!"

"It sure looked like it to me," he drawled.

"Well, you were wrong." She still refused to admit, even to herself, that he might have been trying to help her. Slowly, she lowered her gun. "Angel and I were chasing the phantom, and we were doing just fine. I was going to catch up with him until you came riding out of nowhere and ruined everything!"

"The phantom?" he asked.

"Oh, nothing. Never mind."

"Well, I'm sorry I bothered you. I'll just be on my way." Hawk turned Bruiser around, ready to ride away. He wasn't really going to leave her there, stranded. He fully intended to go after her mount and bring it back to her.

Randi had no idea who this Hawk Morgan was, but she honestly believed he was coldhearted enough to just ride off and leave her on foot.

Not that she didn't deserve it. After all, she had pulled her gun on him. But it would be one really long walk back to the house.

She looked down at the gun she still had in hand.

"Wait a minute!" she called out.

Hawk reined in and looked back to see her holstering her sidearm. "What?"

"You can't just ride off and leave me here!" she declared.

"I can't?" He couldn't help grinning at the look on her face. He could tell it really annoyed her to have to ask him for help. "I thought you didn't need rescuing?"

It irritated Randi to no end that he was mocking her, but she had no choice. She grabbed up her hat and jammed it back on her head. "Well, now I do."

"Then it'll be my pleasure to help you."

Hawk rode back to her side and offered her a hand up.

Randi took his proffered hand and swung up easily behind him. "My name's Randi Stockton, by the way, and this is my family's ranch, the Lazy S."

Hawk had been wondering who she was, and now he had his answer. "Nice to meet you, Randi Stockton. I take it you're related to Jack Stockton."

"He's my father. Why? Do you know him?"

"No, I was just on my way out to speak with him when I saw you."

"Do you always ride after people like that?"

"I thought you were on a runaway. Sorry about the mixup. It won't happen again."

"It had better not."

"Don't worry. I'll know better next time."

"Good," she said with some satisfaction.

"Besides—if there ever was a next time, you probably wouldn't hesitate to shoot me," he said wryly.

Randi's tension finally started to ease, and she managed a grin.

"You're right," she said.

"Let's go find your horse."

"Thanks."

"Hold on," Hawk instructed.

Randi linked her arms around his lean waist. She tried not to notice how broad and muscular his shoulders were as they rode off in search of the runaway Angel.

"Who was this phantom you were chasing?" Hawk asked, now that they were on speaking terms. He was worried that the phantom was an outlaw or someone he should be on the lookout for.

"The phantom's not a person. It's a stallion." She started to tell him the story.

"I remember hearing about that legend," he remarked. "But that was some years ago."

"The tale has been around for quite a while."

"How do you know this is the same stallion?"

"That's what's so fascinating about it. We can't be sure, but whoever finally catches him will find out the truth."

"If anyone ever does catch him." Hawk was skeptical. He knew how elusive wild stallions could be. The horse hadn't earned the reputation as a phantom for nothing.

"I'm going to get him. You just wait and see," Randi declared with certainty.

"But the legend says only the finest warrior can catch him, and you're not a warrior," he pointed out simply.

"I've been known to put up a pretty good fight," she countered.

"That's true." He chuckled.

"I've been trying to find the phantom for more than six years now, and today was the closest I've ever gotten. Angel is fast. If any horse is going to catch him, it would be her." She paused, realizing his horse had run her down. She added, slightly annoyed at having to give him any credit, "Or maybe yours."

Hawk nodded. "Bruiser's fast. Keep an eye out while I'm tracking Angel; maybe you'll spot your phantom again."

"The way he runs, he's probably in another county by now."

Chapter Two

Hawk carefully followed Angel's trail. As they rode along, he found himself looking for an additional set of tracks, but the stallion proved true to his name. He was a phantom. He'd disappeared. There were no tracks but Angel's.

When Hawk finally spotted Angel in the distance, he reined in. He did not want to risk scaring off the runaway.

"There she is," Hawk announced.

"You're a good tracker," Randi said, impressed.

"I've had a lot of practice. Will you need any help with her?" he offered.

"Sometimes she can be skittish, but I should be all right." Randi slipped down from behind him.

"I'll wait back here, just in case."

"Thanks."

Hawk recognized a good piece of horseflesh when he saw it, and Angel was one beautiful palomino. He was impressed, too, by the way Randi walked slowly toward the frightened mount, talking in low tones and making no quick moves. It was obvious she knew how to handle her horse as well as her gun.

Randi made her way to Angel's side, then slowly reached out to grab her reins.

"Good girl," she murmured soothingly.

She took the time to stroke the mare's neck and reassure her. It had been a frightening experience for both of them. She was relieved Angel didn't try to shy away from her, but her relief was short-lived. She quickly discovered Angel had thrown a shoe and injured her leg. Her fetlock was swollen, and she was bleeding from a cut.

Hawk had kept his distance, but when he noticed Randi checking the palomino's leg, he rode closer.

"Is she hurt?" he asked.

"I'm afraid so."

Hawk dismounted and went to take a look at Angel's injury.

"It doesn't look too serious," he told Randi after he'd examined the gash. "But we'd better walk her back, just to make sure."

"All right." Randi hated the thought that Angel had been hurt because of her.

"It might be good, too, if we took her down to the creek and let her stand in the water. She should soak that leg for a while before we head for the house. That should help keep the swelling down. While we're there, I can get my shirt and hat."

"I wondered what happened to your clothes," she remarked, trying not to stare at the broad, tanned expanse of his powerfully muscled chest.

"I'd just stopped to rest and cool off at the creek when I saw you riding past."

"That explains it."

She climbed up behind Hawk again, and they started off at a slow, steady pace, leading Angel.

Randi was getting worried. When she'd ridden out earlier that morning, she'd told her father she was going for a short ride and wouldn't be gone very long. Now that they had to walk Angel back, it was going to take them quite a while to get home. Knowing her father as she did, she was sure he was going to be worrying about her. She knew there was nothing she could do about it, but she hoped he didn't get so worried that he came out looking for her. She was embarrassed enough as it was.

"I understand the Lazy S is one of the biggest ranches in the area," Hawk commented, breaking the silence between them.

"That's right. It's my father's pride and joy. He's worked hard for a lot of years to make it a success."

"Looks like he's done a fine job."

"I'll tell him you said so."

"So do you work on the ranch with him?"

"Oh, yes. I went away to school for a while, but I couldn't wait to get back home. This is where I belong," she said with conviction. "How about you? Where are you from?"

"I was working up in Dry Springs."

"Who was it who told you about the Lazy S?"

"A friend of mine there named Spiller," Hawk answered. "He knows your father and said he was hiring on." Hawk didn't say anything more about what the lawman had told him concerning rustling. If he got the job, it would be up to her father to tell her the reason he had been hired.

"Welcome to the Lazy S."

Hawk couldn't help smiling to himself. "Judging from the way things just got started, it looks like working here might be a real adventure."

"That was a bit of excitement," Randi agreed.

"For both of us," he finished.

Hawk fought to ignore Randi's nearness as she rode double behind him. The feel of her arms linked around his waist and the light press of her body against his left no doubt of her femininity, and he wondered again how he'd ever mistaken her for a boy. He forced himself to concentrate on their conversation as she told him more about the ranch.

"Any sign of Randi yet?" Jack Stockton demanded of his ranch hands as he joined them in the stable.

"We ain't seen her," Rob Harris answered.

"No one has since she rode out this morning," Wade Mason, the ranch foreman, added.

Jack swore under his breath in frustration and concern. This wasn't like Randi—it wasn't like Randi at all. "Saddle up. We're going out to look for her."

Rob and Wade did as the boss ordered. Soon they were ready to ride.

"Which way did she head out?" Jack asked.

"North, toward the creek," Wade answered.

Jack nodded tersely. "Let's go."

When Hawk and Randi reached the creek, they quickly dismounted. Randi turned Angel over to Hawk's care. He led the mare to the center of the shallow stream and stood with her, letting the cool water work its magic on her injured leg.

"How long does she need to stay in there?" Randi asked, concerned about her horse, but also anxious about letting her father know she was all right.

"The longer, the better."

Randi left Hawk to tend to Angel and went in search of his shirt and hat. She found them on the bank farther downstream.

"I think you'll be wanting these before we ride out," she told him, holding them up for him to see.

"Just hang them on a branch there. I'll get them when I'm done."

She did as she was told, then went to sit in the shade on the bank nearby.

Hawk kept Angel in the water for a while longer, then finally started to lead her out of the stream.

"That should be long enough for right now."

"Then we'd better get going. I'm sure my pa's worrying about me."

"Why?"

31

"I told him I wouldn't be gone long when I rode out, and if we walk Angel back, it's going to take us a while."

Randi started over to the tree to get his shirt when she heard the sound of horses coming.

Jack and the men had just topped a low rise when Jack caught sight of what looked like a Comanche warrior leading Angel out of the creek. Terror and fury seized him, for he saw no sign of Randi. He was certain something terrible had happened to her.

"We got trouble, boys!"

Jack drew his gun and galloped full-speed toward the creek. He was ready to fight off an Indian raid. He was desperate to find and rescue his daughter.

Randi looked up to see her father and several of the ranch hands charging their way. She forgot all about getting the shirt and hurried over to stand with Hawk.

"It's my pa," Randi warned Hawk as she waved to let them know everything was all right.

Jack was racing toward the warrior when Randi unexpectedly appeared beside the Indian. She didn't seem to be hurt in any way and was actually waving to them.

"What the hell . . . !" Jack raged in confusion. He was thrilled to see that she was unharmed, but he had no idea who the Indian was or why Randi was with him. He pulled back on his reins to slow his assault.

"What's going on, boss?" Wade asked, riding up beside him. He was as confused as Jack.

"I don't know, but I'm going to find out right now."

He slowed his charge even more, and his men did the same.

Randi went forward to meet them as they finally reined in on the creek bank.

"What the hell is going on?" Jack demanded. He glared down at his daughter and then looked over at the man leading her horse out of the stream.

Up close now, he could tell this man was no warrior, but there was no mistaking his heritage. He didn't know who the stranger was, but whoever he was, he had no business being around his daughter in such a state of undress.

"Pa, it's all right." Randi quickly came to Hawk's defense, and she was relieved when her father and the hands holstered their guns. "This is Hawk Morgan. He's helping me with Angel."

"Helping you with Angel?" Jack snarled, looking over at the horse. "What's wrong with Angel?"

"She's injured her fetlock," Hawk spoke up.

"Hawk was riding in when he saw I was in trouble. He stopped to help me." Randi told herself she wasn't really lying to her father. She was only trying to make their situation more acceptable to him. She knew how bad his temper could be.

This wasn't quite the way Hawk had expected to meet Jack Stockton for the first time, but he appreciated Randi's quick thinking.

Randi continued, "Hawk said if Angel stood in the creek for a while, it would reduce the swelling in her leg. He took her in for me. That's why he has his shirt off."

"Well, put your shirt back on," Jack ordered sharply. He dismounted and went to take a look at Angel's foreleg for himself.

Randi quickly got the shirt and handed it over to Hawk. Hawk wasted no time getting dressed.

"That's an ugly gash." Jack looked at his daughter accusingly. "Just how fast were you riding for her to injure herself this way, young lady?"

"Too fast, Pa," she admitted.

Jack straightened up and looked over at the stranger who'd come to Randi's rescue. He was fully dressed now and looked considerably less like a savage. The sight eased Jack's anger. "I appreciate you helping my daughter."

"I was just glad I came along when I did," Hawk answered, and he realized to his own surprise that it was the truth.

"So, Morgan, what are you doing here on the Lazy S?" Jack asked, still a little suspicious. He couldn't be sure this fellow wasn't one of the thieves who'd been plaguing the ranch lately, stealing stock.

Hawk understood Stockton's suspicion of him. He hastened to reassure him. "Harry Spiller, up in Dry Springs, is a friend of mine. He said you were looking for some help, so I came down to see about working for you."

"You know Spiller, do you?" Jack's gaze narrowed assessingly as he studied the other man. He found it hard to believe Harry would have sent a half-breed for the job, but then . . .

"I've known him for some time. I've got a letter from him in my saddlebag. He said you'd want to see it."

"He was right. I do. I'll take a look at it when we get back up to the house." Jack's doubts about the man were eased when Morgan mentioned the letter. He was relieved, too, that the man had been smart enough not to say anything more about his real reason for coming to the Lazy S. So far, Jack hadn't told anyone, not even Randi, about the request he'd made of his friend in Dry Springs.

"Rob," Jack called to his ranch hand, "bring Angel back. Randi, you ride with me."

"Yes, Pa."

Hawk got his hat, then mounted Bruiser.

Randi cast a quick glance Hawk's way as she swung up behind her father. The complete change in Hawk was surprising. Fully dressed and wearing his Stetson, he no longer appeared the fierce warrior of her first impression. Now he seemed to fit right in. He looked like a ranch hand—but she had to admit to herself that he was a very handsome ranch hand.

Though Jack was grateful Morgan had stopped to help Randi, his mood remained troubled as they rode toward the house. If Spiller had recommended the man, he knew Morgan had to be good, but he had his misgivings about hiring a half-breed. There wasn't a lot of love in the area for anyone with Indian blood. Jack himself had lost many friends to murderous raiding parties through the years. He just hoped Morgan could fit in and do his job without drawing too much attention to himself.

While Jack managed to put his concerns about Morgan aside for the time being, he could not as easily dismiss the memory of seeing Randi standing beside a half-naked stranger. Her explanation of how the scene had come about had been logical, but that didn't make it right.

Randi could have ended up in a lot of trouble today. She was almost a full-grown woman. She was a Stockton. She had a reputation to uphold. He was going to have to have a long, serious talk with her when they got back home.

Hawk was impressed when he got his first look at the Lazy S's main house. The large two-story home had a porch on three sides. There were numerous outbuildings and corrals. All were a testimony to Jack Stockton's success as a rancher.

"Beautiful place you have here," he complimented the rancher.

"Thanks. It's taken years of hard work and sacrifice, but it's been worth it. My goal is to make the Lazy S the biggest, best spread around."

"You're well on your way."

"We're getting there," Jack replied. "Morgan, you come with me up to the house. I want to take a look at that letter you said you had from Spiller." Jack was careful not to say "sheriff." He looked at his foreman and added, "Wade, you let me know when Rob shows up with Angel, all right?"

"Sure thing, boss." Wade left them, riding off toward the stable to go back to work. He wondered if the boss was seriously thinking about hiring on the half-breed. He hoped he didn't. He didn't want any trouble in the bunkhouse.

Jack, Randi, and Hawk reined in before the main house and dismounted.

"Randi."

She recognized the seriousness of her father's tone and looked his way respectfully. "Yes, Pa?"

"You stay here at the house. Don't go running off. As soon as I'm finished with Morgan, I want to talk to you."

It was an order, not an invitation.

She nodded.

"Let's go inside," Jack directed Hawk, and he led the way.

Chapter Three

"I appreciate your help with Angel today," Randi told Hawk as he held the door for her to enter the house ahead of him.

"I'm just sorry she was injured," he said, taking off his Stetson as he went inside.

"Me, too."

"Let's go into my office," Jack said, interrupting their conversation.

Hawk followed the rancher into his office. Jack shut the door firmly behind them.

Randi stood there in the hall only a moment longer, staring at the closed door; then she went on to the kitchen to let the housekeeper know they were back.

"Let's see that letter," Jack directed.

Hawk handed him the envelope he'd retrieved from his saddlebags before they'd come inside.

"Have a seat while I take a look at this." Jack settled in at his desk.

Hawk sat down in the chair facing the desk and waited in silence while Jack read Sheriff Spiller's letter.

"So Spiller thinks you're good enough to catch these bastards." Jack looked up at Hawk when he'd finished reading. His expression was hard as he looked him over. "Are you?"

"Yeah, I'm good enough," Hawk answered, looking him straight in the eye.

Jack respected Spiller's opinion, and it was obvious Morgan was confident of his own abilities. "All right, since Harry recommends you so highly, I'll take a chance on you. You're hired. I want these rustlers stopped. They've been hitting the Lazy S regularly for the past six months now, and I've had enough. Do whatever you have to do to find them—and stop them."

"What do you know about them?"

"Not much. The rustlers have been working mainly off the south range. I'm almost beginning to think someone on the ranch is involved in it, but I can't prove anything—and that's the problem. That's where you come in."

"Is there anyone in particular you suspect might be involved?"

"No."

"All right. Then I'm just another ranch hand."

"Good. I won't even tell Randi or Wade. For now, only the two of us will know what you're really up to."

"That's fine. I will need to get a look at the layout of the ranch, though, particularly the south range, since that's where they've been working."

Jack nodded in agreement. "And you let me know if you see or hear anything—anything at all that might help us. I want these rustlers caught. Nobody steals from the Lazy S and gets away with it." His anger and outrage were real.

Hawk realized all too clearly that Jack Stockton would make a formidable enemy. Whoever was stealing from him wasn't very smart, and that, Hawk knew, was his first clue.

"You go on and find Wade. He's the foreman. He'll help you get settled in at the bunkhouse," Jack directed.

"If I do learn something, how do you want me to get the information to you?"

"Don't worry. I'm always around, and no one will think anything about us talking. I'm always after the men, making sure they get their work done. You won't have to look very far to find me."

Hawk stood to go. Jack got up, too, and followed him out into the hall.

"Miranda!" he bellowed. Without a word to Hawk, he turned and went back into his office.

Hawk was surprised to learn that Miranda was Randi's real name. It was a pretty name, and it suited her. Judging from her father's tone, though, if Randi was as smart as she was good-looking, he knew she wouldn't waste any time showing up in his office.

41

Hawk left the house to seek out Wade and begin his work on the Lazy S.

Randi had been in the kitchen with Wilda, their housekeeper, when she heard her father's shout. Knowing there was no avoiding his fury, she girded herself for what was to come.

"Sounds like he's ready for you," Wilda said, giving Randi an understanding and sympathetic smile. Randi had just explained to her how the stranger had stopped to help her, and how her father had found them together at the creek taking care of Angel's injured fetlock.

"More than ready," Randi said grimly.

She left the kitchen and made her way down the hall, going to stand in his office doorway.

"You wanted to talk to me?" Randi asked, already knowing the answer.

"Yes," he said tersely, not bothering to get up from behind his desk.

Randi went in and sat down before him.

Jack sat for a moment, glowering at her. Then he stood up and walked over to close the door. He moved behind his desk again, and his expression was troubled as he stood there looking down at her.

"There are a few things you need to think about, *young lady*," Jack stated firmly.

Randi met his gaze straight on as she awaited his pronouncement.

"When I rode up to the creek today and saw you with Morgan . . . Why, the man was half-naked!"

He paused, still disturbed by his impression of what he'd seen.

"It was all innocent!" she exclaimed, her tone defensive. "I was just glad for his help."

"I understand that, but I don't ever want you to put yourself in that kind of a compromising position again."

"Yes, sir."

"If it had been someone else riding up who'd seen the two of you together that way . . ." Jack was determined to emphasize his point. "You are a young woman with a reputation to uphold. Do I make myself clear?"

"Very."

"Good." He nodded, satisfied that she would not repeat this mistake.

"So did you hire Hawk on?" she asked.

"Yes, but I've still got my doubts that it's the right thing to do. Some of the boys aren't going to be very happy about having to work with a half-breed."

"We already know Hawk is good with horses. Look at the way he helped me with Angel."

"That doesn't mean things will work out. Keep your distance from him."

"If he's one of our ranch hands, how am I supposed to stay away from him?"

"You're a smart girl. Figure it out."

Randi knew when to pick her fights. "Yes, Pa."

"All right, go on and get out of here. I've got work to do."

Jack watched Randi in silence as she left the office and closed the door behind her. He loved his daughter dearly, and just the thought that something might have happened to her earlier today had left him desperate to know she was safe. It hadn't helped matters any when he'd found her with Morgan, but as it was, everything had turned out all right.

For the first time that day, Jack found himself smiling as he thought about Randi. Headstrong and independent, Randi was definitely his daughter.

Randi let out a sigh of relief as she walked out into the hallway. She'd been lucky her father's anger hadn't been worse. There had been any number of times when she'd had to take the full brunt of his fury, and it hadn't been pleasant. She was thankful today hadn't been one of them.

As she started back toward the kitchen, Randi caught a glimpse of her own reflection in the small mirror on the wall, and her father's words echoed in her mind: *You are a young woman with a reputation to uphold.*

The image staring back at her bore little resemblance to a lady. If anything, the girl in the mirror looked downright disreputable. Her hair was an uncontrolled mass of curls and tangles. Her face was smudged with dirt, and her clothing was wrinkled and soiled.

If her hair had been tied up under her hat, Randi doubted anyone who didn't know her would ever guess she was a female, let alone consider trying to

ruin her reputation. More than likely they'd think
her reputation had already been ruined, or they'd
take one look at her and run in the opposite direction. She thought of Hawk's earlier "rescue" attempt and far too clearly remembered his very real
shock when he'd discovered she was a girl.

Randi frowned at the memory.

She continued to stare at herself. Her mother
had been a lady through and through. Her father
often told her she took after her mother, but at
that moment, the only resemblance she could find
to her mother was the color of her pale blond hair.

Turning away from her troubling reflection,
Randi decided to go up to her room and get
cleaned up a bit. She knew it couldn't hurt.

Once in her room, Randi sat down at her dressing table and went to work taming her hair. It took
a few minutes, but she finally managed to brush all
the tangles out of her thick, golden tresses. With
practiced expertise, she then plaited the now-silky
mass into a single, neat braid that hung down her
back. With her hair done, she went to her wash-
stand, stripped down to her underclothing, and
scrubbed herself clean.

Again, she thought of her father's words as she
washed off the day's dirt and grime: *You are a
young woman* . . .

Randi paused for a moment and glanced over at
her wardrobe, eyeing the dresses that hung there.
She had numerous day gowns and a few fancier
gowns for socials and parties. With all the real

work she did around the ranch, however, the dresses were practically useless to her. She could start dressing like a lady, but she didn't think her father really wanted her to stop working. More important, though, she didn't want to stop. She loved the Lazy S. The ranch was her life.

Closing the wardrobe door, Randi went to her bureau and took out a clean pair of pants and a blouse. Dressed once more in her normal workday clothes, she hurried down to the kitchen to get some lunch.

"So you're all right?" Wilda asked when Randi came into the kitchen. The housekeeper had been wondering how the girl's meeting with her father had gone.

"I'm fine, but I am hungry," Randi replied with a grin.

"Well, good. You just sit down, and I'll get you something," Wilda directed.

Randi did as she was told.

"What happened with the new fella?" Wilda asked.

"Pa hired him on."

"He hired him? But he's a half-breed, isn't he?" Wilda asked sharply. She'd seen the man when he'd left the house after his meeting with Jack and had recognized the Indian blood in him.

Randi heard the disapproval in Wilda's voice and knew there was no point in trying to deny the truth. "Yes, he is."

"I don't know how that'll work out—having someone like *him* on the ranch."

"Hawk's a good man," she defended him.

"There ain't nothing good about a man with Indian blood in his veins," Wilda said in disgust. Years before, her own family's homestead had been attacked by an Apache raiding party, and most of her family had been slaughtered. She witnessed the whole thing. The horror and devastation had scarred her forever and left her filled with hatred for any and all things Indian.

Wilda said no more as she set a plate of food before Randi and returned to her work.

Randi was aware of Wilda's tragic past, and she knew that nothing she could say about Hawk would change the woman's mind. Wanting to get away from the oppressive silence that hung between them, she finished eating quickly and left the house, heading to the stable. There was still work to be done.

Chapter Four

"Rob's riding in!"

Randi heard the shout. Anxious to see how Angel had held up on the trek back, she hurried from the stable. Relief swept through her at the sight of her beloved horse being led in, only slightly favoring her injured leg.

"Did everything go all right?" she asked as Rob stopped before her.

"We took it slow and easy the whole way."

"Good. I'll take her from here. Thanks, Rob."

Randi took the reins and led the mare into a stall in the stable. She had just finished unsaddling Angel when Wade and Hawk came in.

"We heard Rob was back. Hawk wanted to take another look at Angel," Wade said.

"So you're that eager to start earning your keep?" she asked Hawk with a grin.

Randi's manner was so relaxed now and her

smile so genuine that Hawk found himself smiling back at her. "You heard I got the job."

"That's right, and I'm glad my father hired you on. We need all the good help we can get around here."

"Glad to oblige," Hawk said. "Wade's been showing me around. The Lazy S is as impressive as I thought it would be."

"Thanks."

"So how's Angel's leg?"

"It looks like having her stand in the creek worked. The swelling isn't nearly as bad as it could have been."

"Good."

Hawk moved past Randi to kneel down and examine Angel's foreleg. After he'd finished checking the animal, he stood up and glanced Randi's way.

"I'll make up a poultice for Angel. We'll need to keep that leg wrapped up for another day or so."

"Is it that bad?" she asked, worried.

"No, but I just want to make sure the wound heals correctly. It shouldn't take me long. I'll be right back. I've got all the medicine I need in my saddlebags."

Wade stayed with Randi while Hawk went up to the bunkhouse to make the poultice. Randi took a look at Angel's leg herself and knew Hawk had been right. Though the swelling was down, the wound did need some further doctoring.

"I hope Hawk's poultice works fast. Angel's got to be healed by the end of next week," she said.

"Don't tell me you're worried about being ready for the Stampede in town?" Wade knew how much Randi enjoyed competing in San Miguel's annual celebration.

"Of course I am," Randi answered with a conspiratorial grin. "You know Angel and I always enter the race."

"And you win most of the time, too," he finished for her.

"That's right," she declared. She was a fierce competitor. Every summer she looked forward to the challenge. "We have to be ready. I don't know what I'd do if I didn't have Angel to ride in the race."

"You might give someone else a chance to win." Wade laughed.

"I don't want to do that!"

"I didn't think so."

Hawk returned a short time later, ready to apply the healing poultice to Angel's injury.

Randi was concerned, for there were times when Angel was skittish. She was surprised when the mare remained completely calm with Hawk. She displayed no fear of him at all while he worked on her leg.

"That should take care of it," Hawk announced, standing up.

"Do you think she'll be healed enough to run by next week?" Randi asked.

"She should be—as long as no infection sets in."

"Good. It's almost time for the big Stampede.

We have to be ready to run." Randi stroked Angel's neck affectionately.

Hawk had heard of Stampedes, but had never been to one. "You've ridden in them before?"

"Randi and Angel compete every year," Wade explained. "And they're good—real good. There aren't many around these parts who are as fast as these two."

"I can imagine," Hawk said.

At that moment Randi's gaze met Hawk's, and they both were remembering, far too clearly, their first encounter.

Randi was surprised when she felt herself actually blush a bit at the memory of being swept off Angel's back and into his arms. It wasn't like her to blush. She looked away, confused by her own reaction.

"I'm going to take Hawk out and finish showing him around. We should be back by sundown," Wade told her.

"I'll let Pa know," she said.

Randi watched them as they walked away from the stable. Her gaze lingered on Hawk's tall, lean form until he had disappeared from sight.

It was almost dark when Wade and Hawk finally returned. Hawk was more impressed than ever with the ranch. It was obvious Jack Stockton had worked hard to make it what it was today.

Hawk was coming to respect the foreman, too. Wade seemed dedicated to the ranch and his boss. Hawk had been surprised by Wade's easy acceptance of him. He wondered if the rest of the hands would prove to be as good to work with. His past experiences kept him from being too optimistic.

"Our timing's perfect," Wade remarked as they rode in. "They should be getting ready to serve dinner right about now."

"Good. I'm hungry."

"You're not the only one. Come on; let's hurry up and take care of the horses, so we can get us something to eat before the boys finish it all off," Wade encouraged.

A short time later, when Wade and Hawk walked into the bunkhouse, all the hands looked up from where they were eating at the long table in the center of the room.

"We were wondering when the two of you would be getting back," Rob said.

"You know I never miss a meal," Wade said as they joined the others at the table. "I hope you saved us something."

"You ain't gonna starve," Tom Andrews remarked, pushing a big pot of Wilda's stew down the table to them.

"Have you all met Hawk?" Wade asked as he started to dish himself up a serving of the savory stew.

Some of the men hadn't, so he quickly introduced them. Wade noticed the looks several of the ranch hands gave each other when they realized Hawk was a half-breed. He'd known some of the men would hate Hawk for his heritage, but there was nothing he could do to change their way of thinking.

"I'm done eating," Fred Carter said tersely, pushing his plate back and standing up abruptly.

"Me, too," Lew Jones muttered in disgust as he followed Fred from the room.

"Well, that leaves more food for the rest of us," Wade said, taking another helping before passing the dish on to Hawk.

They ate heartily, enjoying the meal and discussing the events of the day with the men who'd remained with them.

"How bad was Randi's horse injured?" Lyle Moore asked, worried now that he'd heard the story of how Hawk had met Randi. "I've been saving up my money to bet on the two of them at the Stampede, but if Angel's hurt—"

"Don't worry. Hawk told Randi Angel would be ready to run," Wade said.

"That's real good to know." Lyle chuckled, relieved at the news. "I'm glad Jack hired you on, Morgan."

Once they'd finished eating, Hawk took the time to get settled into the bunkhouse. He stowed his personal belongings beneath the bunk he'd been given and was about to call it a night when he decided to go down to stable and take one last look at Angel.

Randi had been a little worried when she'd returned to the house at dinnertime. She hadn't been quite sure what to expect from her father. Because he'd seemed to be so angry with her earlier, she'd decided to hurry up to her room and change into a daygown to ease some of the tension between them. She'd also taken an extra moment to unbraid and brush out her hair before going back downstairs to eat.

The look on her father's face when she'd walked into the dining room had been worth it. He'd smiled at her, and for the first time since their earlier encounter she'd managed to relax a bit. The meal and their time together had actually been pleasant. No mention had been made of the events of the day, and she'd been glad.

It was getting late when Randi finally made her way upstairs. She'd planned to just relax and read for a while, but as she started to get ready for bed, she looked out her bedroom window and noticed there was light coming from the stable. It was unusual for anyone to be in there at this time of night, and her first and immediate concern was for Angel. Without hesitation, Randi left the house to find out what was going on.

Hawk had just finished looking at Angel's leg and had left her stall when Randi came hurrying in.

Randi was expecting one of the regular hands to be there, and she was surprised to find it was Hawk.

"Is something wrong?" She looked nervously past him to see Angel in her stall, looking fine.

"No, not at all," he reassured her, amazed by the

change in her appearance. He had never doubted for a moment that Randi was an attractive woman; seeing her dressed this way now only proved how right he'd been. She looked every bit a lady. "I just wanted to take another look at her leg before bedding down for the night."

"Oh, good. When I saw the light, I was afraid something had happened." Randi went over to the stall to pet Angel.

"She's doing fine."

"Thanks for all your help today," she said quietly.

"If it hadn't been for me, you wouldn't have needed help in the first place."

"You thought I was in trouble," she said simply, looking up at him.

"I learned my lesson."

"So you're never going to try to rescue me again?" Randi asked with a smile.

"Are you going to need rescuing? Seems to me you can take care of yourself."

"I try."

"I appreciate what you told your father about how we met."

"I was already in enough trouble. There was no need to make things worse."

"Well, no one will ever find out from me that I mistook you for a boy. I certainly wouldn't have that problem tonight." His gaze went over her, and he felt a stirring deep within him. It surprised him. He hadn't felt this way about a woman since . . .

"Oh . . . thanks." A shiver of physical awareness

trembled through Randi as her gaze met his. It left her a bit nervous, for she wasn't used to feeling that way. "Well, I'd better get back up to the house. Good night, Hawk."

"Good night."

Hawk put out the lamp, then went to stand in the darkness by the stable doorway, watching Randi until she was safely inside the house.

Only then did he start back toward the bunkhouse. As he drew near, he saw that several of the hands were sitting out on the bunkhouse porch.

"Hey, Indian boy," Fred Carter called out to him.

"My name's Hawk," Hawk answered with no emotion as he reached the porch.

"Don't matter what your name is; you just better be careful around the boss's daughter. Ol' Jack don't take kindly to anyone messing with Randi."

The other man with him was chuckling.

Having dealt with people like Carter all his life, Hawk knew the best way to handle them was to ignore them.

"I'll remember that," Hawk said as he walked past them and on into the bunkhouse.

"You'd better."

Chapter Five

Jack was up and out of the house early the following morning. He knew it was important he get over to the neighboring Walker ranch, the Bar W, as quickly as he could to let Pat Walker know what was going on. The pretty young widow had been trying to keep her ranch running since her husband's death the year before. She had managed to hang on this long, but lately she'd been hit by the rustlers, too, and her finances were in a desperate state.

As Jack rode up to the house, Pat came outside to greet him.

"I'm hoping this is a purely social visit, Jack," she called out, smiling in welcome. The Stocktons were good neighbors and good friends.

"I'd like to tell you it is, but we need to talk," Jack said as he dismounted and joined her on the porch.

Pat immediately grew serious. "What did you find out?"

"Nothing yet, but I've hired a man to look into the rustling. His name's Hawk Morgan, and with any luck he'll have some answers for us before too long."

"Good. I have no intention of letting them run me out of business—whoever they are."

"You're the only one I've told so far about Morgan. I haven't even told Wade yet."

Pat was surprised, for she knew how close he and his foreman were. She thought highly of the man, too. He'd been helping her a lot recently, and she appreciated it.

"Why didn't you tell Wade?" Pat asked. "You don't suspect him of being involved, do you?"

"No, I trust Wade. I just thought it best if I kept this quiet. The fewer people who know what Morgan's up to, the better."

"You just let me know if there's anything you need me to do," Pat offered.

"I will, and if I find out anything, I'll send word to you right away."

"I appreciate it, Jack. How's Randi?"

"She's just fine. She's looking forward to the Stampede."

"So am I. Tell her I'll see her in town. It'll be good to relax and have some fun for a change."

"Yes, it will."

As Jack rode from the Walker ranch a short time later, he wondered how long Pat could keep the place going on her own. He'd offered to buy her out after her husband had died, but she'd been determined to make a go of it. He just hoped she could hold on to the ranch. He knew how much it meant to her.

Pat watched Jack ride away and knew she was lucky to have him for a neighbor. He was a smart, powerful man, and if anybody could figure out who was behind all the trouble, he would.

Pat would always remember his kindness over the past year and a half. Jack, Randi, and Wade had checked in on her regularly to offer any help she needed. Her pride kept her from admitting how desperate her situation was becoming, but she was thankful for their friendship.

Pat couldn't wait for the trip to town for the Stampede. It wasn't very often that she got to socialize. It had been almost two years since Al had died in the riding accident. Pat knew she had to move on with her life. She was trying, but it wasn't easy.

"What are we going to do about the breed?" Fred Carter asked Rob in disgust as they worked stock together in the north pasture.

"There's nothing we can do." Rob had been expecting Fred to bring up the subject ever since they'd ridden out earlier that morning. "The boss hired him on. He works here just like we do."

"That don't mean we have to like it."

"Nobody's asking you to be friends with the man; just work with him when you have to."

"I don't want nothing to do with Morgan."

"You don't even know him."

"And I plan to keep it that way."

"Just don't go causing any trouble. The boss has got enough going on right now, trying to catch the rustlers. He don't need you stirring things up in the bunkhouse."

Fred ignored Rob. His hatred of Indians ran deep. Hawk Morgan had better keep his distance from him if he knew what was good for him.

Fred knew he wasn't the only one in the bunkhouse who felt that way. Maybe when he got back to the ranch that night, he'd see what he could do to make Morgan's life miserable. The sooner the breed moved on, the better.

"So what's life like on the Lazy S?" Hawk asked Wade as they rode back toward the house.

Wade had taken him out to show him more of the ranch.

"Most of the time it's quiet," Wade answered. "There are only three rules here at the Lazy S—no drinking, no gambling, and no fighting, and the men don't seem to have any trouble with that. The boys might get a little rowdy every now and then, but once payday comes and they get to go into town for a few nights, they get it out of their systems."

"What about the rustling? Jack mentioned you've had some trouble the last few months." Hawk glanced toward Wade and noticed how grim he looked.

"It's been bad lately. Whoever's behind it has

been hitting us hard. But it's not just us—they hit the Walker ranch just south of here, too."

"Any idea who it might be?"

"No. I wish I did. Keep an eye out and let me know if you see anything suspicious."

"I will."

Though Rob had warned Fred not to cause trouble, Fred wasn't about to ignore the fact that the half-breed was living in the bunkhouse with them. Fred was determined to drive Morgan away, and he knew exactly what he wanted to do.

That evening he went looking for what he needed. He found it easily, then kept watch, waiting for the half-breed to ride in. When he finally saw Morgan and Wade return, he went into the bunkhouse to set his plan in motion.

Fred had told several of his friends his plan, so they settled in at the table or lounged in their bunks, waiting to see what was going to happen. Since it was almost dinnertime, they figured they wouldn't have to wait long for Morgan to show up.

Hawk and Wade returned to the bunkhouse eager for dinner. They'd put in a long day and were looking forward to taking it easy for a while.

"Cook will be bringing dinner out soon," Wade told Hawk as they walked inside. Seeing that some of the men were already there, he greeted them, "How'd you boys do today?"

"Just fine, Wade," Fred answered with a lazy grin.

Rob followed Hawk and Wade into the bunk-house just in time to hear Fred's answer. Fred's seemingly easygoing mood surprised him, considering how angry he'd been about Morgan earlier that day. He wondered if Fred was up to something. He certainly wouldn't put it past him.

Hawk went to his bunk to sit down and wait for the cook to bring in dinner. He noticed that some of his things had been moved from where he'd left them on the bed that morning and wondered who'd gone through his belongings. He had started to take inventory to make sure nothing was missing when he noticed something had been stowed under the blanket on his bunk.

Hawk was expecting trouble. But he wasn't expecting what he found when he pulled the blanket off the bed.

There, in the middle of his bunk, was a live rattlesnake, coiled and ready to strike.

Hawk reacted instantly. He jumped out of harm's way just as the rattler lashed out.

The snake missed and re-coiled on the bed, ready to strike again at him.

Hawk wasted no time. He drew his knife and threw it. His aim was perfect. The rattler was killed instantly, the knife pinning it to the mattress.

At first Fred and the other hands had laughed as they looked on. Fred had hoped the snake would take care of things for them. Now he looked shocked by how quickly Hawk had reacted.

"Who's responsible for this?" Wade demanded.

When the men saw their foreman's fury, the mood in the bunkhouse turned sober.

"We don't know," most of them mumbled.

"There's just no telling what kind of vermin you're going to find in this bunkhouse anymore, is there, boys?" Fred drawled sarcastically.

"Fred . . ." Wade turned on the known trouble-maker.

"It's all right, Wade. I'll handle this." Hawk walked slowly to his bunk. He pulled his knife out of the snake and wiped the blade clean on the sheet. After slipping his knife back in its sheath, he picked up the rattler and turned to Fred.

"I think this belongs to you." He threw the bloody snake directly at the other man.

"Why, you . . . !" Fred tried to dodge the rattler, but it hit him in the face. Furious, he launched himself at Hawk.

The two men crashed to the floor in a violent struggle. Chaos reined as the other ranch hands rushed to get out of their way. Many of the men ran outside and then dashed over to one of the windows to watch from relative safety.

The battle was a fierce one. Fred was a big, strong ox of a man, but he was ultimately no match for Hawk. Hawk's agility and pure strength gave him the advantage. Only Wade's interference stopped the fight.

"Enough!" Wade shouted as he grabbed Fred and hauled him away from Hawk. He shoved him out the bunkhouse door in disgust.

Fred sprawled in the dirt. Cursing and swearing, he charged to his feet, ready to continue the fight, but he found himself standing face-to-face with the boss.

"What's going on here?" Jack demanded angrily, staring at Fred's bloodied face and torn clothing. He'd been out at the stable when he'd heard the commotion.

"Nothing," Fred muttered, frustrated and angry that the boss had shown up.

"Like hell!" Wade said from where he was still standing in the doorway. He disappeared back inside for a minute, then came outside to join them, holding the dead snake. "This is what's been going on, boss. Fred put this rattler in Hawk's bunk— only it was alive when he did it."

"What did you think you were doing, Fred?" Jack turned to the hired hand. It wasn't the first time Fred had caused trouble, but it was going to be the last.

"I was just giving the half-breed a welcome present, that's all," Fred sneered, spitting blood from his cut and swollen lip.

"It's a damn good thing Hawk's fast with his knife." Wade tossed the dead snake aside in disgust. "Somebody could have gotten hurt bad."

Jack looked Hawk's way when he came to stand in the bunkhouse doorway. "Are you all right, Morgan?"

Hawk nodded.

Satisfied, Jack turned back to Fred. He pinned him with an icy glare. "You're fired."

"Fired?" Fred was shocked. Jack couldn't just fire him for a little prank.

"That's right. You know my rules. 'No fighting' is one of them."

"But the breed started the fight!"

"I don't think so."

"He threw the snake at me!"

"You're just lucky the rattler was dead when he threw it!"

"I was defending myself."

"I said, you're fired," Jack repeated in a cold voice that brooked no argument.

"But—"

"Get your things and get off the Lazy S. I want you out of here tonight. Stop by the house when you're leaving, and I'll see you get any wages I owe you."

Fred's fury and humiliation were obvious. He stalked off, never looking back.

Jack turned to the rest of the men who were watching. Though they hadn't said anything yet, he could tell they were shocked by what had just happened to Fred.

"Remember this," Jack lectured them. "You know my rules—there's no fighting, no gambling, and no drinking when you work for me. What you do in town on your days off is your business. What you do here on the ranch is mine. If you want to work here, you follow my rules. It's as simple as that. Any questions?"

The ranch hands knew better than to give Jack any trouble. He was a fair boss, but he was a hard man to deal with if you got on his bad side. They nodded in understanding and moved away, going back inside to wait for Wilda to bring their dinner. None of them went after Fred, and none of them spoke to Hawk.

Jack was troubled as he returned to the main house. He'd been worried that having Hawk around would cause unrest, and now it had. For a moment he considered firing Hawk, too, but decided against it. All that mattered was catching the rustlers, and according to Spiller, whose judgment he trusted completely, Hawk was the man for the job. He just hoped Spiller was right.

Jack went in his office and sat down at his desk. He'd been there only a few moments when someone knocked on the door.

"Who is it?"

"It's me, boss," Wade answered, letting himself in. He stood across the room, waiting to speak.

"What do you want?"

"Why did you fire Fred and not Hawk when they were both involved in the fight?" It wasn't often that he questioned his boss's decisions, but this time he had to, just to make sure he could keep things under control in the bunkhouse. Fred had friends, and they were bound to question Jack's decision.

"This isn't the first time Fred's caused trouble. I've had enough of it."

"But, boss—"

Jack fixed Wade with a serious look. "There's something I haven't told you. There's more to Hawk Morgan than you know."

"I don't understand."

"Hawk came to work here recommended by Sheriff Spiller up in Dry Springs."

"Yeah. So?"

"So, he's here to help me catch the rustlers."

"Hawk does that kind of work?" Wade was surprised by the news.

"That's right. I didn't tell you right off because I thought it would be best to keep this quiet. The fewer people who know the truth about him, the better. I haven't even told Randi yet."

"That changes everything." Wade was thoughtful.

"You can handle it with the boys?"

"I'll come up with something to keep them quiet."

"Good. I knew hiring him on might stir up some trouble, but all that matters to me right now is stopping the rustling. Hawk hasn't caused any problems, has he?"

"No, he's been working out just fine."

"Good. You let me know if anything else happens with the men, and if it does, I'll handle it."

Jack's mood was still dark and troubled after Wade left him. Times were difficult on the ranch.

The last thing he needed was his own men giving him a hard time.

Jack just hoped Spiller had been right about Hawk. The faster they caught the rustlers, the better.

Chapter Six

Wade returned to the bunkhouse to find most of the hands finishing off the dinner Wilda had finally brought out to them. He saw no sign of Hawk, but Fred was there at his bunk, packing up his things and getting ready to leave. Wade went over to talk to him.

"That was a damned stupid thing you did today," Wade said bluntly.

"You can go to hell!" Fred swore at him as he continued to stuff his few personal belongings into his saddlebags.

"I spoke with Jack. I tried to get him to change his mind about firing you, but he wouldn't."

Fred glared at Wade, his expression filled with hate. "Then I guess I'd better get out of here."

"I'll see you around," Wade said mildly as he left Fred to finish up.

When Wade had gone, Tom Andrews and Steve

Parker got up from the table and went to speak with Fred. They were furious about what had happened.

"He shouldn't have fired you," Tom said in disgust.

"What are you going to do?" Steve asked Fred.

Fred looked up at the two of them and smiled thinly. "The first thing I'm going to do is go into town and have myself a fine old time tonight."

"You deserve it," they said.

"You're damned right I do," Fred growled. "I'm not sure what I'll do tomorrow, but I have a few things to settle up around here before I move on."

Tom and Steve could tell by his cold expression and the barely controlled rage in his voice that there was going to be hell to pay somewhere down the line. Fred wasn't a man to forgive and forget; that much was for sure.

Fred picked up his bedroll and saddlebags and started from the bunkhouse. The two men walked out with him to get his horse.

"Don't worry, boys. You'll be hearing from me," Fred said once he'd mounted up.

"Good."

Fred's expression was grim as he rode toward the main house to pick up the last of his pay.

"It ain't gonna be the same without Fred around," Tom remarked, watching him go.

"I wonder what he meant when he said we'd be hearing from him?"

"I don't know, but I bet we find out soon enough."

* * *

Randi sat in her father's study, listening as he told her what had transpired down at the bunkhouse.

"The fight was ugly, and I fired Fred," he finished.

"You didn't fire Hawk?" she asked, surprised.

"No." His answer was terse.

"Why not?" Randi knew how strict her father was about making sure the ranch hands followed his rules.

Jack's expression grew even more serious as he faced his daughter. "There's something you don't know about Hawk."

"What?" Randi was puzzled by the strange way he was acting.

"You know Hawk was recommended to me by a friend up in Dry Springs. Well, that friend was Sheriff Spiller. I'd written to him and let him know how bad the rustling was, and he sent Hawk down here to help."

"Hawk's a lawman?" she asked, amazed by the news.

"No, but Hawk has worked regularly with Sheriff Spiller in the past. Whenever the sheriff needed help tracking down criminals, Hawk got the job done. At first I didn't want anyone to know why I'd hired him on, but now that's all changed. I had to tell Wade the truth, so he could figure out a way to keep peace in the bunkhouse. Since Wade knows, I figured I'd better tell you, too. Just don't spread it around. The fewer people who know what Hawk's here for, the better."

Randi had respected Hawk before, but now she

thought even more highly of him. "I won't say a word, Pa. I promise."

"Good."

They heard a knock at the front door, and Randi got up to go answer it. She opened the door to find Fred standing there.

"Where the hell is your old man?" Fred demanded crudely.

After what her father had just told her, Randi wasn't surprised by Fred's open hostility, but she was surprised by how battered he looked. If he looked this bad after the fight, she wondered how Hawk had fared.

"My pa's—" she started to answer him.

"Right here," Jack said sternly as he came out of his study to confront the troublemaker. "Randi, you go on."

Jack didn't want her anywhere around right now; there was no telling what Fred might say—or do.

Randi wanted to go out to the stable to look in on Angel, so she went outside, leaving her father to handle the angry ranch hand.

When she'd gone, Fred faced his ex-boss, his fury evident.

"You're making a big mistake firing me, Jack. You shouldn't be favoring that half-breed over me."

"You know the rules, and you knew what would happen if you broke them."

The ranch hand was seething. "You'll be sorry for this." The threat in his words was plain.

Jack pinned him with an unwavering regard. "No. I won't. Here's your money."

Fred didn't hesitate. He snatched the cash from Jack's hand.

"Now ride on out of here and stay off the Lazy S," Jack ordered. "I don't want to see you around anymore."

"Go to hell, Stockton!"

Fred stalked out of the house, slamming the door behind him as he left.

Jack Stockton's day was coming.

He was going to see to it.

Randi was on her way to the stable when she rounded the corner of the building to find Hawk washing up at the watering trough. Almost as if he sensed her presence, Hawk stopped what he was doing and glanced her way. It was then that she saw the cut above his eye and a bruise forming along his jawline.

"Are you all right?" she asked worriedly. "I heard about the fight. Do you need anything?"

"No, I'll be fine," he answered.

"If it's any consolation to you, Fred looks a lot worse."

"Good." He managed just a slight grin at the news.

"I'm glad, too. Pa told me what happened. I'm sorry about the rattlesnake. I know the hands can get rowdy sometimes, but—"

"It's all right. I'm used to it."

"You are? But the snake could have struck you."

Hawk shrugged. "It's always been this way for me. I've come to expect it."

"Well, you don't have to worry about Fred anymore. He's gone now."

"That's good to know." Hawk would have liked to believe that Randi was right, but he'd run into men like Fred before. He knew what they were capable of, so he wasn't about to let his guard down yet. "I'd better get on back to the bunkhouse."

Hawk started to turn away.

"Wait!" Randi closed the distance between them and took the towel he'd been using out of his hand. "You're still bleeding."

She pressed the towel to the cut on his forehead and held it there to stanch the bleeding. Randi gazed up at Hawk as she ministered to him. She noticed how his jaw was set, and to her that was a sure sign he was in pain. She wished there were some way she could make things better for him.

Hawk's jaw was set, all right, but it wasn't because of the pain. His jaw was locked because he was fighting for his self-control. The gentleness of Randi's touch deeply disturbed him. He was far too aware of her very nearness for his own good. No other female had affected him this way since Jessie, and his reaction to her troubled him. He didn't want to be attracted to anyone. He didn't want to care about Randi. There could be no future for them.

Hawk deliberately forced his gaze away from her to stare off into the distance, but a moment of weakness overcame him and he looked back and let his gaze drop to the sweetness of her lips. He found himself wondering what it would be like to take her in his arms and kiss her. Heat stirred within him at the thought, putting his willpower to the test. Hawk knew he had to get away from Randi—now. Abruptly, he reached up and took the towel out of her hand.

"Thanks. It'll be all right."

"If you're sure . . ."

"I'm sure." Hawk strode quickly away from her without looking back. The feelings Randi stirred within him were far too dangerous for his peace of mind.

He had to keep his distance from her.

He was on the Lazy S to catch rustlers.

That was all.

Fred wasted no time riding into San Miguel. He headed straight for the Silver Dollar Saloon. He was planning to get good and drunk, and then he was going to figure out a way to get even with his former boss.

"Evening, Fred," Denny Magrane, the bartender, welcomed him. "What are you doing in town? I didn't expect to see you until the weekend, Friday being payday and all."

Fred ignored his small talk as he went to stand at the bar. "Give me a double."

Denny knew from the tone of Fred's voice that something was wrong—very wrong. He quickly set a glass before him and poured him a healthy dose of whiskey.

"Thanks." Fred lifted the glass and took a hearty drink. He sighed out loud when he finally put the empty tumbler back on the bar. "That's better."

"So what brings you to town?"

"Stockton fired me—the bastard," he snarled, lifting his glass to Denny for a refill before taking another deep swig of the potent liquor.

Denny was surprised. "You've been working at the Lazy S for a long time. What happened?"

"A new man Jack hired on—some half-breed—picked a fight with me, and I'm the one he fired."

Denny knew Trey Roberts, the saloon owner, would want to hear this news right away. "Well, it may not be all bad news. Maybe you got better things coming your way."

Fred snorted in derision and emptied the glass again. He pushed it toward Denny for another refill. As the barkeep started to oblige, Fred stopped him.

"I tell you what—just give me the whole damned bottle," he told him.

Denny passed it over. Fred took his glass and the half-full bottle with him and went to sit at one of the more isolated tables near the back of the saloon. He wanted to drown his sorrows in peace.

When he could get away from the bar without drawing any attention to himself, Denny hurried to Trey's office to tell him what he'd learned.

"What is it?" Trey called out, responding to the knock on his closed office door.

"It's Denny. It's important."

"Just a minute."

Denny could hear some shuffling going on inside the office while he waited for Trey to bid him to enter. When his boss finally told him to come in, he opened the door to find Annie, one of the saloon girls, on her way out. Her hair was loose around her shoulders, and her clothing was a bit wrinkled. Denny didn't say a word, but it wasn't hard for him to figure out what he'd interrupted.

"What's so important?" Trey demanded when Annie had closed the door behind her.

Denny quickly related what he'd learned from Fred. He wasn't surprised when Trey cursed the ranch hand soundly.

"How stupid is he?" Trey demanded angrily.

"You know how stupid he is," Denny answered.

"You're right," Trey grumbled. "I do know." Fred was a compulsive gambler. The saloon owner had extended credit to him because up until now, he had always paid his debts on time. "I think Fred and I need to have a talk."

"I thought you might want to see him. That's why I came to get you."

Trey got up, ready to confront the ranch hand. He went out into the saloon and spotted Fred at the table. He was glad business was slow tonight. What he had to say to the fool wouldn't be pretty.

Fred had been sitting in silence, drinking heavily

as he mulled over what to do next. He looked up when he noticed someone walking his way. He wasn't pleased to find it was the saloon owner, but he knew there was no way to avoid him.

"Hello, Trey."

"What's this I hear about you losing your job out at the Lazy S?" Trey didn't wait to be invited; he just sat down across the table.

Fred quickly told him what had happened. "And that's why the bastard fired me," he finished.

"You should have realized what was going to happen before you got in the damned fight!"

"What the hell is Jack doing hiring on a half-breed?"

"Who cares? You owe me a lot of money, and I expect you to pay me back!" Trey looked him straight in the eye. "Do I make myself clear?"

A chill went down Fred's spine at those words. It was true that he'd racked up a large debt gambling, but Trey had gone easy on him—until now. "Yeah, yeah."

Trey leaned forward, piercing him with an even colder and more deadly look. "My money means a lot to me. I'm sure you know that. I don't abide those who don't pay up."

"It's all Stockton's fault! I hate that bastard!" Fred's fury erupted.

"I don't care whose fault it is, and I don't care if you hate him. I only care about my money. Find a way to get what you owe me. I'll be waiting to hear from you, and it had better be soon—real soon."

Fred knew what kind of man Trey was, and he knew better than to mess with him. "You'll get your money."

"See to it." Trey got up and walked away.

Fred poured himself another stiff drink, although he doubted it would do much to improve his mood now. He had to find a way to pay Trey back—and fast.

"Looks like you and Trey were arguing pretty good," purred the raven-haired, red-lipped, voluptuous Sindy as she drew up a chair and sat down close beside Fred at the table. She put her hand high up on his thigh and smiled as she leaned invitingly toward him. "You look worried. You got trouble?"

She pretended to be innocent of his dilemma, even though the barkeep had already told her what was going on.

"Nothing that spending a few hours with you won't help," he said, heat pulsing through him as she leaned in even closer to give him a better view of her ample cleavage. He'd enjoyed having her in the past and saw no reason not to indulge himself again. She would take his mind off Trey for a while, and the prospect appealed to him.

"Let's go upstairs," she invited.

"I'd like that."

Fred groped her generous curves as they left the table and headed to the privacy of her room. He was going to make sure she earned her pay.

And Sindy did.

Sober, Fred was not the most elegant of customers, and drunk, he was even worse. Most of the time Sindy enjoyed her work, but men like Fred were rough and hard to please. Business was slow tonight, so she had to make do with whomever she could get—and right now that was Fred.

Sindy suffered Fred's pawing touch as he quickly stripped away her clothing as soon as they reached the privacy of her room. When she was naked, Fred undressed and then wasted no time tossing her on the bed and taking his pleasure of her. Only when he'd finally collapsed on top of her did she breathe a sigh of relief.

Fred rolled off Sindy, smiling drunkenly. "You're good, darling. Real good."

"Thanks," she said, hoping to sound coy. "You sure were fast tonight."

"I needed it—things are going bad for me right now." He told her what had happened.

"Did you really put a rattler in his bunk?" She was shocked, even though she knew she shouldn't have been. These cowboys were a rough and rowdy lot, and Fred was worse than most of them.

"I sure did."

She shuddered.

"I'm going to get even with Jack Stockton. You just wait and see," he vowed in a deadly tone.

"But how? What are you going to do? You owe Trey a lot of money, and you know how he is about getting paid back."

"I'll find a way. Don't you worry about that."

"Any hope of getting your job back?"

"Hell, no, and I wouldn't work for Jack again anyway. I hate the bastard."

Sindy rolled over on her stomach and lifted herself up on her elbows to stare down at him. "You know the Lazy S real well. Does Stockton keep a lot of cash on hand? You could break into the house and rob him."

Fred smiled at the thought of finding a way to get money out of Jack. He could pay off Trey and then leave town with his pockets full. "I like the way you think, woman, but Jack doesn't keep a lot of cash around. He's too smart for that."

"Then what does he care about?"

"The ranch, mostly, and his daughter." At the thought of Randi, Fred's expression changed. "Now, that might be something. . . ."

"What?"

"His daughter, Randi. Since his wife died a few years ago, she's all he's got left."

Sindy was suddenly becoming worried about what Fred might do. She didn't really know Randi Stockton, but she had seen the young woman around town every now and then. Sindy didn't like the thought that Fred might hurt her somehow. It was one thing to steal money, quite another to harm an innocent girl.

"It wouldn't be smart to mess with his family," Sindy cautioned him.

"What do you know about being smart?" Fred sneered, ignoring her completely. He quickly got up and started to dress. She'd given him a good idea, and he knew what he was going to do. All he had to figure out was how to pull it off.

Sindy was insulted. "At least I'm smart enough to know better than to take on Jack Stockton."

"You just said I should rob him!"

"That's only money. You're talking family now. You'd better be careful, Fred."

"Don't worry. I will be." He finished buttoning his shirt and took some money out of his pants pocket. "You keep your mouth shut about what we just talked about. You hear me?"

"I hear you."

Satisfied that he'd scared her enough to keep her quiet, he tossed the cash he owed her on the nightstand and left the room. He had some serious planning to do.

Chapter Seven

Hawk went to work as a regular ranch hand. The other men told him about the rustling and showed him where some of the missing cattle had been run off. Hawk looked the area over, but found nothing. Too much time had passed. He kept watch as he did his job, hoping for a lead.

The days passed quickly, and soon it was almost time for the Stampede.

It was late one afternoon, and Randi was ready to put Angel to the test. Hawk was there with her as she led the mare out of her stall.

"Do you think she's healthy enough to make the run?" Randi asked him. She trusted his judgment about Angel's leg.

"She's fully healed," Hawk answered, glad Angel had made such good progress in the little over a week since she'd injured herself. He'd checked on her daily and done all he could to nurse her along.

"All right. Let's see just how fast we are," Randi said, still feeling a little nervous.

This was the moment she'd been waiting for. This was the moment she would find out whether she had any chance of winning the Stampede again.

She saddled Angel and walked her out of the stable.

Hawk followed Randi outside to watch.

Randi didn't say a word, but swung up into the saddle and rode slowly over to where Wade and several of the other men were waiting for her. Wade was holding a handkerchief to use as a mock starting flag, and he had his pocket watch in hand to check their time.

"Are you ready?" Wade asked.

"I'm as ready as I'll ever be," Randi answered, her expression serious. "Let's just hope Angel is."

She concentrated on what she had to do, ignoring all the ranch hands who'd gathered around to watch and cheer her on. It didn't matter that she had an audience. All that mattered was running the course she'd laid out for herself in winning time. The Stampede was only two days away. She could delay no longer. She'd let Angel rest up and heal, and now the time had come to find out if she could still compete.

Randi leaned forward and stroked Angel's neck, saying a few soft, soothing words meant for her and her alone. Then she looked up.

"All right, Wade. We're all set."

Wade didn't need any further invitation. He dropped the flag.

Randi reacted instantly. She put her heels to Angel's sides, and they raced off at top speed. They charged toward the far end of the corral and then circled around the back of the stable and the main house. Randi had charted the path carefully. She'd made sure it was as close to the same length and difficulty as the real race would be in town. Leaning low over Angel's neck, she urged the mare on.

As always when she and Angel were moving this fast, Randi felt as if they were flying. The moment was heavenly, and she was smiling in delight when they finally raced to a stop before Wade.

"How did we do?" she asked breathlessly, believing they'd made good time.

Wade glanced down at the watch. When he looked up at her, his expression was troubled. He gave a slow shake of his head before answering, "Not good."

Randi felt heartbroken. She suddenly feared Angel would never be the same, and she knew it was all her fault. "How far off our old time are we?"

Wade tried to keep from grinning as he answered, "You're ten seconds under your best time for last year."

"What?" Randi was shocked, and then immediately burst into relieved laughter. "Why, you . . . !"

Wade and the other hands laughed with her.

"I thought Angel felt good. She hit her stride."

"That she did."

"I guess I know who I'm betting on come Saturday!" Rob called out.

"That's right!" the other men all agreed.

"It looks like we're going to have to save back even more of our drinking money for betting on you!" another hand added.

The men went on back to the bunkhouse to relax, leaving Randi with Wade and Hawk.

"I don't think there's anyone out there who can beat you," Wade told her with confidence, remembering how easily she'd won the race the year before.

"Oh, I don't know," Randi said, looking at Hawk. There was a gleam in her eyes as she remembered their first encounter. "Bruiser's a pretty fast horse. If Hawk enters, I'm going to have to warn the boys about their bets. Bruiser would be a tough one to beat."

"You don't have to worry. I'm not going to enter the race," Hawk answered. He would be going to San Miguel for the Stampede, but only to investigate the rustlers.

"Why not?" Randi was surprised. "Are you afraid Angel and I would beat you?"

"Very funny," Hawk said, smiling in spite of himself.

"The Stampede is quite a celebration," Wade added.

"Have you ever been to one?" she asked Hawk.

"No."

"Then this will be your first," she stated with

conviction. "There's a social on Friday evening. The race and a shooting competition are held during the day on Saturday, and then the big dance is that night."

"It's definitely a good time," Wade told him. "Especially since it's payday."

"I guess I'd better show up. I can't miss Angel's big race."

"That's right. She's expecting you to be there," Randi said, but she realized that she was the one who really wanted Hawk there.

The thought surprised Randi, although she knew it shouldn't have. These past few days she hadn't seen much of Hawk. She knew her father wouldn't be pleased, but she'd actually found herself looking for him. When he'd ridden in with Wade a short time before, she'd been delighted. She had sought him out, for she'd wanted his opinion on the condition of Angel's leg before taking her mare out for the test run.

"When does everybody go into town?" Hawk asked.

"The boss will pay us Thursday night, so most of the boys will head in as soon as we get done working Friday. We have to be there to cheer for Randi and Angel. They're the pride and joy of the Lazy S," Wade said.

"Let's just hope we live up to your high expectations."

"You've never let us down before," Wade said with confidence. "You're going to do just fine."

"We're going to find out real soon; that's for sure."

Randi led Angel back into the stable, leaving the two men outside.

"It's good that we're going to town. You never know what we might be able to find out while we're there," Hawk said thoughtfully.

"That's right. Talk is cheap down at the saloon when all the hands get liquored up. Since it's payday, there will be some serious drinking going on."

"I'll be ready to ride whenever you are."

"I'll check with the boss and find out if there's anything else we need to get done before we go. No matter what, we'll be there in time for Randi's big race."

"You're right. We can't miss that."

Pat Walker was unusually excited about the weekend ahead as she drove her buckboard into San Miguel. She'd left her trustworthy foreman, Ken Gilbert, in charge back at the ranch, and for the first time in ages she was off to be with her friends again. Pat realized she might even have some fun—if she could remember what fun was after dealing with all the trouble she'd been having on the ranch. Of course, Wade was going to be there this weekend, too, so she had the pleasure of his company to look forward to.

The prospect of being with Wade and enjoying herself brightened Pat's spirits as she reined the buckboard to a stop in front of her friend Jeannie

Stewart's home. Jeannie had invited her to stay the night, and she was glad.

"It's about time you got here!" Jeannie called, hurrying out on her front porch to welcome Pat when she saw her drive up. She'd been watching for Pat and was eagerly looking forward to spending the weekend with her longtime friend.

Pat climbed down from the buckboard, and, after tying up the horse, she went to give Jeannie a warm hug. "It's so good to see you. We are going to have so much fun this weekend."

"Yes, we are," Jeannie agreed. "I've been baking all morning for the social tonight."

"Need some help?"

"Of course, I was counting on you! I told the ladies who are running the social that we'd help them box up the dinners for tonight's auction. I love it when the bidding starts. It's always so exciting to see who buys the dinners."

"And this is a payday weekend for the ranch hands. The social should bring in a lot of money."

They laughed, remembering how heated the bidding could get sometimes. Pat was smiling as she got her bag out of the buckboard and followed Jeannie inside.

It was midday when Jack and Randi reached San Miguel. Jack had driven them into town in their carriage with Angel tied to the back. While Jack went to see about checking them into the hotel, Randi drove over to the livery to leave the horse and carriage and to take care of Angel. She wanted to get her settled in.

Tomorrow was her big day. Randi could hardly wait.

She was excited, too, about seeing her friend Sherri Sadowski. It had been more than a month since their last visit, and that had been just a quick conversation after church services one Sunday morning. This weekend they would have plenty of time to catch up on all the latest news and gossip.

After making sure Angel was fine, she started back to the hotel. On the way, Randi stopped by Sherri's father's general store to see if her friend was there working.

"You're here!" Randi said in delight when she found her friend behind the counter.

"Where else would I be?" Sherri teased. "I'm glad you got here early." She looked quickly around, noticed there were a few customers in the store, and then added in a quiet voice, "There's so much I have to tell you!"

"What do you have to tell me?" Randi was surprised and intrigued by Sherri's tone.

"I can't talk about it now. I'll tell you later. Do you want to meet and go to the social together tonight?"

"Yes, why don't you come by the hotel and get me when you're on your way?"

"Fine. The social starts at six o'clock, so let's meet in the lobby about quarter 'til."

"That's perfect. I can't wait to see everyone."

"Me too," Sherri agreed.

Randi was curious. She didn't know what had her friend so excited, but she knew she'd be finding out soon. "How dressed up are you getting for tonight?"

"Very!" Sherri had her reasons, but she couldn't tell Randi about them yet.

"I guess I'd better go back to the hotel and start getting ready."

"That's right. We want to give the boys their money's worth."

The social followed the same format every year. The ladies in town prepared box dinners for the occasion, and each single girl at the social was assigned one of the dinners. When each dinner was auctioned off, the girl had to dine with the one who'd bought it. The funds all went to the church.

The auction was always fun, although there had been a few times when some of the cowboys had gotten good and drunk and made a spectacle of themselves bidding on a certain girl. It had happened to Randi once. Her father had had to step in and outbid everyone to save her from the humiliation of dining with a drunk.

Randi wondered if Hawk would show up tonight—and if he did show up, she wondered if he would bid on her. Deep in her heart, she hoped he would.

"That's right. We have to look good so all the men will bid on us," Sherri said. "I'm just glad I go before you, so they'll still have money left to bid on me!"

"I'll see you in a little while. I have some serious dressing up to do."

"Do you think we'll recognize each other tonight after we get all gussied up?"

"Of course," Randi answered. "We're always lovely. We're just going to be even lovelier than usual tonight."

"I like the way you think!"

Her mood was light as Randi left the store to return to the hotel. She'd brought a pretty gown with her, and she wanted to make sure she looked her best. She had just enough time to get ready for the evening to come.

Jack was meeting with Wade and Hawk up in his hotel room.

"Just remember to pay attention to what's going on while you're here in town," Jack told them.

"Wade and I already talked about it," Hawk assured him.

"Good. Whoever the rustlers are, they're going to slip up sometime, and when they do, we're going to be ready for them." He was disgusted by his inability to catch the thieves so far. "One other thing, Hawk—watch out for Fred. I don't know if he's still in town or not. As angry as he was when he left the ranch, he could still mean trouble for you."

"I'll tell the rest of the boys, too," Wade said as they started from the hotel room, although the foreman knew most of them wouldn't care if Fred wanted to cause trouble for Hawk.

"I'll see you at the social," Jack called as they left his room.

"Are you going to the social?" Hawk asked Wade.

"I wouldn't miss it. It's a dinner auction. We bid on the dinner we want, and each dinner comes with a lady—of course, we know who the lady is before we start." He grinned. "Then whoever bids the highest gets to have supper with her."

"Randi mentioned it, but I didn't know it was an auction. Is she one of the ladies being auctioned off?"

"Oh, yeah. She's done it for about three years now, and she usually does real good. A year or so ago, though, a cowboy got drunked up and bid real high for her. Jack got worried and stepped in with the biggest bid for a dinner ever. Randi ended up having to eat with her pa that year. She still gets teased about that. You're going tonight, aren't you?" Wade asked.

"I hadn't thought about it."

"Start thinking about it. We can show up together," he said, making the decision for Hawk.

"All right."

"Meet me here at the hotel about five thirty."

"I'll see you then."

Chapter Eight

"Randi?" Jack knocked on her hotel room door. "Are you ready to go downstairs to meet Sherri yet?"

"Just about, Pa," Randi called out.

Sitting at the small dressing table, she put the finishing touches on her hair, then stood up to take a critical look at herself in the mirror. Randi smiled at her reflection, impressed by the changes a pretty gown and different hairstyle could make in her appearance. She actually looked like a lady. She hurried to the door before her father got too impatient.

"I'm ready."

"It's about time," Jack said as the door opened. "Well, sweetheart, you were worth the wait."

Randi was a vision as she stepped out of her room. The emerald-colored gown she wore emphasized the color of her eyes and fit her perfectly. With her hair done up in a sophisticated style, she no longer looked like his little girl, Jack realized. His daughter was a woman, and a very beautiful one at that.

"You look lovely."

"Why, thank you," she told him with a smile.

"Your mother would be proud of you."

"What about my father?" she teased.

"I'm always proud of you."

"Let's just hope I don't embarrass the family name tonight at the auction." She laughed.

"When has that ever happened?" he countered, laughing, too. "Besides, as pretty as you look, I'll bet you bring in the highest bid."

They found Sherri waiting for them in the lobby with her parents, Jim and Rosie. The families were longtime friends.

"This is a pleasant surprise," Jack greeted them.

"When Sherri told us she was meeting Randi, we decided to come along with her," Jim told him.

"It's good to see you."

"Don't the girls look pretty?" Rosie said, watching Randi and Sherri walk on ahead of them as they left the hotel.

"They're lovely, but there's no one as beautiful as you," Jim told her.

Rosie laughed at her husband's charming ways, and they followed their daughter outside.

Up ahead, Randi was asking eagerly, "So what did you have to tell me that was so important?"

"Well . . ." Sherri took a quick look around to make sure their parents weren't close enough behind them to overhear. "There's someone new in town."

"So?"

"So—he's the handsomest man I've ever seen! He's got black hair and hazel eyes." She sighed. Her expression turned dreamy as she thought of him.

"Who is he? I haven't heard Pa talking about anybody new."

"His name is Andy Karandzieff. He came here from St. Louis about three weeks ago."

"What's he doing in San Miguel?"

"He's opened up a confectionery called Crown Candy Kitchen. He makes and sells the most delicious candy."

"So you're sweet on him, are you?" Randi said with a smile.

"Yes, I am," she confided.

"Are you sure it's not his candy you're after?" Randi teased.

"Oh, Randi!" Sherri laughed with her friend. "He's just real . . . nice, that's all."

"So you've had the chance to get to know him already?"

"I've spoken to him a few times at church, and he serves lunch at the confectionery, too, so my parents and I all went there to eat one day last week. He's so charming. He's nothing like all the cowboys we get around here. He's a . . . ."

"A gentleman?" Randi finished for her.

"Exactly," she said with a sigh. "A very handsome gentleman."

"Maybe he'll bid on your dinner tonight."

"I hope so. That's my dream, anyway."

"Who won the bidding on you last year?"

"Jed Thompson, but he's moved on. I really haven't been seeing anyone lately. All I've been doing is thinking about Andy."

"Does your Andy know about tonight?"

"He's not 'my' Andy."

"Not yet," Randi said, and they shared a conspiratorial smile.

"Well, I did make it a point to mention the social to him when I saw him last. I didn't say too much, though, because I didn't want it to look like I was begging him to show up."

"It's a church fund-raiser. Pray on it."

"I already have!" Sherri grinned. "What about you? Who do you want to bid on you tonight?"

"Oh, I don't know."

"What do you mean, you don't know?" Sherri asked astutely. She knew her girlfriend very well and could tell when she had something on her mind.

"My pa hired on a new hand last week, and there's something about him . . ."

"What?" Sherri urged, immediately curious about this new man.

"He's different from all the other men."

"How is he different?" Sherri was puzzled. She'd never heard her friend talk this way about a ranch hand before.

Randi knew she might as well tell Sherri the

truth and get it over with. "His name is Hawk Morgan, and he's a half-breed."

Sherri was stunned. "Your father hired a—"

"That's right," Randi interrupted. She didn't want to hear any remarks about Hawk's Indian blood. "Hawk came highly recommended from a friend of Pa's in Dry Springs." She went on to tell Sherri the same version of their first encounter she'd told her father.

"But, Randi, how is he ever going to fit in? You know the way people feel about Indians around here."

"There was some trouble at the ranch," Randi admitted. "Fred Carter picked a fight with Hawk."

Sherri wasn't surprised. She'd heard bad things about Fred before. "What happened?"

Randi told her about the snake. "Pa managed to break up the fight pretty fast; then he fired Fred for starting it."

"I have to ask—who was winning when he broke it up?"

"Hawk, definitely," Randi said with confidence.

"Point him out to me if he shows up. I want to see what this Hawk looks like. He must be special for you to feel this way about him."

"I will, and I want you to show me your Andy, too."

"Don't worry. I'll make sure you get a look at him. Just don't be too obvious about it, all right?" Sherri knew how open Randi could be about things sometimes.

"I'll try to behave myself."

Sherri laughed. "That'll be a first."

Randi laughed, too. They both knew the night ahead was going to be an adventure.

When they arrived at the large, open-sided tent that had been set up to house the dinner auction, Jack, Jim, and Rosie went to join the crowd that was already gathering, waiting to be seated. The girls went in search of Mrs. Washburn, the lady in charge.

Inside the tent, women from the church were busy putting the finishing touches on everything. There was a platform set up in front, and chairs had been arranged inside the tent for seating during the bidding. Tables and chairs were located on the grounds surrounding the tent for the winning couples to enjoy their meals.

"Hello, dears," Mrs. Washburn welcomed them warmly when she saw them coming her way. "This is going to be an exciting night. We have so many wonderful dinners—and so many beautiful girls!"

"We're looking forward to it," Sherri assured her. "Is there anything you need help with?"

"No, we'll be ready to start very shortly. The other girls are waiting out back, if you want to join them."

Sherri and Randi sought out the other girls. In all, there were twelve young ladies who were willing to be auctioned off for the sake of the benefit.

When Mrs. Washburn had finally finished with

her duties and came to get them, she was a bit troubled.

"Oh, my," the elderly woman said with a frown. "Do you know of any other ladies around town who would be willing to help us? We've got twenty dinners boxed up for the sale. Who else could we get?"

Regular meals were served at the social, too. Those who didn't want to get involved in the bidding could purchase dinner at a reasonable price and still be a part of the festivities. The auction of the box dinners, though, had always been an exciting occasion for the town and a great fund-raiser for the church.

"I know!" one girl called out to Mrs. Washburn. "I'll go get my Granny! Everybody loves Granny Dawson!"

"That's a wonderful idea!" Mrs. Washburn agreed. Granny Dawson was a fixture in the community. Everyone thought highly of the opinionated widow.

"If I know my granny, she'll probably bring in the most money!" the girl said with a giggle as she hurried off to find her.

"What about Pat Walker?" Randi offered, knowing their neighbor was going to be in town for the festivities, too.

"I'm not sure. . . ." Mrs. Washburn hesitated. They'd never had a young widow participate before.

"You can ask her. The worst that could happen is that she'd say no," Sherri put in.

"That's true. All right, I'll send someone out to see if she can be found. We've still got a few minutes left before we have to get started."

Several of the other girls suggested additional ladies, and soon they were officially ready to begin.

The tent was opened to the crowd, and it didn't take long for every seat to be taken. Most of those in attendance were high-spirited ranch hands who'd just gotten paid and were anxiously looking forward to the auction. They thought buying dinner with a pretty girl was a good investment of their hard-earned wages.

Wade and Hawk had been waiting with the others to gain entry, and they took seats near the back.

"Think everybody's a little excited?" Wade asked with a grin.

"Is it always this way?"

"Oh, yeah. You haven't seen anything yet. Wait until the bidding gets going."

The crowd was loud and boisterous. Some of the cowboys shouted out their impatience for the auction to start.

"Sherri! Hawk's here!" Randi confided excitedly to her friend as they stood in back waiting for the official opening of the auction.

"Where?"

"He's sitting with Wade. What about your Andy? Has he shown up?"

"No. I haven't seen any sign of him yet." Sherri was disappointed as she looked out over the crowd. She was able to get a glimpse of the man named

Hawk, and she understood why her friend was attracted to him. He was a handsome man—in spite of his Indian blood. The moment she thought it, she scolded herself for her prejudice. If Randi cared about him, then Hawk was special.

Mrs. Washburn appeared at the head table just then, and a respectful silence quickly descended over the crowd.

"Good evening, ladies and gentlemen," she welcomed everyone. "It's our delight to have you here tonight. I know how hungry you must be."

A roar went up from the men.

"We are ready to begin the auction. As you know, all funds raised will go to the church. As you know, too, gentlemen, we expect you to be on your best behavior with our ladies this evening."

"Yes, ma'am!" one cowboy yelled to her.

"Good." Mrs. Washburn smiled brightly at the excitement being generated by the crowd. Judging by how enthusiastic they sounded, it was going to be a very successful night. "Are you ready?"

"Yes!" they called out, applauding.

"Then let's get started!" She turned to the first young woman, a pretty blond who was offering herself up for bid. "We have here Miss Lara Brady, and she has a fried-chicken dinner to serve the lucky winner."

There were cheers and whistles from the men.

"Gentlemen, remember yourselves!" Mrs. Washburn scolded, but she was still grinning. "May I have your first bid?"

The bidding erupted, and soon the price of the meal had reached over ten dollars.

"Going once . . . going twice . . . sold to Ben Fletcher for ten dollars! Congratulations, Ben!"

The eager cowboy raced up front, money in hand to pay the lady who was taking the cash. Lara was looking quite delighted as Ben escorted her to a table outside the tent.

"Next, we have . . ."

The auction was conducted in alphabetical order, so Sherri and Randi knew they had a while to wait. They sat quietly behind the head table while the bidding continued.

Each girl was a bit nervous as her turn to be auctioned off came up. Though there had been occasions in the past when the bidding had been low, that didn't seem to be a problem this evening. The men were more than willing to pay for their dinners—and for the companionship of the lovely ladies.

Randi and Sherri were delighted when they saw Pat Walker coming to wait with them.

"You're going to do it?" Randi asked.

"It's for a good cause, and who knows? Someone might actually bid on me!" Pat laughed good-naturedly.

"I'm sure they will," Sherri assured her.

Sherri turned her attention back to the crowd, and it was then that she saw Andy walk into the seating area.

"There he is!" she whispered excitedly to Randi,

grabbing her arm. "Andy's the one who just came in. He's standing there in the back."

Randi spotted the tall, dark-haired man right away. "You're right; he is handsome. He probably didn't bother coming sooner because you're the only one he wants to bid on."

"I sure hope you're right." Sherri gave her a grateful look.

"Next," Mrs. Washburn announced, "we have lovely Miss Sherri Sadowski. Sherri—"

At her invitation, Sherri went to stand beside her. Cheers erupted from the crowd.

"Sherri's dinner is roast beef and all the fixins. Shall we open the bidding?"

"Two dollars!" one of the men shouted from the crowd.

"All right, we've got two dollars. Anyone else?" Mrs. Washburn asked, keeping the bidding open.

Sherri pasted a smile on her face as the amount slowly crept higher and higher. Even though the dollar amount being bid on her was respectable, she was heartbroken, for Andy had not bid even once. She'd been hoping the attraction she felt for him was mutual, but now she was beginning to believe it had just been her imagination. Sherri glanced Randi's way to see her friend giving her a reassuring look. She nodded back. It wasn't as if no one had bid on her. She girded herself for the rest of the bidding to come.

"We have a bid of twelve dollars!" Mrs. Washburn announced. "Going once . . . going—"

"I bid fifteen," Andy called out.

A murmur of surprise rumbled through the crowd as everyone turned to look at the newcomer who'd just bid.

"Fifteen!" Mrs. Washburn repeated happily. "Fifteen going once . . . fifteen going twice . . ."

The cowboys who had been bidding on Sherri were frustrated, but knew they couldn't match the other man's price.

"Sold for fifteen dollars to the gentleman in back. Sir, if you'll come forward, the cashier will take your payment and you can be on your way to dinner with your lovely lady," she directed.

Sherri's heart was beating a frenetic rhythm as she watched Andy come forward to claim her. Her prayer had been answered! She went to stand by the cashier, carrying their boxed dinner.

"Miss Sadowski." Andy nodded politely her way as he paid for the dinner and the pleasure of her company.

"Sherri, please," she encouraged, coming around the table to join him.

"Let me take that for you."

"Thanks." She handed over the dinner box.

"Are you ready?"

"Would you mind if we waited to see how the bidding goes for my friend Randi?"

"Not at all."

Andy led the way to the back of the tent again, and they stood together, looking on as Randi came forward. Sherri could tell Randi was a bit nervous.

Chapter Nine

"Our next lovely lady is Miranda Stockton, and her dinner is—" Mrs. Washburn started to introduce her.

"Five dollars!" a man shouted before Mrs. Washburn could even finish her announcement.

The elderly lady smiled at his eagerness, knowing his excitement boded well for the sale.

Randi, however, was shocked, for she instantly recognized the bidder's voice. It was Fred Carter!

Randi looked out into the crowd. Across the distance his gaze met hers, and a chill of revulsion shot through Randi at the smirking look upon his face.

At Fred's bid, Jack's expression turned stony, he was about to offer a bid for his daughter when another cowboy spoke up.

"Six dollars!"

Randi's moment of worry was eased by the other man's offer, but her relief didn't last long.

"Seven," Fred countered, still grinning. He didn't have a lot of money left from his final pay, but he hoped he had enough to cause Jack Stockton some grief. He wanted the rancher to worry about him spending the evening with his daughter. He didn't know if he could win the bidding or not, but even if he didn't, if he forced Stockton to bid for his own daughter's meal, he could at least hit him in the pocketbook, where it hurt. He knew his ex-boss would outbid him just to "save" his precious daughter from his company.

"Nine," Jack came back.

"Ten," Fred offered.

"Twelve," he countered.

A murmur went through the crowd again as they sensed the growing tension. If any of the other men had even hoped to win dinner with Randi, it was now out of the question. They couldn't even think about joining in the bidding. They made only twenty-five dollars a month, and that money had to last them until the next payday.

"Fifteen!" Fred returned, sensing the tension in the air and enjoying the feeling of power it gave him.

"Seventeen!" Jack didn't hesitate.

Fred was pushing his luck. He really had only twelve dollars left to his name. If Jack quit bidding against him and left him with the highest bid, he'd be in trouble, but he didn't think that would happen. Even if it did, though, it would be worth it. Owing the church ladies money wasn't nearly as bad as owing Trey. "Twenty!"

Hawk had remained quiet through the auction, but now his attention was all on Randi. He'd always known she was pretty, even from that first day when she'd turned on him with her gun in her hand, but tonight she was more than pretty—she was beautiful. Tonight she was a lady, and the thought that she might end up spending time with someone like Fred angered him.

Earlier when he'd come in with Wade, Hawk had noticed some of the townsfolk, watching him and whispering to one another. Their reaction to his presence hadn't surprised him. That was the way of his life. No one had said anything directly to him yet, but he suspected that was all about to change, because there was something he had to do, and he was going to do it. It didn't matter to him what the good people of San Miguel thought. All that mattered was keeping Randi safe.

Hawk called out his bid for Randi before Jack could counter Fred's last offer.

"Twenty-five dollars," he bid.

"What are you doing?" Wade asked him.

"I'm saving Randi—again," he answered, waiting to see what Fred would do next.

The murmur of shock and surprise Hawk had expected went through the crowd. Most were taken aback that a half-breed would dare to bid on a dinner with a white woman.

Jack, too, was startled by Hawk's offer for Randi. He'd expected to be the one who ended up winning dinner with her. He hadn't even considered that someone else might outbid him. He frowned slightly, waiting to see what was going to happen next.

Hawk was aware that he'd caused a stir, but he didn't care. He cared only about stopping Fred.

Randi was taken by surprise at Hawk's bid, too, but unlike her father, she was delighted. Having dinner with Hawk tonight had been her greatest hope. It looked like this social was going to turn out to be as wonderful for her as it had been for Sherri.

Hawk had hoped his high bid would force Fred out of the bidding, and it did.

"Going once for twenty-five dollars," Mrs. Washburn began, having waited for additional offers and gotten none. "Going twice . . . sold for twenty-five dollars! Congratulations, Miranda!"

Randi was smiling as she took the box containing her dinner and headed for the cashier.

"You want to eat with us?" Hawk invited Wade as he stood up to go claim his prize.

"No, I'm staying on here for a while. There's a little lady coming up I'm interested in bidding on."

"Good luck."

Hawk got up and glanced toward Jack. He saw that Jack was watching him, and he nodded to him in acknowledgment before making his way through the crowd to where Randi was waiting.

"That will be twenty-five dollars," the lady handling the money told him with a genuinely warm smile.

Hawk paid her.

"You're new in town, aren't you?"

"Yes, ma'am."

"This is Hawk Morgan. He works for us out at the Lazy S," Randi quickly introduced him.

"Nice to meet you, Mr. Morgan. Enjoy your dinner."

"We will," Randi answered for both of them; then she led the way to the special seating area for the auction winners.

"Do you mind if we eat with my friend Sherri?" Randi asked Hawk.

"Not at all."

They headed over to the table where Sherri and Andy had just seated themselves.

Jack watched Randi leave the tent with Hawk. He tried not to look too disturbed by the outcome of the auction, but it wasn't easy. The good news was, she wasn't with Fred, but he'd never thought she'd be spending the evening with Morgan.

"Jack!" one of the men sitting nearby called out.

Jack glanced his way.

"Are you going to let your daughter eat with the likes of *him*?"

Jack gave the man a benign smile. "Hawk Morgan works for me."

"But he's a—"

"He's a good man," he finished.

"If you say so . . ."

"I do." His tone brooked no argument or further discussion.

The man turned away to say something to those around him.

Jack ignored them. He didn't care what they had to say. He tried to concentrate on the good news that Fred had been beaten out in the bidding.

"Would you two like some company?" Randi asked Sherry and Andy when they reached their table.

"Of course," Sherri invited. "Andy, this is my friend Randi and—"

"Hawk Morgan," Hawk finished for her.

"It's nice to meet you," Andy told them.

"Well, the hard part is over," Randi said with a sigh as they sat down.

"The hard part?" Hawk asked.

"The auction," Sherri explained.

"It's always a bit scary, waiting to find out who's going to bid on you," Randi said.

"And there's always the fear that no one will!" Sherri laughed.

"Neither one of you ladies will ever have to worry about that," Andy assured them. "You both did very well tonight."

"Yes, but we still got beat," Sherri spoke up.

"You're right. Granny Dawson beat us both." Randi grinned. "Her top bid was thirty dollars."

"I don't think Granny Dawson really counts, though. Her son bought her dinner."

"I guess we did all right—unless somebody

bribed the two of you?" Randi gave both men questioning looks.

"No one had to bribe us," Andy quickly assured them. "It's worth every cent to enjoy the pleasure of your company. Right, Hawk?"

"That's right," he agreed.

"I like you already, Andy. You're not only handsome; you're charming, too," Randi teased; then she turned to Hawk and smiled. "You know, you saved me again tonight."

"I thought you never needed rescuing," he countered.

"I might have if Fred had won the bidding."

"The good news is, he didn't," Sherri said.

"Who's Fred?" Andy asked.

Randi quickly told Andy what had happened out at the ranch. "But enough about that. What about you? Sherri told me you just opened a confectionery in town. How did you end up here in San Miguel?"

"I was in St. Louis for a while, but after hearing all the talk about Texas, I decided this was the place I wanted to build my future."

"Well, we're glad you came," Sherri said, gazing at him across the table. "Just wait until you get the chance to try some of his candy," she told the other two. "It's delicious."

"Thank you."

"You don't need to thank me. It's the truth. Now, Hawk," Sherri went on. "You're new here, too. How did you end up working out at the Lazy S? And what's this about saving Randi 'again'? You mean tonight isn't the first time you've rescued her from the likes of Fred?"

Hawk told her how he'd moved on from Dry Springs after hearing that Jack was hiring for the Lazy S.

"And he saved me on his first day coming out to the ranch," Randi finished for him. "Angel had thrown a shoe, and he helped me get back to the house."

"You were lucky he came by," Andy added.

"Yes," Randi said. Her gaze met Hawk's, and she smiled at him. "I was."

Time seemed to be suspended for a moment as Hawk and Randi regarded each other across the table. Hawk wondered how he'd been lucky enough to end up here with her tonight.

As Randi gazed at Hawk, she remembered how he'd looked the first time she'd seen him and how she'd thought he was a warrior. The change in him tonight was dramatic, but though he looked like the other men who were in attendance at the social, she knew there was a part of Hawk that was very different from them. He was a man who would fight for what he wanted—and not be denied.

"Hawk . . . that's an odd name," Andy said thoughtfully.

"I'm half Comanche," Hawk said tightly.

"Really?" Andy had never met an Indian before, and he was curious about the other man's background. "I've read some dime novels about Indians and half-breeds. There was *Brand, The Half-Breed Scout*, and one about Buck McCade. Was your father Comanche or your mother?"

It took Hawk a moment to realize there was no guile or hatred in Andy's question. There was just honest interest. "My father was a trader. He met my mother when he came to the village, and eventually they married."

"Did you grow up there?"

"Yes, I stayed in the village with my mother while my father traveled."

"Wasn't it dangerous for you? When I lived in St. Louis, there were stories in the newspaper about Indian raids and all the fierce battles that were going on out West."

"There has definitely been fighting between the Comanche and the whites," Hawk said.

"That's for sure," Sherri added, thinking of the terrifying raids she'd heard about through the years.

"Did you ever go on any of the raids?"

"No, I left the village when I was still young, right after my mother died."

"What happened to her?" Randi asked.

"A fever took her. When my father returned from one of his trips and found out she was dead, he took me to live with his sister and her husband on their ranch."

"Did your father stay there with you?" she asked.

"No. He left me on the ranch while he continued to do his trading."

"That must have been hard for you. You were so young," Randi said sympathetically.

"I survived. My aunt and uncle did a lot for me."

"Where's your family now?" Randi asked, curious.

"They're dead."

"They all are?" she asked, surprised.

"Yes." He offered nothing more.

"I'm sorry."

"Did you ever get the chance to go back to your village?" Andy wondered out loud.

"My father took me for visits several times during those first few years. As I got older, I occasionally went on my own."

"Did you miss living there?" Sherri asked.

"I did at first. It was all I knew." Hawk didn't want to talk about those times either.

"Think how different your life would have been if you had stayed in the village," Andy said thoughtfully, then looked at him squarely, "You would have been a warrior now."

"Yes, I would have." When Hawk answered, he glanced Randi's way.

Their gazes met.

"Well, we're glad you're here with us," Andy said.

"We sure are," Randi agreed.

Chapter Ten

Pat Walker was feeling very self-conscious as she went up front for her turn in the auction. Luckily, she'd brought a suitable gown along with her. She knew she was dressed appropriately, but it was still a little unnerving for her, standing in front of so many people. She'd come out of mourning only a few months before.

"Our last lovely lady tonight is Pat Walker," Mrs. Washburn announced.

Pat stepped up beside her.

Mrs. Washburn quickly added the description of the dinner being auctioned off and then asked for bids.

Jack opened the bidding. He liked his neighbor and enjoyed her company.

Wade had been biding his time. Jack might be his boss, but Wade had no intention of letting him win the dinner with Pat. In the past months, he'd had the occasion to help her out on her ranch and to get to know her. Now that she was coming out of her time of mourning, he felt it was safe to try to court her. This church auction was the perfect place to start.

"Ten dollars," Wade offered.

Pat was startled when Wade made his bid, and she was even more surprised that his offer was so high.

In the audience, Jack glanced in Wade's direction. He, too, was taken by surprise at his foreman's bid. He hadn't realized that Wade had any personal interest in Pat. Smiling to himself, Jack dropped out of the bidding.

A few others made offers for Pat, but Wade didn't give up. He topped them all.

Mrs. Washburn finally concluded the sale. "Sold to Wade Mason for fourteen dollars! Thank you, ladies and gentlemen, for making tonight's auction such a success. For those of you who didn't win a meal with one of our lovely ladies, we're selling dinners in the church hall, so please join us there for a festive evening."

Wade strode up to pay for his forthcoming evening with Pat.

"Wade, thank you for buying my dinner," Pat said as he approached the cashier's table.

"It's my pleasure."

"Mine, too." She smiled up at him as he paid the church lady.

Wade took the basket containing their dinner

from her, and they made their way to an open table to enjoy their meal.

Jack was getting ready to leave the tent when he caught sight of Fred heading off in the direction of the Silver Dollar Saloon. He was glad to know the troublemaking ranch hand was out of the way. The night had turned out rather well, considering. Granted, he wasn't overly pleased that Hawk was dining with Randi. He would have preferred it if one of the nice, respectable young men from town had won the bidding, but there was nothing he could do about it now. Determined to enjoy the rest of the evening, Jack went to the church hall to purchase himself a dinner and join in the festivities.

"I really need to know . . ." Pat said to Wade as they ate their meal together. The food was delicious, and it was obvious from watching him that Wade was savoring every bite.

"What?" Wade asked in between mouthfuls.

"Was it me you were bidding on or were you only after the dinner?"

Wade grinned. "I have to admit I'm enjoying the food. I'd be lying if I said I wasn't, but I'm enjoying your company more."

Pat actually found herself blushing a bit at his open praise. She almost felt like a schoolgirl again. She asked, "How many years have you been working for Jack?"

"Over ten now. I've been his foreman for the last six."

"That's a lot of responsibility."

"Yes, it is, especially since the rustling started."

"The rustling . . . I'd almost forgotten about it for a little while."

"Sorry I brought it up."

"No, that's all right. We've got to find a way to stop it. We've got to figure out who's behind it all."

"Jack's doing everything he can. Are you holding up all right?"

The realities of the Bar W's troubles threatened to overwhelm her, and her anxiety showed in her expression. "I'm making it—barely."

"It's that bad?"

"It isn't good," Pat said with a sigh. "I've talked to the boys about the way things are going, and they've all agreed to stay on and keep working for me."

"They're good men."

"Yes, they are. They're very loyal. Al always tried to take care of them, and I'm doing the same."

"We'll catch the rustlers," Wade said, wanting to reassure her. "It's just a matter of time."

"The trouble is, time is the one thing I don't have a lot of. My money's tight—real tight."

"If it gets too bad, I'm sure Jack would help you out."

"Let's just hope it doesn't come to that," she answered with a strained smile. "Now, let's talk about something fun. Let's talk about the weekend. Are you going to compete in the big race tomorrow?"

"No, I'm leaving that to Randi."

"But your Raven is fast. You would do well."

"Raven can hold his own, but after timing Randi and Angel on their practice run the other day, I knew we'd be sitting this one out."

"So you're just going to watch?" She was surprised by his easygoing attitude. Al had always competed in the race no matter how slim his chances of winning.

"That's right—and I'll place a few bets on the side." He grinned. "Randi did all right by me last year, and I'm pretty sure she will again this year."

"I wouldn't be too confident," Pat cautioned with a smile. "Some of my hands are in the running, and they're good."

"They may be good, but I doubt they're any match for Randi and Angel."

"We'll find out tomorrow."

"Will you be at the dance tomorrow night?"

She smiled up at him. "Yes, and I hope I'll see you then."

After finishing his dinner in the church hall, Jack bade his friends good night and went looking for his daughter. He found her still seated with Hawk in the auction dining area, talking with Sherri and the new man in town who'd bid on Sherri's dinner.

"Evenin', Sherri," Jack greeted her as he came up to their table.

"Hello, Mr. Stockton," she replied respectfully. Even though she was grown-up now, he would always be Randi's father to her. "Have you met Andy yet?"

"No."

She introduced them, and Andy stood up to shake the older man's hand.

"It's a pleasure. Welcome to San Miguel," Jack said.

"It's good to be here."

Jack looked at his daughter. "Well, Randi, it's about time to call it an evening."

"Yes, Pa," Randi answered. "We've got a big day coming up tomorrow."

"That we do," Jack agreed.

"Thanks for buying my dinner, Hawk," she said, giving him a smile as she got up to leave with her father.

"You're welcome."

"We'll see you all in the morning," Jack said.

"Good night, Sherri, Andy—Hawk," Randi bade them as she looked Hawk's way one last time.

"Good night," Hawk said.

Hawk watched Randi walk away with her father. Conflicting emotions tore at him. A part of him had wanted the dinner to go on forever, and yet he knew there could never be anything between them. He told himself he'd come to San Miguel to find the rustlers, and he needed to concentrate on that—nothing else.

"Hawk, would you like to go over to the confectionery with us? I'm going to ask Sherri's parents if they'd like to have a second dessert tonight," Andy asked as Sherri stood up with him, ready to go.

"I appreciate the invitation, but I'm meeting some of the hands from the Lazy S."

"We'll see you tomorrow then," Andy told him as he and Sherri left to find her parents in the main hall.

Hawk got up to leave, too. He was heading for the Silver Dollar. Wade had told him it was the most popular saloon in town, especially on payday. He needed a lead.

"Let's stop by the stable. I want to make sure Angel's all right," Randi told her father on the way back to the hotel.

"Good idea. It can't hurt to check on her."

It was almost dark when they reached the livery. Dave Grant was keeping watch and greeted them when they came in.

"How did the social go?" Dave asked.

"From what the ladies were saying, I think it was a great success," Jack answered.

"You'll never guess who brought in the most money at the auction," Randi said.

"Who?" Dave asked.

"Granny Dawson!"

The stable hand good-naturedly laughed out loud. "That's a good one! Ol' Granny would be worth every cent a man paid for her, even without the food."

125

"That she would," Jack agreed.

"We wanted to check on Angel," Randi told him.

"She's in the last stall on the left," he directed.

It was dark toward the rear of the stable, so Randi lit a lantern before going on back. Jack stayed up front to talk with Dave.

"Hello, Angel," Randi murmured, rubbing her nose. "You ready for our big day?"

Angel whickered softly.

"That's what I thought. We'll show them again just how good you are. We're going to fly tomorrow, aren't we?"

After looking the horse over carefully, Randi returned to her father.

"Angel's all ready for the race," she told him with a smile.

"That's good to hear."

"Good luck tomorrow, Randi," Dave said.

"Thanks."

"We'll see you first thing in the morning," Jack said as they left for the hotel.

Hawk ran into Rob as he was leaving the social.

"Where you heading?" Rob asked.

"The Silver Dollar. Want to go?"

"Sure."

"What about Wade? Think he'll be joining us?"

Rob chuckled. "I don't know. Judging from the way he was looking at the widow woman while he was eating dinner with her, we might not be seeing him for a while. He'll know where to find us if he gets lonely."

The Silver Dollar was crowded. They made their way to the bar and ordered their drinks.

"You servin' him?" one drunk slurred, giving Hawk a hate-filled look.

The barkeep turned to the drunk. "He's got money; I'm serving him. If you don't like it, you can get out."

The drunk mumbled something unintelligible, then turned back to his drinking.

Rob looked around. He noticed Fred standing down at the far end of the bar.

"There's an empty table in back. Let's sit there," Rob said.

"Sure."

They settled in to enjoy themselves, speculating on whether Wade would ever show up. Several of the other hands joined them at the table, and eventually Wade came in. After getting himself a beer at the bar, he sat down with them.

"How was your date with the pretty widow?" Rob teased him. "You looked like you were enjoying yourself tonight."

"I was," he answered. "Why didn't you bid on any of the girls?"

"I'm saving my money to bet on the race tomorrow."

"Wise man. Randi's a sure thing. She's going to win, just like she did last year."

"That's what I'm thinking, too."

"What about you, Hawk? You betting on Randi?" Wade asked him.

"Angel is fast. There aren't many around who could take her."

"That's what we're counting on, and it won't be long now. In a little over twelve hours, we'll be right in the middle of all the excitement."

"And you boys do like your excitement, don't you?"

At the sound of Fred's voice, they all looked up to see him standing nearby.

"Evening, Fred," Wade greeted him.

"Wade." Fred pierced him with a hate-filled gaze. He had no use for anybody out at the Lazy S anymore, not even the foreman he'd once considered his friend. He glanced over toward Hawk and smiled thinly. "You may have won the bidding tonight, but we ain't done yet, *breed.*"

Hawk had been watching him carefully, waiting to see exactly what he would try. He was relieved when Fred just turned and walked out of the saloon.

"You'd better watch out for him," Rob warned Hawk.

"I know."

And he did know. He'd dealt with Fred's kind before. He knew how dangerous and deadly men like him could be.

"Good night, Pa," Randi said as she kissed her father's cheek and went into her hotel room.

"Night, little darling. I'll see you in the morning." Jack waited until she was safely inside with the door locked before going on to his own room.

Randi quickly undressed and donned her nightgown. She sat down at the dressing table and began to brush out her hair before retiring for the night.

She was excited about the day to come. The big race was scheduled for eleven o'clock, and she could hardly wait. She got up from the dressing table and laid out her riding clothes for the morning.

There would be no fancy dresses tomorrow. Tomorrow was all about winning.

Randi grinned. The ranch hands were counting on her. She couldn't let them down.

Randi was fairly confident she was going to win, since Hawk hadn't entered with Bruiser. One of these days, though, she wanted to challenge him to a race when Angel was fresh and rested. It would be interesting to see if she could beat him then.

Randi sought the comfort of the bed, but even though she was tired from the long day, sleep proved elusive. She tossed and turned. Memories of Hawk slipped into her thoughts—images of him looking like a warrior, charging out of nowhere to grab her off her horse, of her helping him at the watering trough after the fight with Fred, and of how it had been tonight, having dinner with him. The evening had turned out just as she and Sherri had hoped it would.

Sherri had been with "her" Andy.

And she had been with—

Randi had started to think "her" Hawk, and the realization startled her. She finally admitted to herself that what she felt for Hawk was different from the feelings she had for other men. She tried to tell herself he was just like all the other cowboys who worked for her father, but she knew he was different—he was special.

When Randi was still restless and unable to sleep an hour later, she finally gave up and got out of bed to go look out the window. Though the street was mostly deserted, in the distance she could hear the celebrating of the rowdy cowboys in town for the weekend. As she was standing there enjoying the coolness of the night's breeze, she saw a lone rider coming down the street.

Randi recognized Hawk right away. Since she was clad only in her nightgown, she slipped back behind the curtains to watch him as he passed by. She wondered where he was going at this time of night. Only when he had ridden completely out of sight did she return to her bed.

Randi had not seen the other man who'd been lurking drunkenly in the dark shadows of the night, looking up at her bedroom window, watching her and planning. . . .

Fred had his hand resting on his sidearm as he stood in the shadows, watching Hawk ride out of town. It would have been a simple thing to back-shoot him while there was no one around to witness the act, but he had better plans.

Fred had just started to turn away when he caught a glimpse of Randi standing partially behind the curtain in a hotel room window. He stared up her and smiled.

He knew what he wanted to do.

All he needed was the chance to pull it off.

Hawk bedded down near a stream a short distance out of town. It was a quiet, secluded site, and he was glad for the peace and solitude after all the time he'd spent in the crowded bar. He had lingered at the Silver Dollar for hours, but had heard nothing out of the ordinary.

As Hawk lay staring up at the star-studded night sky, thoughts of Randi stayed with him. He remembered how strong she'd been when she'd fought him like a wildcat. He remembered how gentle her touch had been when she'd tended to his injury after the fight with Fred. He remembered, too, how beautiful she'd looked that very evening when they'd eaten dinner together.

Randi was a lovely woman, but she wasn't for him.

Hawk knew that.

And yet he couldn't get her out of his mind.

He closed his eyes in an attempt to block her from his thoughts, but it didn't work. A vision of Randi still danced before him, tempting him, luring him.

He knew the danger of allowing himself to care about her, and he prided himself on being strong. It had been the only way he'd survived these last years. There could be no future for them. He would leave as soon as the rustlers had been caught.

Hawk rolled over in frustration.

It was going to be a long night.

And it was, for his dreams were filled with images of Jessie and Randi.

Chapter Eleven

Excitement was in the air as the time for the start of the race drew near. The Stampede was a big celebration. Crowds of townsfolk and ranchers wrangled to get the best positions along the length of the route so they could cheer on their favorites.

The Stampede's starting line was on Main Street. It was marked by a big banner hanging across the width of the street. The mood there was growing tense as the riders began to assemble.

Though she'd been dressed up the night before, Randi was back in her normal work clothes today as she prepared for the race. She was just finishing up in the stable with her father and Wade.

"Are you ready?" Jack asked.

"Oh, yes," Randi said as she led Angel outside. She swung up in the saddle and patted Angel's neck. "We're ready."

She looked up just then to see Hawk coming their way. She'd been hoping to see him.

Wade saw Hawk, too, and asked, "Did you come by to wish Randi good luck, too?"

"Do you think she needs it?" Hawk countered. "I've seen these two run. There's no doubt who I'm betting on."

"I'm betting on her, too, and so are the rest of the hands. Don't let us down, Randi," Wade added.

"I'll see what I can do for you," she teased, but she was really thrilled by their faith in her. "I'd hate for you to all end up broke and blame me."

"It's almost time," Jack said, interrupting their banter.

"I'd better go. We don't want to miss the start."

"Randi . . ."

She recognized her father's serious tone and looked back at him. "Yes, Pa?"

"You're going to do great," he encouraged her, "but be careful."

"I will, Pa."

She rode off toward the starting line on Main Street, ready to take on all comers.

"Riders! Are you ready?" called out Judd Bartlett, the town's mayor, addressing the twenty riders who had lined up before him.

"Yeah!" they yelled in response.

The crowd that had gathered around cheered in anxious anticipation.

Hawk stood with Wade and Jack, watching

Randi. He knew how fiery and competitive she was, and her fierce determination was evident in her serious expression as she focused on Judd Bartlett, watching and waiting for him to drop the starting flag.

"Get on your mark! Get set!" Judd paused for effect. *"Go!"*

He dropped the flag.

In that instant Randi and Angel charged off, galloping away at top speed.

A roar of excitement tore through the spectators as the riders raced past them.

Randi leaned low over Angel's neck as they battled for position. Speed meant everything. They tore through the town, racing neck and neck with cowboys from neighboring ranches, heading for the first turn.

"How much did you boys bet on Randi?" Wade asked Rob and Lew as they joined the throng.

"Half my pay!" Rob answered.

"I only bet five dollars," Lew told him. "I just hope I don't lose it."

"You won't," Hawk said with confidence.

The race was too close to call as the contestants circled the town. The other riders were challenging her, staying close beside her. As they started back toward the far end of Main Street, Angel and Lightning, rancher Pete Turner's stallion, were running neck and neck.

"Go, girl!" Randi urged Angel on, pushing the

mare to her limits when she saw the finish line some distance ahead of them.

Angel responded to her urging with a surge of power, giving them just the edge they needed to take the lead.

Pete savagely spurred Lightning, trying to keep up with Angel's breakneck pace. He had no intention of losing to Randi Stockton again. He hated the Stocktons. He had for years. He wanted to get the best of them, but it looked like there was nothing he could do. Randi and Angel were pulling away from him.

Randi was exhilarated as they gained half a length on Lightning. She was smiling widely as they neared the finish line, and she let out a shout of victory as they crossed it just ahead of the challenging rancher.

"She did it!" Jack yelled, running forward to congratulate his daughter.

Wade and the other men were cheering, too. They had just made a goodly sum off their bets.

Hawk stood back and watched as Randi rode up and dismounted before the mayor. Her father came to stand proudly at her side.

"Congratulations, Randi," Judd told her as he awarded her the winning prize money. "Here's fifty dollars. You and Angel proved you were the best again!"

"Thanks!"

"Remember, folks," Judd went on, addressing the crowd as they began to disperse, "we've got the shooting competition coming up at one o'clock. Don't miss any of the fun this afternoon."

"I'll meet you back at the hotel after I take care of Angel," Randi told her father.

"Do you need any help?" Jack offered.

"No. I shouldn't be too long."

"All right. We'll get something to eat, and then I think I'll enter the shooting competition."

Hawk had hung back when the other ranch hands hurried forward to first congratulate Randi. While he was biding his time, he noticed that the rancher who'd come in second in the race was still mounted up, looking on as Randi was congratulated by all the men. The expression on the man's face was one of pure fury, and Hawk could tell he was a bad loser.

When the ranch hands had finished congratulating Randi, they headed for the Silver Dollar to collect on their winning bets.

Randi began leading Angel toward the stable. It was then that Hawk sought her out.

"That was some fine riding," he complimented her.

"This race was a lot closer than last year. Last year we beat Lightning by a full length."

"All that matters is that you won."

"It was exciting," she agreed. "Lightning is fast, but Angel just proved she's still faster."

"Who was riding Lightning?"

"That was Pete Turner. He's a neighboring rancher."

"He didn't look too happy."

"He'll get over it. He always does," she told him with an impish grin. "Are you going to enter the shooting competition this afternoon?"

"I hadn't thought much about it."

"Pa always does."

"Has he ever won?"

"No, but he enjoys the challenge."

"Why don't you enter?" Hawk asked. "I've seen how you handle a gun. You should try."

She grinned at him. "No. I won the race. That's enough competition for me today."

"Randi!"

She turned around at the sound of Sherri's call, disappointed at the interruption. She was usually glad to see her friend, but she had been enjoying the time alone with Hawk.

"I just heard that you won the race! Congratulations!" Sherri hurried over to join them.

"I've got to take Angel down to the stable. You want to come with us?"

"Sure," Sherri answered.

"I'm going to go find Wade," Hawk said. "I'll see you at the shooting competition."

"You're entering?"

He nodded.

"Good. We'll cheer you on," Randi and Sherri promised.

Though it was before noon, Hawk found Wade already settled in and relaxing with several of the other hands at the Silver Dollar. He joined them at their table.

"What'll you have?" Sindy asked, coming up to them.

"Nothing for me, thanks," Hawk answered.

"Are you sure?" She gave him a suggestive look and leaned toward him to give him a better view of her cleavage.

"I'm sure."

His answer was so indifferent that Sindy was a bit put off. She wasn't used to any of the cowboys ignoring her or turning her down. She quickly left.

"She wasn't just selling liquor, you know." Lew chuckled.

"I know," was all Hawk said.

"Why aren't you drinking with us?" Rob asked.

"I'm going to enter the shooting contest."

"That contest is a good one," Lew added.

"That's what Randi said. Are any of you entering?"

"No. Jack usually does, though. Fred always did, too, but I haven't seen him around yet today," Wade told him.

"How good is Fred?"

"He's real good," Lew answered. "He's come close to winning a couple of times."

"How good are you?" Wade countered.

"I guess we'll be finding out soon enough," Hawk told them.

They lingered in the saloon until the time came

for the competition; then they all went down for the action.

The shooting contest was held on the outskirts of town. Targets were posted, and in each round, the entrants got three shots with their revolvers. Those coming closest to the bull's-eye went on to the next round.

A crowd had already gathered to watch. Randi and Sherri had made sure to get there early enough to have a good vantage point.

Over forty men had entered the contest, but after three rounds, the number was down to less than ten. Fred, Jack, and Hawk were among them.

The next round progressed.

Fred went first, then stood back to watch. When he'd learned that both Jack and Hawk had entered the competition, he'd been pleased. Today he was going to show them—and everyone else in San Miguel—just who was the best gunman in these parts.

After Milt Cramer, the man who was serving as judge, checked the targets, he turned to the crowd to announce who would continue. "We're down to our final two now, folks."

A murmur of surprise went through those gathered that so many contestants had already been eliminated.

"Who are they?" someone yelled excitedly.

"Well, I was about to tell you," the judge joked. "Our two finalists are . . . Fred Carter and Hawk Morgan."

Jack's disappointment was obvious as he went to join Randi and Sherri.

"Who do you think is going to win, Pa?" Randi asked, knowing there had to be tension between Hawk and Fred.

"Fred's good, real good. I don't know about Hawk."

"Hawk will win," Randi said with quiet certainty. "He has to."

Two more targets were posted by the judge.

"Fred, you go first," Milt directed.

Fred glanced toward Hawk and smiled arrogantly at him. He walked slowly up to the mark and took aim. He got off his three shots and then confidently holstered his gun. He strode easily back toward where Hawk and Milt were standing.

Applause came from the crowd.

"Your turn, breed," he sneered in a low, mocking voice.

Hawk ignored him. He walked forward, never looking away from his target. With a calm, yet fierce determination, he drew his gun and fired.

Randi, Sherri, and a few others cheered for Hawk.

Milt went to get the targets.

Everyone waited anxiously to learn the results.

"We have a winner!" Milt called out, coming back to make the announcement. "Congratulations go to . . . Hawk Morgan. You hit the bull's-eye dead-on."

Fred was cursing vilely as he stormed over to the judge. "Let me see those damned targets!"

Milt held them up for Fred to see. There was no mistaking who the winner was. One of Fred's shots had missed the center by over an inch. He had lost.

Fred swore violently and stalked off in humiliation. He was going to enjoy every minute of his revenge when the time finally came—and it wouldn't be long now, if he could help it.

Everyone ignored the sore loser. They cheered Hawk as he was presented the winning prize money.

"That was some fine shooting, Hawk!" Jack praised him.

"Yes, let's celebrate!" Randi said. "We can go to Crown Candy Kitchen, Pa. Sherri's friend Andy owns it, and she says he has delicious treats there."

Sherri was delighted that Randi had suggested going to Andy's place.

"That sounds wonderful," Jack agreed.

They started for the new candy shop.

"Where did you learn to shoot like that?" Jack asked Hawk as Randi and Sherri walked on ahead of them.

"My uncle taught me while I was living with him on his ranch. He always said a man had to be able to handle a gun if he wanted to stay alive on the range."

"He was right about that."

They reached the store, and Randi and Sherri hurried inside. It was a one-room establishment. There was a counter and a large glass case filled with all sorts of delectable treats. Several tables and chairs were set up on the other side of the room for those choosing to have a meal there.

Andy was busy working behind the counter, wearing an apron over his clothes. He smiled the moment he saw them coming through the door.

"Good afternoon, ladies," he welcomed them. "Hawk . . . Mr. Stockton. Good to see you again."

"Call me Jack, please," he said easily, eyeing Andy's wares with open interest. "This is some fine-looking candy you've got here."

"What would you like?" Andy asked. "We've got rock candy, pulled molasses candy, lemon drops, gumballs—"

"Gumballs?" Sherri was curious. "What are they?"

"Try one," Andy took one from the bowl and handed it to her. "But don't swallow it."

Sherri was intrigued. She cautiously started chewing on the candy, and her frown turned to a delighted smile. "What is it?"

"It's made of chicle, and I add the flavor to it."

"It's really different."

"I'll have some rock candy," Randi said, knowing how delicious the sugar-based treat on a string was.

Andy handed her the candy, then waited for Jack and Hawk to make their decisions.

"Did you know Randi won the race this morning?" Sherri asked Andy.

"One of my customers told me about it earlier. Congratulations," he complimented her.

"Thanks, and Hawk just won the shooting contest," Randi told him.

Andy was truly impressed. "Then your candy is on me."

"I can pay," Hawk offered.

"No, allow me."

"Well, if they gave awards for the best candy in Texas, you'd be the winner today," Sherri said.

"You'll have to tell them to hold that contest at the Stampede next year." Andy laughed.

They were just starting to leave the store when Randi brazenly decided to ask the question she knew was haunting her friend.

"Andy?"

At her call, he looked their way.

"Will be you at the dance tonight?"

"I'll be there," he answered, his gaze focused on Sherri.

"We'll see you then," Randi said.

Sherri only smiled in delight.

Chapter Twelve

"Are you ready, Randi?" Jack asked as he knocked on the door to her hotel room.

"I'll be a minute longer," she called out.

"I'll meet you in the lobby." Jack did not want to stand around in the upstairs hall.

"How are you doing this evening, Mr. Stockton?" Paul, the hotel clerk, asked cordially.

"Just fine, Paul."

"You all set for the big dance?"

"As soon as my daughter comes down, we'll be on our way."

"Have a good time, and think of me while you're there. I have to work all night."

"Why don't you just shut the place down and come with us?" Jack joked.

"I'd like to do that, but I think my boss might get a little angry with me."

They both shared a good laugh.

* * *

Randi checked her appearance in the mirror in her hotel room one last time before leaving to meet her father. She made her way down the hall, her thoughts on the evening to come. She knew Sherri was thrilled about the dance because Andy was attending, and she was happy for her friend, but she wondered if Hawk was going to show up. She hoped so. She reached the top of the steps and paused, looking around for her father in the lobby below.

Jack and Paul were still chatting when Randi appeared at the top of the steps. Both men stopped talking to stare at her.

Randi was a vision of femininity. She had styled her hair down around her shoulders in a mass of golden curls. Her turquoise gown was modestly low-cut and fit her perfectly, showing off her figure to advantage. She was stunning.

"You look lovely," Jack said as he went to meet her at the foot of the stairs.

"Thank you, Pa." She was glad he approved.

"We'll see you later, Paul," Jack said as he offered Randi his arm and proudly escorted her from the hotel. He was looking forward to a very pleasant evening.

The hotel clerk watched them go, wishing all the more that he could shut down and attend the dance after getting a look at Randi.

Hawk was sitting alone at a table in the back of the Silver Dollar. After leaving the candy store he'd met up with Wade, and they'd come to the saloon to pass the time, hoping to hear something that might help them track down the rustlers. They'd met with no success, though, and Wade had left about an hour earlier to get cleaned up for the dance.

Hawk knew the foreman was looking forward to the evening to come. Wade had told him that the widow Walker was going to be there; at the social the night before she had promised him a dance.

Hawk lingered at the saloon for a while longer, but the place was pretty much deserted. Most of the cowboys had gone to the dance, eager for the chance to be with the ladies from town.

Across the room, Sindy was sitting with the other working girls, eyeing Hawk with interest. Business was slow that evening—very slow—and she was bored. She always liked a challenge, and since there was nothing else to do, she decided to try to entice Hawk to go upstairs with her. She'd never bedded a half-breed before, and she wondered if he would be a savage lover. The idea brought a sensuous smile to her lips.

She stood up and slowly walked over to stand before him. She was ready to do whatever it would take to get Hawk upstairs and into her bed.

"Evening, Hawk," she said slowly, her inflection telling him all he needed to know about her motive in seeking him out. Her gaze went over him, visually caressing him.

"Evening," he answered.

"Looking for a good time tonight?" she asked, making sure her tone was alluring.

The men who frequented her bed at the Silver Dollar knew what a wild and passionate lover Sindy was. She earned every cent they paid her, and she was ready to give Hawk more than his money's worth tonight. Since it wasn't crowded, they could take all the time they wanted.

Hawk looked up at the saloon girl and managed a half smile at her brazen ways. "I appreciate the offer, but I have to be going."

Sindy found his lack of interest in her to be a challenge. She moved closer and spoke in a low, soft voice. "I can take you places you've never been before."

"Like I said," Hawk began, snaring her wrist as she boldly reached down and attempted to fondle him, "I have to be going."

He held on to her wrist as he stood up.

"You don't know what you're missing," she countered a bit angrily.

Sindy wasn't used to being turned down. The men of San Miguel wanted her. They lusted after her. Some of the cowboys had even fought over her, and most of the time she loved every minute of their attention. There were a few she wished would leave her alone, but this one . . . this one wasn't one of them. She watched Hawk as he kept walking toward the swinging doors.

Hawk didn't stop or look back. He left the saloon and stood outside on the sidewalk for a moment, glad for the fresh air and the coolness of the night.

Hawk intended to ride out, to leave town, but the sound of the music and laughter coming from the dance drew him. He made his way toward the grassy area at the center of town where the dance was being held.

A low, wooden dance floor had been constructed there, and festive lanterns were hung around it. The musicians were seated off to one side, and what they lacked in talent, they made up for in enthusiasm. It was obvious that all those in attendance were having a good time.

Hawk saw Randi right away. He'd always known she was lovely, but this evening she was more stunning than ever. His gaze lingered on her as she danced with a man he'd never seen before. She was laughing at something he'd said and gazing up at him as he whirled her around the dance floor.

Hawk was troubled by the feelings that the sight aroused in him. He told himself Randi meant nothing to him. He hadn't allowed himself to care about anyone since Jessie's death. Even so, as he looked on, a part of him wanted to be the man holding Randi in his arms.

Hawk knew he should mount up and ride out of town.

But he didn't.

He stayed where he was, watching from the shadows.

"Thank you for the dance, Miranda," Glenn Hathaway said when the music ended. He walked with her from the dance floor.

"Thank you, Glenn," she returned with a genuine smile. He was a nice young man who worked as a teller at the bank.

"Would you like something to drink?"

"That would be fine."

He escorted her to the refreshment table. As they were getting their cups of punch, Sherri and Andy joined them.

"Are you having a good time?" Sherri asked her in a low voice as Glenn and Andy spoke of other things.

"Yes, but I haven't seen Hawk anywhere around tonight. Have you?"

"No. Maybe he decided to go back to the ranch."

Randi tried not to show her disappointment at the prospect, but Sherri knew her too well.

"Take another look around for him. He might still be here somewhere," Sherri encouraged her. She knew how she would have felt if Andy had not shown up that evening.

With Glenn busy talking to Andy, Randi had the opportunity to slip away unnoticed. She had already disappeared into the crowd gathered around the sides of the dance floor when the music started up again.

Hawk had lost sight of Randi after the dance had ended. When the musicians began to play once more, he expected to see her return to the dance floor, but there was no sign of her.

"I was wondering where you were."

The sound of her voice so close behind him startled Hawk. He turned to find Randi gazing up at him.

"What are you doing here?" he asked, smiling at the sight of her in spite of himself.

"I was looking for you," she answered simply. "What are you doing over here by yourself? Why aren't you up with the rest of us having fun?"

"Dances have never been fun for me."

"Why? Don't you know how?" She was teasing.

"No, actually, I don't."

"Then I think it's time you learned, don't you?"

Without waiting for him to say anything more, Randi took his hand and led him a few steps away into the sheltering privacy of an alleyway.

"I'll teach you," Randi said softly.

"I might prove to be a slow learner," he said.

"Then we'll just have to practice more." Randi went into his arms.

The sound of the music drifted around them as they stood there unmoving, gazing at each other in the soft moonlight.

Excitement coursed through Randi, and she instinctively lifted her arms around his neck to draw him even closer.

For the first time in years, no thoughts of Jessie haunted Hawk. He was aware only of Randi, of how beautiful she was and how much he wanted to hold her close. He gave no thought to learning to dance. Instead, with utmost tenderness, he bent to her and claimed her lips in a cherishing kiss.

The kiss was gentle—for a moment. Then the power of the attraction they could no longer deny overwhelmed them both.

A deep, abiding hunger filled Hawk. He crushed Randi to him. His mouth moved hungrily over hers, and Randi responded without reserve. She met him in that passionate exchange, reveling in his nearness, glorying in the hard press of his body against hers.

Any thought that they might be discovered was forgotten. They clung together, thrilling in the excitement of their newly acknowledged need for each other.

It was only the two of them, alone in the sweet, blissful heat of the night.

Randi was lost in the pleasure of Hawk's embrace. His kiss was heavenly. A fire of need was sparked within her, and she moved closer to the strength of him. She wanted to be as close to him as she could.

At her unspoken invitation, Hawk stifled a groan. Randi was in his arms, and she wanted him as much as he wanted her. It was heavenly. . . .

And then the sounds of drunken laughter suddenly echoed loudly around them as a staggering cowboy moved past the entrance to the alleyway.

Hawk and Randi were both instantly jarred

back to complete awareness of where they were and what they were doing.

They broke apart and stood staring at each other in breathless confusion as reality intruded.

"I enjoyed your dancing lesson," he said with a smile when the drunk had finally moved out of sight.

"You were a fast learner," she told him. She was amazed by the way his smile transformed him. She'd thought him handsome before, but this way, he left her breathless.

"I had a good teacher," Hawk returned.

Randi wanted to go back into his arms and stay there. She wanted to kiss him again, but she knew this wasn't the time or place. Anyone might come upon them there in the alley.

"If I'm so good, let's go see how much you really just learned," she challenged him, boldly taking his hand in hers. "Let's have a real dance."

"You sure you want to do this?"

"I'm sure."

"All right," he agreed. Any possible embarrassment he might suffer over his own lack of dancing skill was worth it if it meant having Randi in his arms again.

Randi drew Hawk along with her away from the alley; they reached the side of the dance floor just as the music ended. The musicians started a new song almost right away.

"Are you ready?" she challenged.

"I'm ready," he answered in a low, sensual voice.

A shiver of awareness trembled through Randi as Hawk took her hand in his and drew her out onto the dance floor with the other couples. They had eyes only for each other as they began to move together.

Hawk was tentative at first, but only for a moment or two. Then he found his rhythm. They moved slowly but smoothly around the floor.

Dancing with Hawk was heavenly for Randi, and it ended too quickly, as far as she was concerned. As she was forced to move out of his arms, she felt almost bereft. Before she had the chance to say anything, though, Abe Ryan, one of the men from town, sought her out.

"I've been waiting all night to have a dance with you," Abe said eagerly.

Randi liked Abe, but she wanted to stay with Hawk. She started to respond, but Hawk spoke up, taking charge.

"It looks like you're going to have to keep waiting," Hawk said, stepping between them.

Abe wasn't a man who liked confrontation. He backed off and hurried away.

She smiled as Hawk led her out onto the dance floor again. "So you like to dance that much, do you?"

"With you."

They said no more. They gave themselves over to the pleasure of the moment.

Jack had been keeping track of his daughter. He realized how much time she was spending with

Hawk and that she wasn't dancing with any of the other men. Knowing he had to do something, he waited through one more dance, then approached them on the dance floor.

"If I may?" Jack said, cutting in.

Hawk reluctantly handed Randi over to her father.

He walked from the dance floor, pausing only once to glance back before disappearing into the crowd.

Chapter Thirteen

When the dance ended and her father was escorting her over to join Sherri and Andy, Randi looked around for Hawk. She saw no sign of him anywhere. Somehow she managed to keep smiling, even though disappointment filled her. She wanted to be with Hawk.

Jack left Randi with her friends, while he went off to speak with another rancher.

"I think you owe me a dance," Andy told Randi.

Randi laughed as she glanced at Sherri. "You're not going to get jealous, are you?"

"Absolutely not. Enjoy yourself. Andy's a very good dancer," Sherri said. She knew Randi well enough to be able to tell that she was a bit unhappy right then and needed some cheering up.

"I know he is. I've been watching the two of you tonight," Randi said.

"Well, now it's our turn. Shall we?" he invited.

"I'd be delighted."

"Where did Hawk go?" Andy asked as they moved smoothly around the floor together. "I saw the two of you dancing earlier."

"I don't know. He didn't say." She kept her tone light and indifferent. Sometimes she surprised herself by what a good actress she could be.

"It's too bad he left. I would have enjoyed talking to him some more. He's a very interesting man."

"Yes, he is," Randi agreed. She kept an eye on the crowd, but instinctively she knew Hawk was nowhere around.

When the dance ended, they found Sherri talking with Ernie Jackson, one of the men who worked on Pat Walker's ranch.

"Here comes Randi now," Sherri said as they walked up. "You have to tell her!"

"Tell me what?" Randi asked, wondering what her friend was so excited about.

"Go on, Ernie," Sherri urged.

Ernie looked at Randi and explained, "She wants me to tell you about the phantom stallion."

Sherri had been right. Randi did want to know.

"What about him?" she asked eagerly.

"I saw him. It was just a few days ago, out in the Black Canyon area."

"Did you get up close to him?"

"No. He was gone before I even realized what I was looking at. I tried to track him down, but I couldn't find his trail anywhere. It's too rocky up there. From what little I did see of him, though, I can tell you he is one magnificent horse."

Excitement grew within Randi. She hadn't been crazy after all when she'd thought she'd seen the phantom the day Hawk had ridden in. The stallion really did exist.

"One of these days I'm going to catch him," Randi said with certainty.

Ernie just chuckled at her. "I know Angel's fast. She just proved that at the race, but even as quick as she is, I don't think she has any hope of catching up with the phantom."

"We'll see," Randi replied. She was already thinking about how she would try to locate the elusive stallion.

"Good luck to you, Randi," Ernie said, grinning as he moved off. "I know you're going to need it."

Andy looked from Sherri to Randi, confused. "All right, what's the story about this phantom horse?"

Randi quickly related the tale of the fierce Comanche warrior and his magnificent white stallion.

"That's fascinating, but if the legend says only the finest warrior will catch him . . . you're a lady. Doesn't that rule you out?"

Sherri laughed good-naturedly at his observation. "I have to tell you, Andy, legend or not, when Randi makes up her mind to do something, she usually does it. She's a match for any man."

He was impressed anew with Randi. "Good luck

to you. Maybe at next year's Stampede, you'll be riding the phantom stallion instead of Angel."

"Wouldn't that be wonderful?" Randi smiled. "I won today on Angel, but imagine how big my lead would have been if I had been riding the stallion. He's incredibly fast. That's why no one's been able to catch him."

"Yet," Sherri emphasized for her.

"That's right. I'm just going to have to take a ride up to Black Canyon and see what I can find."

"Evening, Pat," Wade said as he sought her out where she was talking with friends at the side of the dance floor.

"Why, good evening, Wade," she greeted him.

"Would you like to dance?"

"I'd love to. Thank you."

Pat allowed him to lead her onto the dance floor as a fluttering sensation filled her stomach. She'd been thinking about him all day. They'd had a wonderful time together at the social the night before. She'd felt young and carefree being with Wade, and now he was here, wanting to dance with her.

Pat went willingly into his arms. It had been a long time since she'd danced, but after the first few steps she discovered that she hadn't forgotten how.

"Have you been enjoying your time in town?" Wade asked.

"Oh, yes. It's been such fun."

"That's good."

"You're right. It has been good for me. I've been so worried about what's going on at the ranch that I'd almost forgotten how to relax and enjoy myself."

"Things will get better for you," he reassured her.

"They already are," she said. Then she looked up at him as she finished, "I'm here with you."

Pat smiled at Wade.

He returned her smile. Everything was going just as he'd hoped it would.

Wade spent the rest of the evening with Pat. When it was almost time for the festivities to end, he escorted her back to her friend's house. It was nearly midnight as they walked up the path to the porch steps.

"Thank you for a wonderful evening," Wade told her, still holding her hand.

"No, thank you," Pat said softly. Wade made her feel like a woman again. Her heart was pounding excitedly in the hope of what might be to come. Gazing up at him in the moonlight, she almost believed she was beginning to care for him. He had helped her so much on the ranch, and this weekend, just being with him had been a delight.

The soft tone of her voice was all the invitation Wade needed. He bent down and kissed her.

As starved as Pat was for affection, she didn't hesitate to respond. She eagerly embraced him and kissed him hungrily in return. Excitement surged through her at the intimacy of the exchange. When they finally broke apart, she was breathless—and smiling.

"I'd better go in now."

"Good night," Wade murmured. He stayed where he was, watching until she was safely inside.

He was feeling most satisfied as he walked away. Things were definitely working out just right.

He headed for the saloon. There was one more thing he had to do before he could call it a night.

The Silver Dollar was crowded when Wade got there, just as he'd expected it to be. A lot of the cowboys had shown up there now that the dance was over. Wade took a look around and spotted neighboring rancher Pete Turner drinking at the bar.

"Evening, Pete."

"It's about time you showed up," Pete remarked, his irritation obvious. He'd been in a bad mood all day since losing the race to Randi and Angel.

Wade ignored his censure. "I've been working."

"That's good to hear."

"I thought you might appreciate it."

"I do, but I want to know what's happening. What's going on?"

"This isn't the place," Wade quickly cautioned him, very aware that men from the Lazy S were there at the saloon, too. "I'll meet you out back in a few minutes."

Wade paid the bartender for the whiskey the man had set before him. He picked up the glass and took a deep drink before casually moving away to mingle with the ranch hands for a while.

Pete remained standing at the bar a little longer. He finished off his own drink, then called it a night. Without drawing any attention to himself, he left the saloon and went to wait for Wade in the alley. It was dark and there was no one around, so he knew it would be a safe place for them to talk.

Time passed, and Pete got even more aggravated. He was about to go back in and get Wade when the other man finally showed up.

"What the hell took you so long?" Pete demanded. "I don't pay you to keep me waiting."

"No, you pay me to get the job done, and that's exactly what I'm doing. There are a few things you need to know."

"Like what?"

"Jack hired that Hawk Morgan to try to stop the rustling. We're gonna have to be even more careful from now on."

"Damn!" Pete swore under his breath.

"There's one other thing, too."

"What?" he asked in disgust, knowing it had to be bad news from the way Wade was talking.

"Fred went and got himself fired."

"Son of a . . ." Pete swore under his breath.

"I know. It was stupid, but there's nothing we can do about it."

"How is everything going with Pat?"

"Just fine." Wade smiled in the darkness. "No one suspects a thing. Jack and the boys think I'm sweet on her, so they're not going to question my spending time at her place whenever I get the chance. I'll keep her distracted, so she'll never figure out we're using that box canyon of hers for our work."

"Good." Pete was glad that something was going right. He looked at Wade with a little more respect. "That canyon worked out just fine the last time."

"Yes, it did, but now that Hawk's here nosing around—"

"Get rid of him," Pete interrupted. His tone was cold and deadly. His meaning was clear.

Pete hated Jack Stockton and all his success. He wanted to cause the other rancher as much trouble as he could. One day, he hoped—if he was lucky enough—he might even drive Stockton out of business. That was why he'd recruited Wade to help him with the rustling. He liked having an inside man. He paid Wade handsomely, and he expected to get results in exchange for that money.

"Pete, I'm no killer," Wade protested immediately.

"Do you want to hang?"

"No." Wade was beginning to realize just how serious and complicated their situation was. Cattle rustling was a hanging offense, and they couldn't risk being caught.

"Then find someone who can take care of this. We don't need that half-breed ruining things for us." It was an order.

"All right," Wade finally answered.

"Good. Let me know what's going on."

"I will."

Together they walked out of the alley, then went their separate ways.

As Wade started off across town to the Ace High Saloon, he didn't notice Hawk watching him from a secluded, night-shrouded spot down the street.

Hawk had been heading out of town when he'd seen Wade come out of the Silver Dollar Saloon. He'd almost called out to the foreman, but before he could, Wade had quickly disappeared into the alley behind the building. Puzzled by his behavior, Hawk had reined in a little farther down the street. He found a place where he could keep watch without drawing any attention to himself. He didn't know what the foreman was doing, but he wanted to find out.

Hawk hadn't had long to wait. The foreman had emerged from the alley with Pete Turner. Hawk had watched as the two men split up and went in different directions. Something wasn't right, but he knew this wasn't the time to approach Wade.

Hawk had planned to spend the night at his campsite and then ride out to the ranch at first light. After seeing Wade's odd behavior, he changed his mind. He was going to come back into town in the morning and try to learn what connection there was between Wade and Turner. There had to have been a good reason they'd met in secret that way, and he was going to find out what it was.

* * *

The Ace High was almost as busy as the Silver Dollar had been. It catered to a far rougher crowd than the Silver Dollar. The cowboys who frequented the Ace High were mostly drunks who were out to do some serious gambling and have a good time.

Wade found Fred Carter right where he had thought he would be—playing poker. Wade went to stand at the bar and watch the ex–ranch hand play. He didn't say anything until Fred had thrown down his hand in disgust and gotten up from the table.

"Bad night?" Wade said when Fred stalked up to the bar and ordered a drink.

Fred glanced his way. "You have no idea. What are you doing here?"

"Looking for you."

"Why?"

"You still need money?" Wade knew all about Fred's debts in town, and, from the way the poker hand he'd just played had gone, it looked like nothing had changed.

Fred eyed him in disgust. "You know I do."

Wade nodded. "Then we need to talk. I may have a job for you."

Fred was curious but cautious. Wade's offer was intriguing, but he had already figured out how he was going to get the money to pay off his debt to Trey. On the other hand, it couldn't hurt to be open to other possibilities.

"All right," Fred answered. "Start talking. I'm listening. What have you got for me?"

"Let's go over here." Wade directed him to a secluded corner of the rowdy bar.

It was much later when Wade returned to the hotel, a satisfied man.

Everything was going to work out all right.

Chapter Fourteen

Hawk was in a serious mood as he rode to his campsite. Wade's secret meeting with Pete Turner troubled him, but what disturbed him even more were the feelings that Randi's kiss had stirred deep within him. No matter how hard he tried, he couldn't forget the beauty of her embrace.

Since Jessie's death, Hawk had hardened himself to any tender emotions. He had had to. The pain of losing those he'd loved in the raid that day had overwhelmed him. Since then, he'd only existed emotionally.

But now Randi had come into his life, and she was threatening what little inner peace he'd managed to find.

Randi had touched his heart.

Holding her in his arms had been heavenly for him—and it had also been his hell. Logic told him to protect himself—to stay away from Randi because caring about her would only cause him pain—but there was nothing logical about the way he felt. He wanted to be with her.

Frustration and confusion ate at Hawk as he reached his campsite. He built a small fire and got ready to bed down for the night. Even as he sought what comfort he could find in his bedroll, he knew he would get little rest. His thoughts were only of Randi and the memory of their heated embrace.

Randi lay in her bed in the hotel room, thinking back over the night just past and missing Hawk. She didn't know where he'd gone, but she sure wished that he had stayed longer at the dance with her. She had danced with Andy and several other men during the course of the evening, but none of them had stirred the feelings within her that dancing with Hawk had.

A vision of Hawk the way he'd looked smiling down at her that night drifted through her thoughts and sent a thrill coursing through her. She sighed. No other man had ever affected her this way. And even though they hadn't known each other for very long, Randi believed, as she relived in her mind the touch of his lips upon hers, that she had fallen in love with Hawk.

The realization didn't surprise her. If anything, finally coming to understand her feelings for him calmed her.

She loved Hawk.

Acknowledging the truth of her love, Randi rolled over and closed her eyes. A smile curved her lips as she drifted off to sleep. She hoped to dream of Hawk.

Hawk returned to town early the next morning. He was a man on a mission. He wanted to find some of the other Lazy S ranch hands, have breakfast with them, and try to find out if they had any idea why Wade would have met so secretly with Pete Turner the night before. Hawk reined in and tied up Bruiser before the hotel, then went inside. As he'd hoped, Rob and Lew were already seated in the hotel's restaurant, so he went to join them.

"Mind if I eat with you?" Hawk asked.

"After watching you shoot yesterday, there's no way I'm ever telling you no," Rob chuckled.

"Sit down," Lew invited, gesturing toward an empty chair.

"Thanks."

The waitress appeared and took Hawk's order.

"How about that Randi? I can't wait to see her today and thank her. I won fifty dollars yesterday, betting on her and Angel!" Lew said when the waitress had gone.

"Randi did a fine job," Rob agreed. "But we all knew she would. She likes to win; that's for sure."

The men talked easily, rehashing the events of the exciting weekend.

"And now it's back to work for all of us," Rob concluded. "I wonder where Wade is this morning? I expected him to be here with us."

"I saw him earlier," Lew put in with a grin. "He was all dressed up and heading to church with the widow woman."

Rob was truly surprised. "I knew he was sweet on her, but I didn't know he was sweet enough on her to go to church with her! This could be getting serious."

Both men laughed. They'd never considered Wade the churchgoing type.

The waitress served them their breakfast, and they dug in.

"Did you have any trouble with Fred after the shooting match yesterday? I know he was mad—real mad," Lew asked Hawk.

"No."

"That's good. He can be one mean—" Rob started to use a word that wasn't appropriate for Sunday morning, so he stopped in midsentence.

"I figured as much." Hawk knew what Rob was saying.

They spoke of other things for a while, and then, finally, Hawk found the opening he was looking for. He spotted the man Wade had met last night entering the restaurant with a pretty woman on his arm. The man nodded in greeting as he escorted the lady past their table.

"That's Pete Turner, isn't it?" Hawk asked as casually as he could, once the man had moved out of hearing.

"Yeah, he owns the Flying T. It's just on the other side of the Walker spread," Rob offered.

"He wasn't too happy when Randi won the race yesterday," Hawk said.

"No, he lost last year to Randi, too. Pete's got a temper. He ain't one to mess with," Lew added.

"Is his ranch a big place?"

"It's no Lazy S, but it's decent. He's been here for quite a few years. He and Jack go way back."

Hawk was satisfied with what he'd learned.

"You want to ride back to the ranch with us?" Rob asked as they finished eating and got ready to leave the restaurant. "We'll be riding out shortly."

"No, I've got a few things to take care of first. I'll see you back at the bunkhouse."

Hawk paid the waitress for his meal and left. Mounting up, he rode for the Lazy S, but this time he took a circuitous route. He wanted to take a look around the area between the Lazy S and the Turner and Walker ranches. With any luck, he would find some sign of the rustlers.

"I have to ride out to Black Canyon when we get home," Randi told her father as they rode for the Lazy S.

"And why is that?"

She quickly explained what Ernie had told her. "I've just got to take a look around."

"I don't know what I'm going to do with you, young lady." Jack chuckled. "Last night you were all ladylike, dancing with the men in town, and to-day you want to try to track down and capture a renegade stallion."

"Want to ride with me?" she asked, laughing, too.

"Not today. You go on and have fun, but I don't know what you'll do if you ever do manage to get a rope on him."

"Why, I'll bring him back to the ranch and break him in myself," Randi said with easy confidence.

"If he can be broke." Jack had his doubts. "After running wild for all this time, that stallion may be too hard to handle."

"Let's hope I get the chance to find out." Randi always loved a challenge.

Fred was ready and waiting, passing time in his hotel room in town. Wade had said that he'd send word when everything was set, so for now, all he had to do was sit around. He hoped Wade didn't take too long. He was eager to get this done and have some money in his pocket.

. Smiling at what he considered his bright prospects, Fred stretched out on his bed and relaxed. He regretted that it was Sunday, and the saloons were closed. He could have used Sindy's company. He was in the mood to do some celebrating.

Hawk had learned the boundaries of the Lazy S from Wade during his first days there. When he reached the south range, he followed the creek that marked the property line with the Walker ranch. He searched for some sign that the rustlers might have passed through there. The going proved tedious. The ground was rocky and hard. If the rustlers had crossed this way, they had left nothing behind to mark their passing.

Hawk finally reined in and dismounted to give Bruiser a rest and let him get a drink. He sat down in a shady spot to relax and study the landscape. He was looking around, taking in the lay of the land, when he noticed what appeared to be the remains of a campfire on the far side of the creek.

Hawk wasted no time crossing the shallow creek to check it out. The campfire had been there for a while. He sifted through the ashes, hoping for a clue of some kind, but found nothing. Still, this was a start. Someone had camped out in this spot. He'd have to find out from Jack if he'd known of any activity in the area.

Returning to Bruiser, Hawk mounted up. He was encouraged by his find, but knew this was just a beginning. He rode on, keeping a careful eye out for anything else that might help him learn the identity of the thieves.

Randi was excited as she rode for Black Canyon. The canyon was actually on the Walker ranch, but not too far over the property line. She knew Pat wouldn't care if she trespassed while looking for the stallion. She just hoped the horse was still in the area. If he was, she was going to find him.

Keeping Angel to a steady, ground-eating pace, Randi covered the miles with ease. It was a beautiful day for a ride, and she was enjoying the peace of being alone. It gave her time to think about the events of the night just past and her feelings for Hawk.

Randi had looked for Hawk in town that morning, but she hadn't seen him. Rob and Lew had mentioned on the ride back to the ranch that they'd had breakfast with Hawk, but that he'd ridden off on his own. She couldn't help wondering where he'd gone.

Randi and Angel topped a low rise, and it was then that she spotted another rider far off in the distance, heading her way. She reined in and tried to make out who the lone cowboy was. She was still on the Lazy S, so she figured it was probably one of the hands taking the long way home.

It didn't take Randi long to recognize Hawk and Bruiser, and she smiled. She watched him coming toward her, her gaze hungry upon him. Randi hadn't thought it was possible for Hawk to look any more handsome to her than he had last night, but today, as he drew nearer, she could see the slight shadow of a day's growth of beard and she thought it gave him a more rakish look. Her heartbeat quickened as he rode up.

"This is a pleasant surprise," Hawk said easily as he stopped beside her. "What are you doing way out here?"

"Looking for the phantom. I was talking to one of Pat Walker's men at the dance last night, and he told me that he'd spotted the stallion up by Black Canyon this past week. What about you? I missed seeing you in town this morning."

"I left ahead of the other men. I'd ridden through here with Wade when I first hired on and he was showing me around, but I wanted to check it over again."

"Did you learn anything new in town?" She wanted the rustlers caught as badly as her father did.

"The only thing that seemed out of the ordinary was seeing Wade meeting late last night with Pete Turner out in back of the Silver Dollar Saloon. I was riding out of town when I saw them together. How do Turner and your pa get along?"

"All right, I guess," Randi answered, surprised by this news. "But you know, Wade and Pete have known each other for years. I don't think there's anything too strange about their drinking together on the Stampede weekend."

"I just thought it was worth mentioning. Whoever is behind the rustling knows exactly what they're doing."

"Do you think we'll ever catch them?" Randi worried.

"Yes, we will. They'll make a mistake eventually, and when they do, we'll be ready," Hawk told her.

She felt reassured by his words.

"How far away is this Black Canyon you're wanting to ride to?" Hawk asked.

"Come on. I'll show you," she offered. "As good a tracker as you are, maybe you can help me find the phantom's trail."

"We can give it a try." Hawk wasn't about to pass up the opportunity to spend more time with her.

Chapter Fifteen

Randi and Hawk rode side by side along the trail that led toward the canyon.

"I missed you after you left the dance so early last night," Randi told him.

"I thought I'd better take a look around town, check out the saloon and see if I could learn anything."

"It's too bad you didn't have better luck."

"You're right."

They crossed the stream and kept on riding.

"We're on Walker land now," Randi told him.

"Pat Walker's a good neighbor to you, isn't she?"

"Yes, she is, but I don't know how long she's going to be able to hold on to the place. Times have been hard for her. Pa's even had to send Wade and some of our men over to help her out."

"What about her own ranch hands?"

"Some of them quit on her because she can't afford to pay them very much. Pat loves that ranch.

She keeps hoping things will turn around for her, but the rustling has hurt her even more than it's hurt us."

They fell silent as they continued on. Hawk studied the trail, looking for clues to the rustling, while Randi kept watch over the hills around them for some sign of the elusive stallion.

"I think, starting right now, I'm just going to begin calling him Phantom," Randi said in frustration as they neared the entrance to the dead-end canyon. "The name really suits him."

"That stallion's no phantom. He's just smart."

"Then I hope he's smart enough to know that I'm never going to give up. What would you do if you were after him? How would you catch him?" she challenged Hawk.

Hawk had been thinking about just that. "The first thing I'd try to do is box him in. We already know he's too fast to run down. Angel's good, but she's no match for your Phantom."

"So there's hope we might catch him today, since we're here at Black Canyon."

"That's right. If we see Phantom, we can herd him into the canyon. Once we've got him boxed in, we should be able to rope him."

"I like the way you think." Randi was impressed with his plan. "But first comes the hard part of all this—we have to find him."

"We will."

Hawk's confidence in her gave Randi even more

hope that this time, with his help, she just might really be successful.

"I'm going to need to rest Angel for a while when we reach the next watering hole."

"All right," he agreed. "We've still got plenty of daylight left."

"There is one thing, though." She tried to sound serious as she cast Hawk a sidelong glance.

"What?" He had no idea what was troubling her.

"You have to keep your shirt on today. As you remember, my pa wasn't too happy that first day when he found us down at the spring."

"So you think he's going to be showing up here?" Hawk asked, smiling.

"You never know. Pa could show up anywhere, anytime."

"It was good that he came looking for you when he did that first day. It made getting back to the house a lot easier for us."

Randi knew he was right, but she had missed riding back to the ranch with Hawk. Riding double with her father just hadn't been as exciting as riding with Hawk.

"It's amazing that Angel healed so quickly. She was wonderful in the race. Without your help, we probably wouldn't have won."

"Don't give me too much credit. I'm the reason she hurt herself in the first place." Hawk still felt responsible.

"Don't even think that way. As fast as I was

chasing Phantom, Angel might have injured herself anyway."

"Well, the good news is she didn't suffer any lasting damage."

"And once she gets a little rest here, she'll be ready to run again," Randi said as she led the way off the main trail down to a small, shaded watering hole.

They dismounted and led their horses to the water's edge to drink. Once the horses had had their fill, they tied them to a nearby tree and then sat down in the shade a slight distance away to relax for a little while.

"Did you have a good time at the dance last night?" Hawk asked Randi. He was very aware of her beside him.

"I did while you were there. I was just sorry that you had to leave so soon."

"If I'd stayed . . ." He looked over at her, remembering the pleasure of having her in his arms. "You could have given me more dancing lessons."

"Did you need more lessons? I thought you were doing well."

"It never hurts to practice."

The deep sound of his voice sent a thrill of awareness through Randi. Their gazes met. Her breath caught in her throat at the heated look in his eyes.

Suddenly the idea of tracking down the phantom stallion didn't seem quite so important anymore.

All that mattered was being with Hawk.

Slowly Hawk leaned toward Randi. He lifted one hand to cup her cheek as his lips sought hers.

Randi didn't hesitate to meet him fully in that kiss. It started out tender and gentle. It was a sweet taste of the ecstasy they knew could be theirs. Then Hawk deepened the kiss, wanting more, needing more, and she responded hungrily.

Encouraged by her passionate response, Hawk crushed Randi to him. They lay back on the ground, wrapped in each other's arms, glorying in their closeness. Kiss after hungry kiss stoked the fire of their desire.

Randi had been kissed by several other men, but she had never experienced anything like the passion Hawk aroused in her. She clung to him, reveling in the power and heat of his body. When his lips left hers to press kisses along the side of her neck, she arched against him in an instinctive, sensual invitation.

Hawk moved up over her and claimed her lips again in a deep, devouring kiss. Randi held him close. She caressed his shoulders and his back, tracing paths of fire upon him.

Hawk was caught up in the power of his need for Randi. His strong-willed self-control was quickly slipping as she responded so eagerly to him. He swept the sweet curve of her body with an intimate caress.

His bold touch sent a shiver of anticipation trembling through Randi. She had never known such intimacy before. His heated caress shocked her even as it thrilled her.

Any doubt Randi had had before about her feelings for Hawk was vanquished in that moment. She loved him. No other man had ever aroused her this way. No other man had ever filled her with such excitement. She wanted to be close to him, to hold him to her heart and never let him go.

And then, suddenly, Bruiser and Angel whickered and stirred restlessly.

Jarred from the depths of their passion, Randi and Hawk went still. They lay unmoving, aware of where they were and what had just transpired between them.

The press of Randi's body was a searing brand against Hawk, and he fought to bring his runaway desire under control. Randi, too, was on fire with her need to stay in his arms, but when Angel stirred again, they forced themselves to break apart.

Hawk got up and deliberately moved away from her. After her remark about her father earlier, he would take no chances with her reputation. He wanted to make sure she wasn't in any kind of compromising situation should someone be riding in. It pained him to leave her, but, at least, he told himself with an inward smile, he did still have his shirt on.

As Hawk walked toward the horses to take a look around, Randi called out excitedly, "Hawk! Look!"

He turned Randi's way to see her pointing farther down the canyon. There, standing in a small clearing about a half a mile away from them, was Phantom.

"Let's ride!" he said, trying to keep his voice down so the stallion wouldn't be spooked.

She jumped up and ran to join him. As soon as they were mounted on Angel and Bruiser, they raced after their elusive prey.

Phantom immediately sensed that these two meant trouble. He took flight. He charged off and disappeared down the trail that led deeper into the steep-walled, rocky canyon.

Hawk and Randi exchanged a quick look of triumph.

They had Phantom right where they wanted him.

Angel was fast, but Bruiser was faster. Hawk urged Bruiser on, eager to catch up to the mysterious stallion. He caught occasional glimpses of Phantom far ahead of them as they gave chase. Hawk shook his head, for they didn't appear to be gaining on him at all. Phantom was living up to his reputation.

Hawk's chase came to an abrupt halt when he rounded a bend in the trail and found himself at the canyon's end. He reined in harshly, causing Bruiser to balk uneasily at the sudden stop.

"Where did he go?" Randi asked breathlessly as she and Angel rode up beside him.

"I don't know," Hawk replied in frustration, bringing Bruiser back under control. "Phantom was right in front of us; then suddenly we were here, at the end of the canyon."

"And he's gone. He disappeared again."

"He couldn't have just vanished." Hawk dismounted and walked around, looking for the stallion's tracks. "He's got to be here somewhere."

Randi actually found herself smiling as she watched Hawk. His fierce determination to find the stallion was obvious.

"Now you know what I've been going through all these years. I'd see him, and then he'd be gone."

Hawk swung back up in the saddle and retraced the way they'd just come. The stallion had to have a hiding place somewhere along the way, since he'd been able to disappear so quickly and so completely. Hawk was going to find it.

He scoured the trail. The ground was rocky, making tracking difficult, but he finally found what he was looking for—a small broken branch on some thick, tangled brush.

"Did you find something?" Randi asked.

"He went through here," he said with certainty.

Hawk led the way again, walking Bruiser slowly through the brush. The going was rough as they picked their way through the overgrowth.

"Have you ever been back here before?" Hawk asked as they rode out of the brush to find themselves near some huge boulders and a craggy outcropping of the canyon wall.

"No. I didn't know this was here."

"Phantom knew. Let's go see what else we can find."

Leading her, Hawk carefully rode through the rocky narrow opening between the boulders. Bruiser was skittish at first, but finally calmed down and moved forward.

Randi urged Angel to follow. She was amazed by what Hawk had discovered. She'd been in this canyon many times through the years, but up until now she'd always believed it was a dead end. Everyone had always said there was only one way in and one way out of Black Canyon. She was beginning to think they'd all been wrong. The path Hawk had discovered looked like it actually led somewhere.

Hawk knew he was on to more than just tracking the mystery stallion. Markings on the walls of the narrow passage, along with the well-trodden ground, made him believe that cattle could have passed through not too long ago. He tried not to get excited about the discovery. He had no proof of anything yet, but soon he would know whether his guess was right or not—and if it was, it explained why Jack had had such a hard time finding the rustlers.

"Do you think we have much farther to go?" Randi asked, growing wary as they continued on. She wasn't frightened, but she definitely was feeling uneasy about where they might end up.

"It's hard to say. Is Black Canyon completely on the Walker ranch?"

"Yes, but Pete Turner's place, the Flying T, isn't too far away. It's just west of here."

Hawk said nothing more as they rode on. They covered almost another half mile before the trail finally led out into the open.

"No one knows this is here!" Randi said, shocked as they emerged from the canyon. Looking around, she tried to figure out exactly where they were.

"No one except Phantom—and the rustlers," Hawk told her, dismounting to check a dead campfire nearby.

"So this is how they managed to get away without being caught!"

"That's right."

"We're still on Pat's ranch, but I know she's not involved in any of this." Randi frowned and tried to make sense of everything they'd just learned.

Hawk continued to scour the area.

"We'd better head back. It's going to be dark in another few hours, and we need to let Pa know," Randi told him.

The shortest way back home was the way they'd come, so they reentered the passage. This time they were far more confident as they followed the winding route back to the canyon's interior.

"We still didn't catch Phantom," Randi said with a grin.

"No, but we're a lot closer to catching the rustlers."

"All thanks to Phantom," she added. "You were right. He's one smart stallion."

They reached the end of the passage and rode

out into the canyon. As they passed the watering hole, a thrill went through Randi at the memory of being in Hawk's arms.

"Too bad we don't have time to stop and water the horses again." Randi glanced Hawk's way.

"You're right," he said, his voice deep with meaning. "It is."

Chapter Sixteen

When Hawk and Randi returned to the ranch, they immediately went in search of her father. They found him at the stable with Wade and several of the other hands.

Jack looked up as they came in. He asked with a grin, "Where's your phantom stallion?"

"We saw him."

"But he got away?"

"Yes, he did—as usual, but Pa, Hawk and I need to talk to you. It's important."

"What is it?" Jack stopped what he was doing and walked over to them.

"Let's go up to the house," Randi said, remembering what Hawk had said about Wade's meeting with Pete. She told herself there wasn't anything to worry about, but still, she wanted to err on the side of caution.

Wade frowned as he watched them go. He

looked over at Lew when they'd disappeared inside the house.

"I wonder what that was all about?" Wade asked.

"Hard to say. Randi rode up to Black Canyon to look for that stallion," Lew answered.

Wade displayed no outward interest in the news, but inwardly he was suddenly very worried. He wondered where she'd met up with Hawk. If the two of them had been up to the canyon, there was no telling what they might have discovered. Needing to know exactly what she was about to tell her father, Wade hurried to finish his work, then left the hands to their chores as he went outside.

From the secretive way Randi had acted, Wade knew he wasn't welcome to participate in their conversation. If Jack had his study window open, though, he was pretty sure he might be able to hear what they were saying, if he was standing close by outside. It was worth a try. The important thing was not to be caught listening in.

"You found what?" Jack was stunned at Randi's revelation as they stood together in his study. He looked between Randi and Hawk in disbelief.

"A secret passageway out of Black Canyon," she repeated.

"We traveled the passage both ways, and it's definitely been in use," Hawk offered. "There were several dead campfires in the area, too."

Jack was still in shock. "No wonder I couldn't find anything," he muttered in disgust.

"Exactly," Hawk agreed. "And if it hadn't been for the phantom stallion, we wouldn't have found it today."

"How did you find it?" Jack asked, curious.

"Hawk and I were chasing Phantom. We thought we had him boxed in the canyon. We thought it would be easy to rope him, trapped as he was, but when we reached the end of Black Canyon, there was no sign of him anywhere. That's when Hawk started tracking him. It took a while, but he found the entrance to the passage hidden behind some rocks and heavy brush."

Jack was still mulling over all they'd learned. "Let's keep this quiet for right now. We'll ride out there first thing tomorrow morning. After I've had a chance to look things over, we'll go pay Pat a visit."

"You don't think she knows about this, do you?" Randi asked, worried.

"No, her situation there is too desperate. If she was involved in the rustling, she'd have some money."

Relief swept through her. "You're right then; we have to tell Pat about this. She needs to know someone's using her land. But we still don't know who," Randi said in frustration.

"We're closer than we were, thanks to Hawk." Jack looked over at the tracker, impressed with his discovery.

Hiding outside the window, Wade had heard every word. When they finished talking, he quickly moved off. He knew what he had to do—he had to get word to Pete. Pete would know how to handle this.

It was time for dinner when Wade made his way back to the bunkhouse, but instead of eating, he called Rob aside.

"I'm going to sneak off for a while," Wade told him with a knowing grin.

"Where are you going?"

"There's this pretty little widow who said she'd like to see me tonight." Wade left it at that, letting Rob draw his own conclusions.

"How soon will you be back?"

"I'll have to be back before dawn," he said. "I don't think Jack would appreciate my missing work."

"That's right. We don't want to have to do your share, too," Rob said teasingly, thinking that Wade was one lucky man to be going off to see the pretty widow.

"I'll be back."

Wade was glad that he'd managed to keep his manner casual. He went out to the stable and was able to ride away without anyone else noticing. Once he was out of sight of the ranch house, he cut across country. It was a long ride to Pete's ranch, and he didn't have a lot of time.

It was over an hour later when he reached the

Turner ranch house. One of the ranch hands had let Pete know that someone was riding in, and Pete was standing on the porch, watching and waiting, as Wade reined in out front.

"What the hell are you doing here?" he demanded.

"We have to talk—now." Wade dismounted, quickly tied up his horse, and joined Pete on the porch.

"Inside," Pete said.

They went into his office and shut the door.

"You know better than to show up here like this!" Pete raged at Wade.

"Shut up and listen to me!" Wade snarled back. He'd never spoken to Pete that way before, but it got the man's attention. "Hawk and Randi were out riding in Black Canyon today, and they found the passage. They told Jack. I heard him say he was going to check it out himself in the morning, and then talk to Pat."

"We have to stop him."

"But how?"

"How do you think? We've got no choice—unless you want to hang?"

"Hell, no."

"Then take care of it, and don't come back here again until I say so."

"I've got the perfect fellow lined up for the job, but I'll need money."

Pete unlocked his desk drawer and counted out a

generous amount. "Here. That should be enough."

Wade grabbed up the cash, stuffed it in his pants pocket, and headed for town.

Fred lay in bed with Sindy in her room above the saloon, exhausted from the hours of seemingly endless passion they'd just shared.

"You are one hot woman," he told her as he ran a hand boldly over her naked breast.

"So I got you all fired up, did I?" Sindy asked with a throaty chuckle.

"You know it," he growled, sitting up and moving away from her. "But it's time for me to go. You probably got some other fellas waiting on you downstairs."

"You never know," she said, pleased that he was through with her.

Fred got dressed and tossed money on the table beside the bed. "You earned every cent."

He looked down at her where she lay, stretched out sensuously on the bed, and he couldn't resist. He reached out to caress her breast one last time, then strode from the room.

Sindy waited until he'd closed the door, then jumped up and counted out the cash. The money was the only thing that made suffering Fred's touch worth it. He did pay her nicely. It was getting late, and she decided to call it a night. She'd made enough for one evening.

Fred returned to the saloon, went up to the bar, and ordered a drink. He was feeling pretty satisfied as he downed a gulp of his whiskey. He lifted his gaze to look in the mirror hanging on the wall behind the bar, only to see a reflection of Wade sitting at a table in the back of the saloon, watching him. Taking up his glass, Fred made his way to join him. Since it was a weeknight, he guessed Wade had come specifically to see him.

"What are you doing here?"

"Looking for you. Denny told me you were upstairs."

"What do you want?"

"We need to talk—somewhere private. It's time to do that job we talked about, and it pays good."

"All right, we can go to my hotel room." He was more than eager to earn his money.

"Fine."

They quickly finished off their drinks and didn't say anything more until they were alone in Fred's room.

"What have you got for me?" Fred asked.

Wade took the wad of bills from his pocket and counted them out for Fred. Fred smiled up at Wade.

"Nice, very nice."

"The breed found the passageway out of Black Canyon."

Fred nodded in understanding. "So what do you want me to do?"

Wade explained what needed to be done.

It was the wee hours of the morning when Wade returned to the ranch. Rob stirred and woke up when he came into the bunkhouse, but he didn't say anything. He figured the foreman must have had one real good time with the widow to have stayed out that late.

Hawk was lying in his bunk, still awake when Wade returned. He had been aware of the foreman's absence and had heard the talk going around that he had gone off to see Pat that night. Hawk remembered how Wade had courted Pat in town during the Stampede, so he knew it wasn't too surprising that they wanted to see more of each other. He just couldn't help wondering if that was where Wade had really gone.

Hawk sought sleep, but none came. His doubts about Wade bothered him, but it was the sweet-hot memory of holding Randi in his arms that disturbed him the most. Remembering the pleasure of her kiss was enough to keep him awake all night. He knew he needed his rest, but more than rest, he needed Randi.

Sleep proved elusive for Jack, too. It was not the first time, he'd lain awake long into the night, trying to figure out who was behind the rustling. Now that they knew where the secret passage was, they would have to set a trap for the rustlers. It would require Pat's cooperation, but Jack didn't think that would be a problem. Still, he couldn't make any definite plans until he'd spoken to her about the situation the following day. Frustrated and worried, he passed the long, dark hours of the night just waiting for the first light of dawn.

Randi lay in bed, staring out the window of her bedroom. The moon was low on the horizon, and the clear sky was star-spangled. It was a beautiful night—almost perfect. And it would have been perfect if she'd been with Hawk.

The time they'd spent together by the watering hole had left her even more convinced of her love for him. His every kiss and caress had made her long for more.

Randi could hardly wait to see Hawk again the next morning. The only trouble was that they wouldn't be riding to the canyon alone. Pa would be riding along with them. She told herself that catching the rustlers was the most important thing, but a part of her yearned for the chance to be alone with Hawk again. Somehow she had to find a way to tell him of her feelings. She had to let him know she loved him.

Fred packed what he needed and got ready to ride out of town hours before sunup. He wanted to get to the canyon and find the best place to set up the ambush.

He smiled to himself as he envisioned picking off Jack and Hawk as they rode into Black Canyon. Hawk might have won the shooting match in town, but this time he was going to win. It was going to be a very good day.

* * *

Jack was a driven man as he rode out with Hawk and Randi at dawn. His mood was solemn.

"Randi tells me that you and Pete Turner have been friends for a long time," Hawk spoke up.

Jack nodded, looking over at Hawk. "We have. We both settled here at about the same time. Why?"

"I was just trying to figure out who might be involved in this."

"Why Pete?"

"His ranch is close by, and late Saturday night, Wade met him in the alley behind the saloon. I saw them there talking together."

"Wade met with Pete in an alley?" Jack frowned.

"That's right. Any idea why they'd have to sneak off that way to talk?"

"No." Jack was grim, wondering what the two men had to say to each other that couldn't be said in the saloon.

"Wade can't be involved in any of this. He's worked for us for years," Randi protested.

"I know you trust Wade," Hawk said.

"Up until now I have. Up until now I never had any reason to doubt Wade was a good man," Jack said, his anger growing as he considered the alternative. "But we know it's someone on the inside—and who better than my foreman? I've always trusted him. I hope like hell I'm wrong about this."

They didn't say any more as they rode on toward the canyon, but Jack and Randi both began to realize that if their suspicions were right about Wade, Pete Turner might be involved in this, too.

Fred was ready. He'd positioned himself near the canyon's entrance high up in a rock-strewn area that gave him a perfect, unobstructed view of anyone riding in. Rifle in hand, he waited. Wade hadn't been too certain who'd be showing up that day, but it didn't matter. He would handle whatever came his way. He'd let them ride past him and then he'd open fire. They'd be trapped in the canyon. It was going to be very simple.

The time passed slowly for him. Fred distracted himself with thoughts of Sindy. He fully intended to seek her out once he finished here. He wanted to enjoy another night like last night. If things went as he hoped they would today, he'd definitely have reason to celebrate. He would have gotten his revenge and his debts would be paid off. Life would be good.

Finally Fred spotted three riders in the distance, heading his way. He'd expected Jack and Hawk, but he wasn't sure who the third rider was. As they drew closer, he finally recognized the third rider as Randi.

Fred smiled. After such a run of bad luck, things were finally starting to go his way. He liked that. He had already made plans for Randi—big plans— and now she'd served herself up to him, riding right into the trap he'd set for her father and the half-breed.

First, though, he had to take care of Jack and Hawk.

Then Randi would be all his.

Jack Stockton was going to pay for the grief he'd caused him.

Lifting his rifle, Fred took aim and waited. Once they'd passed by, he would have the perfect shot.

Jack and Hawk were riding slightly ahead of Randi, and she found her gaze drawn to Hawk. She couldn't look away from the broad width of his powerful shoulders. The memory of the way he'd looked bare-chested the first day they'd met was seared into her consciousness. She remembered how she'd ridden double with him, and she found herself wanting to ride that way with him again. Recognizing the wayward direction of her thoughts, Randi forced herself to concentrate on the real reason they were there.

Hawk was alert and on edge as they rode toward the entrance to Black Canyon. He didn't know why, but for some reason he felt very uneasy this morning. He'd learned early in life to trust his instincts, and he took care to study the surrounding hillsides. He looked for any sign of trouble as they rode farther down the trail.

"Randi," Hawk began as he glanced back her way, wanting to tell her to keep up with them.

It was then, out of the corner of his eye, that he caught sight of the glint of sunlight off metal, high on the hill behind them. He knew what it meant.

"Ride!" he shouted.

Chapter Seventeen

Fred took careful aim. His mood was deadly. He might have come in second in the shooting competition at the Stampede, but today he was going to hit his target. He had no doubt.

Just as Fred started to pull the trigger, he heard Hawk shout and realized he'd been seen. He began to fire.

The first shot hit Jack in the chest. He cried out as he fell from his horse. He lay unmoving, facedown on the ground.

"Pa!" Randi shouted.

"Randi! Get out of here! *Now!*" Hawk ordered, drawing his gun to return fire.

Randi went for her gun, too, as she spurred Angel on. Hawk rode after her, looking for cover, but there was none nearby. They were trapped and vulnerable. Whoever had planned this ambush had known exactly what he was doing.

"Ride for the passage!" Hawk shouted to her, knowing it was their only hope of escape.

Fred was not about to let them get away. He got Hawk in his sights, and, with steady determination, he fired. He smiled in satisfaction as he saw his bullet find its mark. Hawk was knocked from his horse.

"Hawk!" Randi screamed in complete horror as she saw him fall.

Hawk lay still on the ground. Blood from a head wound covered his face.

Randi was in shock. This couldn't be happening! Hawk and her father couldn't be hurt. They couldn't be! She refused to think they might be dead. She had to get to them to help them.

Fred was feeling quite proud of himself. He fired off several more rounds aimed to hit in front of her to panic Angel.

It worked.

Angel balked and reared. Randi held on for dear life. When more shots rang out around them, Angel bucked and twisted violently in her fright. Randi lost her seat and was thrown. Her gun flew from her grip as she hit the ground hard and was knocked unconscious.

Fred was worried. The last thing he'd wanted was for Randi to be injured. She was worth more money to him unharmed. He hurriedly mounted his own horse and raced down to check on her condition.

Dismounting beside Randi, Fred knelt down

and made sure she was still breathing. Relief flooded through him when he found out she was alive. Fred went back to his horse and got his rope. Since she was unconscious, he had no choice. He stripped her of her gun belt, then bound her wrists and ankles and gagged her with his bandanna. That done, he went after Angel.

The palomino had run a slight distance away. He walked slowly toward her, talking in a low voice to keep her from running off. He'd often seen Randi approach Angel this way, and he knew it usually worked. He was quite proud of himself when he was able to grab up Angel's reins and lead her back to where he'd left Randi.

It took some effort, but Fred managed to lift Randi up and lay her facedown across Angel's back. He secured her there. Fred didn't know how soon she might regain consciousness, but he knew what a wild woman Randi could be, and he wasn't going to take any chances with her.

Mounting up on his own horse, he started down the canyon trail leading Angel. He was headed for the passageway. It was the fastest way out.

Fred glanced back one last time at Jack's and Hawk's lifeless bodies.

He smiled.

He had definitely won the shooting contest today.

Some days were better than others.

Blinding pain racked Hawk as he slowly regained consciousness. He groaned and lay unmoving. He fought against the agony that tortured him and tried to understand what had happened.

It took a moment for his thoughts to clear and the memory of the ambush to return. When it did, he sat up suddenly. He feared the man who'd ambushed them was still there, and he was ready to go for his gun. He remembered that Jack had been shot, too, and he was worried about Randi. He needed to make sure nothing had happened to her.

Hawk hadn't reckoned on the excruciating torment that tore through his head when he moved so quickly. He sagged weakly back, bracing himself on one arm. He reached up and tentatively touched the wound at his temple. His hand came away covered in blood.

As much as the wound hurt, Hawk knew he was lucky to be alive. Desperate to help Randi and Jack, he tried to ignore the pain, but it wasn't easy. He staggered to his feet and swayed unsteadily. He spotted his gun on the ground nearby and went to pick it up. The throbbing in his head intensified as he bent down to retrieve it. In silent agony, he locked his jaw against the torment and fought to focus on what he had to do.

Straightening up, he looked around. There was no trace of Randi, but he spotted Jack lying on the ground a short distance away. He made his way over to kneel down beside him. With great care, Hawk rolled Jack over. The front of his shirt was blood-soaked, and for a moment Hawk thought he was dead. He was surprised when Jack moaned and slowly opened his eyes.

"Hawk," Jack managed, looking up at him and seeing Hawk's bloody head wound. "The shooter . . . ?"

"He's gone."

"Randi . . . is she . . . ?" His words were tortured. He expected to hear the worst.

"She's not here," Hawk answered.

"Maybe she got away in time." He sounded hopeful.

"Maybe." Hawk knew better. Whoever had been after them hadn't been about to let her get away.

"We have to go after her! We have to find her!" Jack agonized.

Painful memories of Jessie's abduction suddenly returned to torture Hawk, and a fierce, grim determination filled him.

"I will," he said solemnly.

"But what about your head?" Jack knew Hawk had to be in pain.

"I'll be all right."

"I have to go with you!" Jack insisted in spite of the seriousness of his own wound.

"You'll only slow me down."

"I'm going!" he repeated.

Hawk didn't waste time arguing with him. He opened Jack's shirt to take a look at his wound and realized how lucky they both were to still be alive.

Hawk was thankful the man who'd ambushed them hadn't been a better shot.

Taking off his own shirt, Hawk used his knife to cut a piece from it. Quickly, he bound up his own wound, then made a bandage for Jack out of the rest of it. He helped Jack to sit up and then wrapped the makeshift bandage tightly around his chest.

Jack grimaced in pain as he moved.

"The bullet's still in you, but I don't want to risk trying to dig it out here," Hawk told him. "Are you feeling strong enough to get back to the ranch on your own?"

"I told you"—Jack ignored Hawk and tried to get up, determined to find his daughter—"I'm going with you."

Jack was intent only on saving Randi. He couldn't worry about himself when his daughter was in danger. He was ready to find his horse and start the search, but as he tried to get to his feet, he found he was so weak he almost collapsed.

Torment ate at Jack. He sat back down heavily on the ground. Hawk had been right. He was too weak from loss of blood to try to track her, and he wouldn't get any better until the bullet was removed.

It was the most painful thing Jack had ever done when he looked at Hawk and told him, "Go find Randi. I can make it back alone."

Hawk nodded. "Wait here while I find our horses."

Jack prayed it wouldn't take him long. Whoever

had taken Randi already had a good head start on him.

Randi was in danger. Hawk had to rescue her before any harm came to her.

Hawk set out after their horses. He hoped they had run deeper into the canyon, for then he'd have a chance to catch them. If they'd fled the canyon, he and Jack were in trouble.

Hawk hadn't gone far when he found Randi's gun and gun belt lying on the ground; he had the answer he'd dreaded. Just as he'd suspected, she hadn't escaped. Something terrible had happened to her.

Taking the gun with him, Hawk continued to search the area. It wasn't easy, but he finally found fresh tracks leading toward the passageway, and it looked like one of the horses had been Angel.

Whoever had ambushed them had taken Randi captive, but why? It hadn't been an Indian raiding party. There was only one other set of tracks with Angel's.

Hawk whistled and called out for Bruiser as he moved on, looking for the missing horses. On foot the going was slow, but he finally found both the animals near a small watering hole farther back in the canyon. He was relieved that they didn't run off as he approached them and got their reins. After tying them to a nearby tree, Hawk stowed Randi's gun in his saddlebag, then took time to wash the blood from his hands and face. The pain in his head was still severe, but he couldn't let it stop him. Nothing mattered except going after Randi as quickly as he could.

He rode Bruiser back to where Jack awaited him, leading Jack's horse behind him.

Jack was sitting down, leaning against a rock when he saw Hawk approaching in the distance. Jack realized then that with his shirt off, Hawk once again looked as he had the first time he'd seen him. He looked like a true Comanche warrior. The moment he thought it, he grew angry with himself. He knew and respected Hawk. Hawk was no murderous savage. He was the man who was going to help save Randi.

"Thank God, you found them," Jack said when Hawk reined in before him.

"I found Randi's gun, too. Whoever ambushed us took her prisoner."

Jack was sickened by the news. "Who would do this?"

"I'm going to find out," Hawk told him with certainty.

Hawk dismounted and went to help Jack to his feet. He knew how weak the rancher was and that he was going to need help.

Hawk was right. It was a struggle for Jack to get on his horse even with help, but somehow he managed.

Still, man that he was, Jack wasn't about to let anyone know how bad he was feeling. He looked over at Hawk once the younger man had mounted up on Bruiser.

"Be careful," Jack said.

"I will."

"Hawk—find her."

Their gazes met in painful understanding. Hawk nodded to him, then wheeled Bruiser around and galloped off at top speed toward the passage. There was no time to waste.

Jack watched him go, and he prayed for Randi's safe return.

Fred was feeling pleased with himself as he rode across country. He was traveling as fast as he could with Randi tied down across her saddle. It wasn't easy going, but she was bound to come to sooner or later.

Fred knew eventually some of the hands from the ranch would go looking for Jack, Hawk, and Randi, but he figured he had close to a full day's head start on any search party. Of course, once they found Jack's and Hawk's bodies, they would come after him and try to track him down, but by then he'd be long gone.

He'd been riding for almost an hour when he finally heard Randi groan. He stopped and dismounted to take her down from Angel's back.

"You finally woke up, did you?" he said coldly.

Randi had regained consciousness to find herself bound and gagged, and tied facedown on Angel's back. She'd struggled to get a look at the man riding the horse ahead of Angel, and when she'd seen that it was Fred, she'd been stunned. She tried to free herself, to break loose, but bound as she was, she was helpless.

Fred came back and released the ropes that held her on Angel's back. When he reached up to pull her down, she kicked him in the chest.

"You bitch!" Fred snarled. He yanked her down from the horse's back and shoved her to the ground. He'd wanted to backhand her, but controlled the urge. He didn't want to risk bruising her face.

Randi lay sprawled at his feet in the dirt, glaring up at him. She deliberately tried to act defiant as she struggled to hide her fear from him. She couldn't let him know she was terrified.

Fred bent down and untied her ankles.

"Now get on your horse and don't try anything stupid."

She stood up and mounted Angel.

Fred took Angel's reins and got ready to ride. He glanced over at Randi and saw that she was looking back the way they'd come.

"Don't go getting your hopes up. There ain't nobody coming after you. Your Pa and the half-breed are both dead." He saw her eyes widen in shock and pain, and he enjoyed the feeling of power her reaction gave him. He grinned. "Yeah, I made sure of that. So it's just you and me, now."

Putting his heels to his horse's sides, Fred started off again. He kept a tight hold on Angel's reins. He wasn't taking any chances.

Tears streamed down Randi's cheeks as she held on tight to the saddle horn.

Hawk and her father were dead.

Memories of the ambush, of seeing her father and Hawk gunned down in cold blood, assailed her. She had tried to go to them and help them. She had tried to return fire, but then Angel had panicked and she remembered nothing after being thrown.

Desperation filled Randi.

She was alone.

Hawk rode out of the passage and picked up their trail. He had no idea where they were headed, and it didn't matter.

The only thing that mattered was saving Randi.

He had to find her.

He couldn't let anything happen to her.

Forcing away thoughts of what had happened to Jessie, Hawk concentrated only on his tracking. Whoever had taken Randi captive had close to a two-hour head start on him. Every minute counted. He pushed Bruiser to his limit as they raced on. Time was of the essence.

Chapter Eighteen

The ride back to the Lazy S was torture for Jack. When the main house finally came into view, he was swaying weakly in the saddle. Encouraged that he was so close, he held on as tightly as he could and kneed his horse to a faster pace. He had to get home. He had to let the men know what had happened, so they could ride out and help Hawk find Randi.

As anxious as he was to have the men go after Hawk, Jack was tortured by thoughts of Wade and his possible betrayal. Could he trust his foreman? Did he dare let Wade head up the men who would go to help Hawk? He didn't know. If Wade was involved—if Wade had betrayed him—there would be grave danger in including him. He wasn't sure what to do.

Jack had almost reached the house before anyone spotted him. A shout went out among the men when they realized something was wrong, and they rushed out to meet him.

Wade was one of the first to reach Jack's side.

"Jack! What happened to you?" Wade asked, helping Jack as he collapsed and half fell out of the saddle.

"We were ambushed in Black Canyon," he managed.

"Where are Hawk and Randi?" Rob asked, looking around to see if they were following him in.

"Whoever shot us took Randi. Hawk's gone after them. He's trying to track them down. You have to go help him." There was desperation in his voice.

"Let's get you inside." Wade stepped up and took charge. "Rob, you ride into town and get the doc."

"There's no time for that!" Jack protested angrily with all the fierceness he could muster.

"You need a doctor," Wade countered.

"I'm not worried about me. Wilda can take a look my chest. She may be able to get the bullet out. The rest of you men"—he looked up at the hands who'd gathered around—"get ready to ride."

"Come on. We need to get you inside," Wade urged. He appeared concerned as he helped Jack up the walkway, but, in truth, he was furious. Fred had been told to take care of things. He and Pete hadn't paid the fool that money to miss!

Jack allowed Wade to help him, but, troubled as he was by his suspicions, he was repulsed by his touch. Still, he knew he couldn't allow his reaction to show. He didn't know anything for sure—yet.

Wilda heard the commotion outside and was just coming to see what was wrong when they entered through the front door. Rob and Lew followed them in, while the rest of the men waited anxiously outside on the porch.

"Jack! What happened?" She was shocked by the sight of his bloodied shirt.

"He's been shot," Wade told her.

"Let's get him upstairs and into bed," she directed, leading the way to turn back his bed for him.

They followed her down the hallway into Jack's bedroom and helped him sit down on the side of the bed.

"Rob, I'm going to need hot water, and a lot of it," Wilda ordered.

He hurried off to tend to it.

She stripped away Jack's bloodied shirt. Once she had it off of him, she helped him to lie back. After carefully removing the makeshift bandage, she quickly examined his wound.

"You need to have the doc look at this," she said, her expression grave as she glanced up at him. The gunshot wound was serious. She knew Jack was lucky to be alive. If the bullet had been any closer to his heart, he would have been a dead man.

"All right," he groaned, "but don't send Rob. He's one of the best trackers we have. I want him to help find Randi."

"Where was Hawk headed?" Wade asked.

Rob had returned from the kitchen by then, and Jack looked up at both of them as he answered, "Hawk found a secret passage out of Black Canyon."

"What?" Everyone in the room appeared shocked by his claim.

"That's why we haven't been able to catch the rustlers in all these months," he explained; then he quickly told them about the passage and its location. "Whoever took Randi must have ridden out that way, and Hawk went after them."

"We'll ride out right away," Rob promised him.

"Good." A sense of relief filled him. "But be careful. Whoever did this is out for blood."

"I'll go tell the boys to saddle up," Wade said, starting from the room.

Lew followed him. Wilda went down to check on the water Rob had put on to heat, leaving Rob alone with Jack. Rob started to go.

"Don't leave . . ." Jack began in a faint voice. He could tell that what little strength he had was rapidly fading.

"What is it, Jack?" Rob went to stand at the bedside.

Jack looked up at Rob and reached out to grab his arm. As weak as he was, his hold on the other man was fierce, and he braced himself up on one elbow to speak. "Be careful."

"We will," Rob promised.

"No, you don't understand." He paused to draw a ragged breath. "Watch out for Wade."

"What?" Rob was completely shocked.

"I don't know for sure," he said in a low voice, "but he might be involved in this. Watch him. Don't turn your back on him."

It was an order.

Rob nodded, but he doubted Jack's suspicions. He knew for a fact that Wade had been at the ranch all day. There was no way he'd had any part in the shooting.

"Good. Now, go on—go. Hurry—help Hawk find Randi." Jack sagged back on the bed and closed his eyes. He was totally spent by the effort of speaking.

Rob rushed from the room, passing Wilda on her way back in with a basin of hot water.

"We'll be back," he told her, "with Randi."

Wilda tended to Jack's wound as best she could while they waited for the ranch hand they'd sent to town to return with the doctor.

Fred was glad when he saw a spring up ahead. The horses needed a rest. There was no need to run them into the ground. They were making good time, and nobody would be coming after them anytime soon. Reining in on the bank, Fred dismounted and looked up at Randi.

"Get down." It was an order.

Randi's gaze was cold upon Fred as she did what she was told. Hatred for him filled her. He had killed Hawk and her father in cold blood and actually seemed proud of it.

Fred walked slowly behind her. Randi tensed and wondered what he was doing. She was surprised when he removed the kerchief he'd used to gag her.

"Here," he said, getting his canteen and shoving it at her.

"Untie my hands," Randi said, holding her arms out to him.

"Hell, no. I know you too well." He smirked at her. "Drink up while you can. We got a lot of miles to cover today."

Randi took the canteen from him and drank thirstily. It was awkward to do with her wrists tightly bound, but she managed.

As she drank, Randi looked around for a way to escape. She'd been tempted to take off when he'd first dismounted at the spring, but Angel was so tired now, she knew they wouldn't have gotten very far. Still, she was sure the opportunity for escape was going to come. It had to! And when it did, she would be ready. She just wished she hadn't lost her gun.

"Things have turned out real good for me," Fred bragged as he led both horses down to the water's edge, leaving her standing there on the bank. "Yeah, good old Wade should have paid me double for the way I pulled everything off today."

"Wade!" She hadn't meant to say anything. She'd wanted to ignore Fred completely, but his mention of the foreman proved Hawk had been right in his suspicions. Rage and even more pain filled her at the knowledge of Wade's betrayal.

"That's right. Me and Wade, we been working together for a long time. Your pa never figured it out. Wade's slick—real slick. He has everybody fooled."

"He doesn't have everybody fooled!" she countered, unable to control her fury any longer. "Hawk knows!"

"But that don't matter now, does it?" he said snidely, enjoying tormenting her. "Your precious half-breed is dead—and so is your pa."

The agony in her heart tore at her, but more than the agony, uncontrolled fury erupted within her. No longer caring if she lived or died, she ran at Fred and attacked him. She hit him and kicked him as hard as she could, and she did manage to land a few blows.

Fred was infuriated by her attack. He grabbed her by the arms and hauled her up against him, holding her pinned so she couldn't move.

Randi twisted and turned, frantic to break free of his vile hold. She hated him with every fiber of her being.

"It's a damned pity I already have plans for you," he snarled in her ear. "Otherwise, I might just be seeing how much of a fight you'd put up if I spread them pretty legs of yours right here and now."

She shuddered at his words.

He felt her tremble and laughed aloud. Then he bent to her and pressed a hot, wet kiss to the side of her neck.

"Leave me alone! Don't touch me!"

Fred laughed even more at her reaction. He shoved her away from him.

She pivoted around to glare up at him in fury and disgust.

"Don't you worry, Randi. I won't be using you. I'm taking you to a nice little place near the border. There's a fella there who pays a lot of money for pretty little virgins like you."

Randi was horrified by what he'd just told her. She wanted Hawk to come and save her from the terrible fate that awaited her. She longed to look up and see him riding toward her at full speed, coming to rescue her as he had in the past.

But Hawk would never be coming to save her again.

Hawk was dead.

Regret and agonizing pain filled her, for she'd never had the chance to tell him she loved him.

Randi went numb inside, overwhelmed by all that had happened to her.

Fred eyed Randi hungrily as she stood there before him. She was a pretty one, all right. He'd secretly watched her all the time on the ranch. He liked the way she looked in those pants of hers. He was enjoying her feeling of helplessness, too. On the ranch, she'd been the boss's daughter, someone they all had to listen to. Out here with him, she was nothing. Having her all to himself this way made him feel powerful.

He smiled and went to get the horses ready to

ride. The sooner they got back on the trail, the sooner he'd get the rest of the money he was wanting.

Hawk and Bruiser raced across the countryside, following the double set of tracks. He knew Bruiser was growing tired, but he wanted to keep going as long as he could. When he finally found a small watering hole, he stopped only long enough to let Bruiser get a drink and rest up a little.

Hawk couldn't sit still while Bruiser rested. He was too worried about Randi. He paced tensely, staring off in the direction the trail led. Though Angel was fast, Bruiser was faster. He had to be gaining on them, but without a sighting he had no idea just how far ahead of him they were.

Once he was sure Bruiser was rested, he rode out again. It was then that he thought of Jack. He hoped the rancher had made it safely back to the house.

Jack lay rigidly on the bed as Dr. Murray worked to extract the bullet from his wound. Sweat beaded Jack's brow. His hands were clenched into white-knuckled fists by his sides.

"You are a very lucky man, Jack," Dr. Murray told him, finally speaking after removing the bullet. He held up the bullet for his patient to see.

"I'm not feeling real lucky right now," Jack said in a hoarse voice as some of the tension went out of him.

"You should. If this bullet had been an inch farther over, Wilda would have been sending to town for the undertaker instead of me."

The doctor set the bullet in a dish on the night table and went back to cleaning out the wound. When he finished, he looked down at Jack, his expression serious.

"You really have no idea who shot you?"

"No, none, but I intend to find out," he said grimly.

Dr. Murray knew Jack, and he warned him, "You're in no condition to go anywhere for a few weeks. You can't start moving around too soon."

Jack didn't respond; he just turned his head away to stare out the bedroom window.

"When your ranch hand came into town to get me, I left word at the sheriff's office that there had been some trouble out here at the ranch. Sheriff Johnson wasn't there at the time, but I'm sure he'll be riding out to check in with you when he gets back."

Jack looked over at him. "Thanks, Doc."

Dr. Murray nodded. "You're welcome. You stay in bed and let that would heal. I'll come back out tomorrow and look in on you again," he instructed as he got ready to leave.

It was midafternoon by the time Wade, Rob, Lew, and the other men who'd ridden with them reached Black Canyon.

Rob hadn't understood the reason for Jack's

warning, but he took it seriously. Jack wasn't a man who spoke rashly. As they rode into the canyon, looking for the hidden passage, he watched Wade to see if the foreman did anything unusual. He expected him to be able to find the passage reasonably quickly, since Jack had given them directions. Wade was leading the way, and he rode on past the area where it was supposed to be.

"Wade," Rob called out, reining in at the hidden entrance. "This is it here."

"Are you sure? I thought Jack said it was farther back." Wade stopped and looked back at Rob.

"Yeah, this is it. Follow me," Rob directed the men as he guided his horse through the thick brush and into the narrow passage.

Wade rode back to follow Rob and the others. He'd deliberately ridden past the entrance to make their search take longer. He wanted to give Fred as big a lead as possible.

Chapter Nineteen

Sheriff Johnson made it out to the Lazy S late that afternoon.

"We're so glad you're here," Wilda said, showing him the way up to Jack's room.

"Dr. Murray told me some of what happened, but I wanted to hear the whole story from Jack."

"He's been resting since the doc left, but I know he'll be glad to see you." She stopped before the bedroom door and knocked lightly before going in. "Jack, Sheriff Johnson is here."

"Come on in," Jack said.

"I'll leave you two to talk. If you need anything, I'll be downstairs." She let herself out of the room.

"Jack, sorry to hear what happened," the lawman began after she'd gone. "Are you doing all right?"

"As well as I can be, I guess," he answered, hating his own weakness. He wanted to be out searching for Randi, not lying there in bed.

"The doc said you were ambushed?"

"That's right—out at Black Canyon." Jack went on to tell him all he could remember about the shooting. "I'm damned lucky to be alive. Hawk, too."

"Where is Hawk?"

"He rode out after Randi, straight from the canyon, but whoever took her had at least a two-hour lead on him. I sent Wade and Rob and the boys out to try to help him. We've got to find her!"

The sheriff understood his desperation. "I'll get some men together from town and have them ride out there, too."

"There is one other thing." Jack looked at the lawman. "Wade may be involved in this. I can't prove it yet, but I've got my suspicions."

"I'll remember that, and I'll get back to you if I find out anything."

"Thanks, Sheriff." All the talk had exhausted Jack.

"And if you hear back from your hands, send word to me right away."

"I will."

With that assurance, the lawman headed back to San Miguel.

Sherri showed up at the store to go to work and found her mother and father in serious conversation behind the counter. When they saw her walk in, they both went quiet, and she immediately suspected something was wrong.

"What is it? Did something happen today? You both look worried," she said.

Her father nodded. He looked concerned as he answered her. "One of the deputies was in a while ago to tell us there was trouble out at the Lazy S."

"What kind of trouble?" Sherri looked between her parents, wondering at their guarded expressions.

He related what little he'd learned. "Talk has it Jack and Hawk were ambushed and shot, and Randi was kidnapped."

"Randi? Kidnapped? But why? Who would have taken her?" Sherri demanded, aghast.

"The deputy didn't have any idea. Sheriff Johnson is out at the ranch right now talking to Jack."

"What are we going to do?"

"There's nothing we can do but wait."

"And pray," her mother added.

Sherri was tormented by what she'd learned. She went about her work at the store, but her thoughts remained on Randi. She hoped her friend would be found, and she prayed she was all right.

Sindy was bored. The day had been quiet at the bar, and she liked a little excitement in her life. When a few cowboys came in, she was glad for the distraction and hoped they'd liven things up for her. She worked her wiles on them, trying to get them upstairs, but they seemed intent on talking about the big news in town.

"What big news?" she asked, irritated that she couldn't get their undivided attention.

"You ain't heard?" one of the cowboys said. "There's been big trouble for Jack Stockton." He quickly related the talk he'd heard around town.

"His daughter was kidnapped?" Sindy repeated in disbelief, remembering her conversation with Fred and knowing he might be the one responsible.

"That's right, and there ain't no telling if they'll ever be able to find her."

"I gotta go." She was angry and disgusted at the same time.

"Where are you going, Sindy? I was just about ready to take you upstairs and have some fun with you."

"Wait for me. I won't be gone too long. I'll make it worth your while and show you a real good time when I get back."

Sindy left the Silver Dollar and hurried toward the sheriff's office. She didn't care that she was wearing her working clothes from the saloon. She ignored the open, disapproving stares of the townsfolk. She just wanted to let the lawman know about Fred. She thought it might help the search party find the girl. She'd always suspected Fred was really stupid, and he'd just proven it.

When she got to the office, only one of the deputies was there.

"Where's the sheriff?"

"He's out at the Stockton place," he told her. "Why? You got trouble?"

"No, but I need to talk to him. Tell him to come see me at the Silver Dollar as soon as he gets back."

"I will."

The deputy watched Sindy go, admiring the view.

Randi lay huddled and unmoving under the blanket Fred had thrown her way when they'd made camp. She'd wanted to try to escape from him tonight, but he'd tied her hands behind her and bound her ankles again before he'd bedded down for the night. She'd been struggling to free her hands for hours now, but with little success. She had no intention of giving up, though. Sooner or later she would find a way to break loose, and when she did, she would claim her revenge.

Fred was going to pay for killing her father and Hawk.

She'd see to it.

Randi closed her eyes as the pain of losing the two men she loved most tore at her heart. She had loved her father her whole life. He had always taken care of her and he had always been there for her. She would miss him for the rest of her life.

Her thoughts turned to Hawk, and a deep, abiding pain filled her. She'd waited all her life to fall in love, and she finally had—with Hawk, only to have him torn from her so violently. Tears filled her eyes.

Memories of the time they'd spent by the watering hole swept over her. No other man had ever touched her heart the way he had. She remembered the ecstasy of his embrace and kiss. Being held in his arms had been wonderful. He had been strong, and yet incredibly gentle with her. Hawk had been everything she'd ever wanted in a man, and now he was lost to her forever.

She began to cry again in silent mourning.

Hawk didn't stop tracking Randi until darkness had completely claimed the land. He'd hoped to sight a campfire in the night, but found nothing. Frustration swamped him as he bedded down for the night. He had nothing with him to eat, and he didn't care. He just wanted the long hours of the night to pass quickly, so he could be on their trail again.

Hawk lay, staring up at the night sky, reliving the events of that morning. Over and over in his mind, he saw the glint of the sun off the rifle barrel as the first shots were fired, and he saw Jack being hit.

Hawk was furious with himself. He'd sensed something wasn't right, but he'd never suspected someone would be waiting to ambush them. He would never make that mistake again.

Who was it who had ambushed them?

Who would have known they were riding for the canyon that morning and had time to set it up?

Hawk remembered that Wade had gone to see the widow the night before—or so he'd said. But Wade hadn't known that they'd discovered the secret passage out of the canyon.

Frustrated, Hawk closed his eyes and tried to

sleep. He needed to get what rest he could, for he planned to be back on Randi's trail at first light.

It wasn't often Hawk prayed. After Jessie's death, he hadn't had much to say to God. As he lay there this night, though, he silently offered up a prayer, asking for help in finding Randi.

Dawn found him saddling up Bruiser and on the trail again.

The terrain grew more rugged with each passing hour, and Hawk knew he'd be lucky if he didn't lose the trail. He pushed Bruiser to his limits. They were riding at a good pace near midday when the horse suddenly stumbled and came up lame.

Hawk was immediately worried, for Bruiser was usually surefooted. He couldn't afford to have anything happen to Bruiser, not when they were out there in the middle of nowhere.

Hawk dismounted and quickly went to check his hoof to see what was wrong. What he discovered left him filled with useless rage. Bruiser had thrown a shoe, and when it had come off the shoe had torn a damaging chunk out of his hoof.

Frustration filled Hawk as he stood up and stared off in the direction Randi and her kidnapper had ridden. He had been gaining on them. He'd hoped to catch up with them the next day at the latest, but now in the condition he was in, Bruiser would be lucky if he could even make it back to the ranch. There was no way for them to continue their pursuit.

Hawk realized Jack would have sent men from the ranch after him to help with the search, but he couldn't just sit there and wait for them to show up. They were too far behind him. It would be long hours before they caught up with him, and by then there was no telling where Randi might have been taken.

Hawk didn't like the idea of turning Bruiser loose on his own, but he had no choice. Trying to lead the horse as he continued tracking would slow him down even more.

Hawk spotted what looked like a secluded grassy area ahead of them. There had to be a spring nearby, so he knew he could leave Bruiser there, and the horse would at least have food and water.

After taking the time to remove Bruiser's other shoes so it would be easier for him to walk, Hawk led the horse toward the grassy area at a slow, hobbling pace. There was a small spring, so after unsaddling Bruiser and taking off his bridle, he turned him loose. Bruiser limped down to the water's edge to get a drink.

Hawk filled his canteen. Carrying only his saddlebags and the basics he needed to survive, he started back on Randi's trail once more.

It was hot. The sun was beating down mercilessly, and Hawk noticed it much more now that he was on foot. He missed his Stetson, but knew he wouldn't have been able to wear it anyway. The pain from his head wound was still fierce, and his hat would only have aggravated it more. Grimly determined never to give up his search for Randi, he followed her trail, walking as quickly as he could.

Hawk looked back only once to see Bruiser standing near the spring, watching him go. He was glad Bruiser wasn't trying to follow him. The horse would be safer there.

The going was rough for Hawk. The heat and the pain took their toll, but he never let up. He covered several miles before stopping for the first time to rest.

Doubts were beginning to torment him, and clouds forming to the west worried him. If any heavy rains came, they would wash out the trail. Knowing he had no time to waste, that he had to get on the move again, Hawk took a deep drink and started out once more.

Hawk had been on the trail for another hour when he discovered the tracks led into a small canyon. After what had happened at Black Canyon, Hawk approached the entrance warily. He moved forward cautiously, keeping a careful watch for any sign of trouble.

And it was then that he heard it: farther up the canyon, the sound of a horse neighing.

Hawk drew his gun as a torrent of emotions raced through him. He had lost so much time with Bruiser's injury, he couldn't be sure it was Randi and her captor up ahead. Hope swelled within him, but he knew better than to get too excited.

Hawk moved forward, expecting trouble. He was ready for a showdown.

What he found astounded him.

There in the center of the canyon just ahead of him stood Phantom.

Hawk stopped to stare at the elusive stallion. Of all the things Hawk had imagined finding there, Phantom had been the last he'd expected. He was disappointed that there was no sign of Randi, but the hope that had filled him earlier returned. If ever a horse was fast enough to help him reach Randi in time to save her, it would be the phantom stallion. All he had to do was figure out how to capture him.

Only the finest of warriors could ride Phantom. . . .

The elusive stallion's legend played in Hawk's thoughts as he slowly holstered his gun and dropped the gear he'd been carrying with him. Hawk knew he was about to find out just how good a warrior he really was.

Phantom stood unmoving, watching Hawk as he walked slowly toward him.

Hawk made no sudden moves, and he began talking to Phantom in the Comanche tongue.

The stallion cocked his head at the sound of his voice and tensed a bit as he drew closer.

Hawk saw his reaction, so he deliberately stopped and turned away. He knew stallions were as curious as they were brave, and if he were to have any hope of catching Phantom, he had to lure him in. Hawk stood there waiting.

Phantom eyed the man suspiciously, then took several steps in his direction. When the man remained still during his approach, the stallion ventured even nearer.

Hawk knew Phantom was coming closer. He turned slowly to look at him, then once again turned his back to him.

The stallion was made even more curious by his actions. The horse boldly stepped forward and nudged the man in the back.

It was then that Hawk made his move. In one smooth motion he turned and grabbed a handful of Phantom's mane, then vaulted onto his back. He felt the stallion tense beneath him.

"Easy, Phantom," he soothed in his native language.

The big, powerful horse trembled, but didn't buck. Hawk knew that if he held on tightly, it would only make the stallion more nervous. Instead, wanting to calm him, Hawk sat him easily and continued to talk as he stroked his neck and withers.

It took a few minutes, but Hawk finally felt some of the tension ease from the horse. Gently, he urged him to move. Phantom responded. They rode around the area, slowly getting used to each other.

Hawk was worried that Phantom might run off when he stopped to pick up his gear. Even so, it was a chance he had to take. Bringing the stallion to a stop, he dismounted. He kept stroking his neck and talking to him in even, unthreatening tones while he bent down and picked up his rope.

The stallion eyed the rope a bit nervously, but Hawk reassured him. He quickly fashioned a makeshift halter and put it on the horse. Phantom did not balk, and Hawk was greatly relieved. Hawk gathered up the rest of his things, then swung back up onto the stallion's back.

As fast as Hawk knew Phantom could be, he was certain they would make up the time he had lost traveling on foot. They charged down the canyon, riding as one.

Only the finest of warriors could ride Phantom—again Hawk remembered the legend.

It had been years since Hawk had felt as if he belonged in the Comanche world, but at this moment, leaning low over Phantom's neck, he was a true warrior on the hunt.

Chapter Twenty

It was almost noon when Wilda saw Sheriff Johnson riding up to the house. She hurried upstairs and knocked on Jack's bedroom door, then opened it to tell him the news.

"Jack—Sheriff Johnson's riding in!"

"Is he alone?" Jack asked hopefully.

"Yes, he's by himself."

His hopes were dashed.

"Bring him on up when he gets here," he ordered. Wilda went down to greet the lawman.

"This is a surprise—you coming back out here so soon," Wilda said as he entered the house.

"I've got some news for Jack."

He sounded so solemn that Wilda grew worried.

"He's upstairs. You can go on up." She watched him go, fear for Randi's safety filling her.

"Jack?" Sheriff Johnson called out just outside his bedroom door.

"Come on in," Jack responded. Then he quickly asked, "Have you found my girl?"

"No, Jack, I'm afraid not, but I do have some news I thought you might find interesting."

"What is it?" He was eager to hear anything that would help find Randi.

"Sindy, one of the girls who works over at the Silver Dollar, paid me a visit. She heard what happened, and she thinks she knows who did it."

"Who?"

"Fred Carter," he answered. "Sindy heard him talking about how much he wanted to get even with you for firing him."

Jack scowled. "It makes sense. I know Fred was furious, but there's no way Fred could have known on his own that we were riding out to Black Canyon. Someone had to have told him ahead of time." Again he thought of Wade, and his mood grew even darker.

"You think Wade was the one?" the sheriff asked, remembering their earlier conversation.

"I can't be sure. We didn't tell anyone here at the ranch where we were going. I don't know how Wade could have found out. I need more proof before I can go outright accusing him of anything," Jack said solemnly. He looked up at the lawman. "Hawk will be back. He's going to find Randi and bring her home to me, and when he does, we'll know the truth."

"Well, you let me know if you need me." Sheriff Johnson started from the bedroom.

"I will. And Sheriff . . ."

The lawman looked back at Jack.

"Thanks for riding out."

When a violent thunderstorm broke overhead, Wade, Rob, and the other men sought cover near a rocky overhang. Lightning flashed and thunder roared around them. Heavy rains pummeled the land.

Wade acted upset, but he was really delighted with this turn of events. He had no doubt, as the fierce rain poured down, that there would be no trace of Hawk's trail left when the storm finally passed over. They would be forced to return to the ranch empty-handed. Things couldn't have worked out better for him.

Huddling close to the rocks, the men from the Lazy S held on to their horses and waited for the storm to pass. They all knew what the heavy downpour meant, and they were angry at being so thwarted. They cared about Randi and were worried about her. They wanted her safely returned to the ranch. When at last the rain started to let up, they ventured out, more than a little damp, but still ready to ride. Wade's first comment stopped them cold.

"There's no point in going on, boys." Wade sounded disgusted as he looked out over the rain-scoured land.

"We can't give up, Wade," Rob insisted. "We've got to keep looking for them."

"What are you going to follow? There's no trail left."

"We can ride on a ways and see if we can pick up their tracks farther out."

"Yeah," Lew agreed. "It might not have rained a few miles on. We might get lucky."

Wade was already feeling lucky. He was more than ready to cut and run, but since the others were putting pressure on him to continue the search, he couldn't quit looking just yet.

"We can try," Wade finally agreed.

The men from the Lazy S mounted up and rode off in the general direction they'd been heading before the storm had hit. It was several hours later when, after serious and intensive searching, the rest of the men were ready to give up, too. There was no trace of Hawk's trail to be found anywhere.

"All right," Rob said, looking over at Wade in defeat, "let's head back."

"Jack ain't gonna like this," Lew remarked. He thought they should keep going awhile longer. "He ain't gonna to like this at all."

"Hell, I don't like it," Wade told them. "But there's nothing more we can do. Even if we split up, I don't see any hope. We could keep at it for days, but there's no guarantee we'd ever pick up the trail again."

"I know. You're right," Rob said, turning his horse back toward the Lazy S. He could just imagine how upset their boss was going to be when they returned without Randi. He sure hoped Hawk had better luck finding her than they had.

Randi had had enough as she rode along with Fred near sundown on the second day. She didn't know exactly what she was going to do just yet, but tonight was the night. Tonight she was going to take action. Somehow she was going to get free, and when she did, she was going for Fred's gun. He had murdered her father and the man she loved. She wanted revenge.

Randi realized it would be dangerous, possibly deadly, but at this point she no longer cared much about staying alive.

She had no future.

Her future had died with Hawk.

While they'd been riding today, Fred had taken great pleasure in describing what her life was going to be like once he'd sold her off. Randi knew she'd rather be dead than live through what he had planned for her.

"We'll camp here," Fred declared.

His words interrupted Randi's thoughts, and she was forced to play the obedient captive again—for a while. Docilely, she did as she was told, dismounting and sitting down in the small clearing while he tended to their horses and built a small campfire. She kept hoping he would let his guard down, since she seemed so willing to do whatever he told her to do.

Fred handed her some food and the canteen. He sat down across from her to eat, too.

"In another few days we'll be there. Then once I get rid of you, I can start living the good life," he said with a smile.

She had been trying to ignore him, but her hatred of him got the best of her. "What kind of life can you have, knowing you're a murderer?"

"I did what I had to do."

"Kill two innocent men?"

Fred's expression turned ugly. "You're old man was hell to work for! He worked us long days and didn't pay us much of anything, and then he went and fired me just for trying to get rid of that damned half-breed!"

"Hawk was a good man." Fury welled up inside her.

He looked at her and sneered, "Yeah, he's good—good and dead—just like every Indian and half-breed should be."

Fred got up and went over to Randi to get her ready to bed down for the night. He needed to retie her arms behind her back and bind her ankles again. He needed to know she wasn't going anywhere while he was trying to sleep.

But Randi had other ideas. Her anger with him was so great, she was barely able to control herself. She scratched up two handfuls of the sandy, gritty dirt, and just as Fred hunkered down in front of her, she threw the dirt right in his face, deliberately aiming for his eyes.

"You bitch!" Fred yelled, temporarily blinded.

Randi lunged forward and shoved him as hard as she could. Fred lost his balance and fell backward. She made a grab for the gun in his holster. He anticipated her move and hit out at her. He managed to knock her away from him.

Spotting his rifle on the far side of the campfire near his bedroll, she ran to it. She picked up the rifle awkwardly and started to spin around to face him. With her hands bound, it was hard to keep a grip on the rifle, let alone fire it, but she had to try. She knew this might be her only chance.

Randi looked up to find that Fred was already right behind her.

She didn't hesitate. She pulled the trigger.

Randi knew an instant of satisfaction when she heard Fred shout out in pain as the bullet hit him in his left arm.

Even though she'd shot him, it didn't stop him from coming after her. Fred tackled Randi with brute force as she tried to flee. The power of his assault knocked the rifle out of her hands and left her pinned beneath him on the hard, rocky ground.

"You're gonna pay for this," Fred raged at her. He violently backhanded her. Right then he no longer cared if she had any bruises on her or not.

The fierce power of his blow left Randi dazed. She tried to fight back, but her efforts were weak and futile.

Fred dragged her bodily over to her blanket and

shoved her down. He was bleeding from the gunshot wound in his upper arm, but he still managed to tie her up so she wouldn't be able to move for the rest of the night.

Fred got up and staggered away, clutching his wounded arm. He had to get the bleeding stopped. He knew he'd been lucky. It was only a flesh wound, but it still hurt like hell.

The sound of the single gunshot had echoed eerily through the night. Miles away Hawk heard it and was instantly alert. He got up and stood there in the night, staring off into the darkness. An even greater fear for Randi's safety filled him when total silence followed. He continued to wait, but heard nothing more.

Hawk didn't bother to lie back down. There was no point in trying to sleep.

When at last the first light of dawn brightened the eastern sky, he was already on Phantom continuing his pursuit. He was even more worried now about what he would find on the trail ahead.

Fred's arm was hurting him when he got up at dawn. He walked over to Randi and nudged her with the toe of his boot.

"Wake up."

She opened her eyes to find him standing over her. She could see the hatred he had for her in his expression, but she didn't care. She was just sorry she hadn't been able to get off a better shot.

"You look real pretty this morning," Fred sneered, enjoying the sight of Randi's bruised cheek. She damned well deserved it.

He knelt down, untied her feet and hands, then tied her hands in front of her again so she could ride. He went to saddle the horses, but kept an eye on her while she got ready. His wounded arm slowed him down, so it was later than usual when they finally rode out.

A sense of hopelessness overwhelmed Randi as she faced yet another day in captivity. Never before in her life had she felt so completely devastated. She had tried her best to escape and she had failed. She rode along in silence, staring off in the distance.

Comanche warrior Running Wolf and several other warriors from the tribe were on their way back to their village when they caught sight of two riders in the distance. They positioned themselves on top of a nearby rise to watch their approach and be ready to attack.

Fred was completely unaware of the danger that lay ahead of them. He was concentrating only on covering as many miles as possible that day. He was in pain, and he just wanted to get rid of Randi as fast as he could and collect as much money as he could get for her. He was mad that the damned woman had almost gotten the best of him. Of course, this was Randi and she wasn't just any woman. He was going to be real glad when he was through with her.

Randi saw them first—Comanche warriors silhouetted against the sky in the distance.

"Comanche!" she gasped.

"What?" Fred was surprised that she'd spoken, and he was even more alarmed when he realized what she'd seen. Absolute terror filled him at the sight of the warriors. He knew what kind of fate would await them at the hands of the Comanche.

Fred forcefully wheeled their horses around and took off, galloping back the way they'd come. They had passed a rocky area not too long before. He knew that if he could reach that, he'd at least have some cover from which to return fire.

Running Wolf and his band wasted no time giving chase. Their chilling war cries filled the air, echoing across the land as they rode.

Fred and Randi reached the rocks in time. He threw himself from his horse's back and ran for cover. He didn't care what happened to Randi now. All that mattered was saving his own skin. He left her to fend for herself.

Randi took cover, too, but as far away from Fred as she could. Huddling down behind a rock, she started to work at freeing her hands. She stayed down low, rubbing the rope against a sharp edge on the rock. If she got her hands free, she would have a little bit better chance of surviving.

Running Wolf and his men attacked the white man from a distance, drawing his fire. They shot back at him, but did not close in. It was only a matter of time before he ran out of ammunition, and then they would overrun him.

Fred expected this to be a fight to the death, so he was determined to take as many of the Comanche with him as he could. He was shocked when the Comanche suddenly stopped firing. Their war cries no longer rent the air. Everything was completely and eerily silent.

Fred couldn't imagine why they'd stopped their attack. He carefully peeked out from behind the rock where he'd taken refuge to see what had happened. He knew the Comanche didn't just stop an attack for no reason.

Randi, too, was confused. She looked out from her hiding place to see that the Comanche had reined in and were staring off in the direction from which she and Fred had just come. She shifted her position to look that way.

It was then that Randi saw him. There on top of a low rise not too far off was a lone warrior mounted on a magnificent white stallion.

Randi's heart lurched painfully. The stallion seemed to be Phantom, and the warrior looked a little like Hawk.

Randi told herself it couldn't be Hawk. Hawk was dead; Fred had said so.

The fierce-looking warrior started riding toward them at a slow, measured pace.

As he drew ever closer, she suddenly realized the warrior wasn't wearing the traditional loincloth. He was wearing long pants and boots! She hadn't been wrong. It was Hawk, and he was actually riding Phantom!

Unspeakable joy filled her, and tears came to her eyes.

Hawk was alive! He was alive!

And he'd come for her!

Randi wanted to jump up and run to him. She wanted to throw herself into his arms and stay in his embrace forever.

But reality intruded.

The danger was still there. She was unarmed and threatened by Fred on one side and fierce hostile Comanche warriors on the other.

Randi stayed where she was, trying to figure out what do to. The fact that the Comanche had stopped their attack and were watching Hawk meant something.

Only the finest warrior could ride the phantom stallion.

She remembered the legend then, and for the first time, she felt hope grow within her again.

Hawk was here.

He had come to save her—again.

Everything would be all right.

It had to be.

Hawk had been a driven and desperate man as he'd continued his search for Randi that day. He'd ridden Phantom hard and fast, pushing the stallion to his limit following the trail. He'd frantically tried to find some trace of her and had feared the worst.

When he'd first heard the sounds of the battle, Hawk had raced to the top of the rise. He had seen the fighting below, and it was then that he'd spotted two horses running from the rocky area and recognized that one of them was Angel.

Hope had surged through him, for he knew that meant Randi was somewhere close by.

He'd looked among the rocks, and that was when he'd seen Randi, hiding out there. He'd seen Fred, too, using the rocks for cover as he'd returned the warriors' fire.

Fury had filled Hawk.

Fred was the one who'd ambushed them and taken Randi captive!

Hawk had known he had to stop the fighting somehow. He'd just started forward when the Comanche caught sight of him. He'd reined in, unsure how they would react to his presence, and he'd been surprised when the warriors had suddenly stopped their attack to stare up at him.

Hawk had been puzzled for a moment, but then he'd remembered that the Comanche believed the tale of the phantom stallion, too.

Torn between the thrill of finding Randi alive and the agony of knowing just how dangerous the situation was, Hawk lifted one arm in greeting and rode slowly toward the gathering of warriors.

Chapter Twenty-one

Running Wolf tensed as he watched the mysterious warrior riding toward them on what looked like the phantom stallion. He was shocked when the rider drew close, and he recognized him as Hawk. He had not seen his friend since his last visit to the village, and that had been many years before. He knew Hawk was living in the white world, and he wondered what had brought him there that day, dressed as he was.

"Who is this warrior?" one of the braves asked.

"He is one of us," Running Wolf assured him.

"You know this one?" Broken Knife asked, more than a little in awe. He could see that the warrior was wearing the pants and boots of a white man, but he also knew the legend about the stallion.

"He is the finest warrior," Running Wolf answered with certainty. "He is Hawk."

When Hawk reached the group of warriors, he

reined in before them. His tension had eased when he'd recognized Running Wolf among them.

"It is good to see you, my friend," Hawk greeted him in the Comanche tongue. Though they had not seen each other in a long time, they had been good friends during the years he'd lived with the tribe.

"It is good to see you," Running Wolf returned. He eyed the horse with great interest, then looked up at Hawk with respect and admiration. "You are riding the stallion of the legend."

"He has served me well in my quest," Hawk praised Phantom.

"You are on a quest?"

"Yes, I have come to rescue the white man's captive."

Running Wolf had wondered why only one of the white riders had returned their fire. Now he understood.

"Who is this captive?"

Hawk answered, "She is my woman."

"We will help you."

Fred had grown even more terrified as he'd watched the warrior on the white stallion ride up to join the other Comanche. And when he finally recognized that it was Hawk, his fear turned to insane fury.

He'd shot Hawk!

Hawk couldn't still be alive!

He had to be dead!

But even as he tried to deny the reality of Hawk's presence, he couldn't.

Desperate and willing to try anything to save his own skin, Fred stayed low and scrambled through the rocks toward the place where Randi had taken cover. Using her as a shield would be his only hope for escape.

Randi had finally managed to free her hands, and she was ready to do whatever it would take to get away from Fred. Soon this would all be over. Soon she would be with Hawk again!

In her heart, she prayed that if Hawk had survived the ambush, maybe her father had, too. She looked out again to see what was happening, only to catch sight of Fred working his way toward her.

"No!" Randi was frantic to protect herself from Fred. She looked around and grabbed up a good-sized rock, then threw it at him. Her aim was true.

Fred had been concentrating on staying down low, so Hawk couldn't get a shot at him. He hadn't expected Randi to attack. The thrown rock caught him off guard. He tried to dodge it at the last minute, but it still hit him in his wounded arm.

Fred swore loudly as pain racked him, and his hatred for her grew even stronger. He charged after her.

Randi turned to make a run for it, but Fred was there before she could get very far. He grabbed her and jerked her forcefully back to him.

"Thought you were gonna get away from me, did you?" he snarled in a threatening voice.

Randi fought him with all her strength, but even with his injured arm, his hold on her was brutal. Fred drew his gun and pressed it against her side.

"Stopping fighting me now or you're dead," he said harshly.

She felt the cold metal of the gun against her and went still. "What do you want? What are you going to do?"

"You'll see."

"But Hawk's here—and the Comanche. You can't get away from them."

"Oh, yeah? Watch me!"

He dragged her back to where he'd left his rifle. If he were to end up dead, so would she.

Hawk rode with the other warriors toward the rocks where Fred had taken refuge. They reined in a good distance away.

"Give it up, Fred! Throw down your guns!"

"Like hell!" he shouted back. He was tempted to open fire on them, but he had only a little ammunition left and they were still far away. He knew he had a better chance of bargaining for his freedom as long as he had his gun and Randi.

"There's no way out for you now."

"You wanna bet?" He stood up and dragged Randi to her feet in front of him. He held the gun on her. If even one of the Comanche took a shot at him, she was going to die. "You let me ride out of here, and maybe—just maybe—I'll let Randi live!"

Hawk closed in on Fred. He knew better than to try to bargain with him.

"Let her go—now." It was an order.

Running Wolf and the other warriors followed Hawk's lead. They spread out on either side of him in a show of force.

Fred looked around, trying to figure out the best way to end the standoff.

"Listen to him, Fred. It's over," Randi said.

"It ain't over! I still got you!" He tightened his hold on her even more to emphasize his words. "And I got Hawk right where I want him."

Fred started to lift his gun to take a shot at Hawk.

Randi suddenly realized what he planned to do. She didn't hesitate. Praying silently for strength, she violently twisted free of his hold. She deliberately hit out at his wound as she tried to knock the gun out of his hand.

Fred grimaced in pain and reacted instinctively. He shoved her from him and pushed her violently down. When he did, his gun went off.

Hawk saw him shove Randi down and heard the sound of the gunshot. Fearing the worst, he drew his gun and fired.

Hawk raced to the scene and all but threw himself from the stallion's back. Gun in hand, he made his way through the rocks to find Fred lying on the ground. Hawk kicked his gun away from his hand, then rolled him over to make sure he wouldn't be shooting at anybody anymore. He wouldn't be. He was dead.

Hawk turned to Randi.

She lay unmoving, facedown in the dirt.

Hawk knelt beside her and carefully turned her over.

Relief and excitement swept through him when Randi gave a low, pained moan. She was alive! There was an ugly mark on her forehead where she must have hit her head on a rock when Fred had shoved her down, but she hadn't been shot.

With great care, Hawk took Randi in his arms and got to his feet. He suddenly realized he'd left Phantom untethered and feared the stallion might have run off. He glanced back to see Phantom standing quietly, waiting for him.

Hawk carried Randi to where Running Wolf and the other warriors had reined in by Phantom.

"Your woman is alive?" Running Wolf asked, concerned.

"Yes, but she's been injured. How far are we from the village?"

"Not far. We will go there."

"Thank you, my friend."

"You have been injured, too?" He noticed the dried blood on the cloth Hawk had used to bind his head wound.

"It is nothing." Hawk knew he would be all right. All that mattered now was Randi.

"The stallion did not run off," Running Wolf remarked, impressed. "You are truly the finest of warriors."

Hawk said nothing. His only concern was taking care of Randi. He had her back again, and he would never let her go.

Running Wolf dismounted and went to help Hawk. He took Randi from him so he could mount up, then handed her up to his friend. He swung back up on his own horse.

"Let us ride."

They headed for the village.

Hawk cradled Randi protectively against his chest as he followed his friend's lead.

It had been many years since Hawk had visited the tribe. After his grandparents' passing, he had not had any reason to return. He'd had a few friends there—Running Wolf among them—but his life had been in the white world.

Hawk was thankful now that the tribe was camped nearby. With Randi injured, he needed the haven the village offered to tend to her.

The ride to the village took less than an hour. When the word spread that a warrior on the phantom stallion was riding in with Running Wolf and the other braves, the villagers rushed from their tepees to watch them approach. All were in awe of Hawk as he rode into their midst.

Running Wolf dismounted and helped Hawk with Randi again. When Hawk got down, he took her back in his arms and followed the warrior to a tepee near the center of the village. Running Wolf went in first, and Hawk followed. Hawk laid Randi on a blanket there.

"I will get the medicine man," Running Wolf told him.

Hawk stayed there by her side, praying that her head injury wasn't serious. There was a small container of water in the tepee, so he carefully bathed her face as he waited for the medicine man to come.

It was only a short time later when the flap of the tepee was thrown back and Running Wolf entered with another man.

"This is Sun Chaser," he told Hawk. "He will help your woman."

Hawk looked at the older man and nodded. "Thank you."

Hawk quickly explained to the medicine man what had happened to her; then he and Running Wolf left him alone with Randi.

Tense and worried about Randi, Hawk went to tend to Phantom, wanting to keep busy. He found that a large number of the villagers had gathered around the stallion, studying him with great interest. Hawk went up to Phantom and stroked his neck. He spoke to him in low tones.

"You saved Randi today," Hawk praised him. "Without you, I would never have reached her in time."

Phantom stood calmly before him and whickered softly, almost as if in response to his words.

The villagers were amazed at the ease with which Hawk handled the stallion and believed now that he truly was the warrior who fulfilled the legend.

Hawk led Phantom down to the nearby spring to drink. He fettered him and left him to graze with the other horses. He returned to the tepee to find Running Wolf there, watching for him. His friend offered him food, and they sat together, eating. Running Wolf spoke of the adventures they'd shared as young boys, and while Hawk joined him in those reminiscences, his thoughts were on Randi. He kept glancing toward the tepee, anxiously waiting for the medicine man to emerge.

When at last the flap was thrown back and Sun Chaser came out of the tepee, Hawk immediately stood up and went to him.

"How is she?" he asked, nervously looking past him into the tepee.

"She will be well," the medicine man assured him, "but she will need rest."

Sun Chaser stepped aside to allow him to enter, and Hawk hurried inside to see Randi.

He knelt down beside her and bent to gently kiss her.

Randi lifted her arms to him in invitation, wanting to hold him, needing to be as close to him as she could.

"You saved me again."

Hawk gathered her close. His relief at knowing she was alive, at knowing she was going to be all right, nearly overwhelmed him.

"I was afraid I'd lost you," he told her with deep emotion.

"And I was afraid I'd lost you. Fred told me you were dead. He told me that he'd killed you—and Pa."

"Your father is alive. He was wounded, but he should be all right. He's back at the ranch."

Randi started to cry with joy at the news. Hawk held her to his heart.

"I love you, Randi," he swore. He drew back to seek her lips again in a kiss that told her all she needed to know about the truth of his words.

"And I love you," she told him when they finally ended the embrace and moved slightly apart.

Hawk wanted to keep her in his arms and never let her go. He wanted to hold her and kiss her and spend the rest of his life showing her how much he loved her, but this was not the time. He knew he needed to let her rest and regain her strength. He started to get up, but she reached out to hold his arm.

"We have to get back to the ranch," she said in desperation.

"Why? What's wrong?"

"I know who is behind all this—it's Wade. Fred said Wade paid him to shoot you and Pa. We have to get back to the Lazy S. With Wade there, anything might happen." Her plea was frantic, and the exertion left her pale and exhausted.

"We'll ride for the ranch as soon as you're strong enough," Hawk promised her.

"All right." Randi knew he was right. She wouldn't last five miles, feeling as weak and dizzy as she did now. She closed her eyes against the pain, emotional and physical, that threatened to overwhelm her.

"Rest now," Hawk told her. He stayed by her side until he was sure she was asleep. Only then did he leave the tepee.

Hawk saw Running Wolf standing with some of the other warriors, watching Phantom, and he walked over to join them.

"Who is this Hawk that he could catch the phantom?" Red Eagle, one of the youngest warriors in the tribe, was asking Running Wolf. He had always been fascinated by the legend and had chased the stallion several times, trying to catch him, but with no success. He wanted to see the man who'd finally caught him.

"Hawk is the finest warrior," Running Wolf told them. He glanced toward the tepee and saw Hawk coming their way. "This is Hawk."

Red Eagle and the others who hadn't been riding with Running Wolf earlier turned to look at him. They immediately realized that Hawk wasn't a full-blood Comanche. They were shocked.

"How can he be the one?" Red Eagle challenged. "He is a white man!"

Running Wolf fixed him with a commanding glare. "Hawk is Comanche. He has claimed the phantom and proven himself as a warrior."

Red Eagle fell angrily silent. It infuriated him

that this man—this white man—had claimed the horse he had wanted so badly.

"How is Phantom?" Hawk asked as he came to stand with them. He was unaware of the younger brave's anger.

"Your stallion is fine. Many are impressed with your skill and want to hear the tale of how you claimed him." Running Wolf nodded toward those standing nearby.

"The phantom claimed me," Hawk told them. He recounted the story of how Bruiser had thrown a shoe and how he'd been forced to continue tracking Fred and Randi on foot. "I didn't know if the stallion would let me ride him, but he did. He's fast, faster than any horse I've ever ridden before. It's no wonder no one was ever able to catch him."

"What will you do with him now?" Red Eagle asked, wondering if Hawk was going to set the stallion free again.

"I plan to keep him."

"I will trade you for him," the young brave offered, willing to pay handsomely for the beautiful animal.

"No."

Red Eagle was irritated by Hawk's refusal. The legend said only the finest of warriors could ride the phantom stallion, and he wanted to prove to everyone just how good he was.

Red Eagle considered stealing the phantom and just riding away. If he were mounted on the stallion, he was certain no one would ever be able to catch him. The young warrior smiled at the thought, but knew he couldn't steal another warrior's horse. Somehow, some way, though, he was determined that he was going to ride the phantom.

Chapter Twenty-two

"Who is this man?" Moon Flower asked her friend Dove Song. Her voice was a little breathless as she watched the handsome stranger walking through the village with Running Wolf.

"I don't know, but I'm going to find out," Dove Song said. She was just as intrigued as her friend.

"He has a woman with him," Moon Flower reminded her.

"I know, but I have not heard that she is his wife."

"We will have to see. If he is the one who tamed the stallion from the legend, then he is a great warrior." Her eyes gleamed with delight and interest.

"I could tell that just by watching him," Dove Song agreed with a quick smile. She began to plan a way to find out more about the new man in the village.

* * *

It was growing dark outside when Hawk returned to the tepee to find Randi asleep on the blanket. He was hard-pressed not to lie down next to her and take her in his arms. He wanted to hold her close. He wanted to reassure himself that she was going to be all right. Instead he forced himself to sit down across the tepee from her. It was enough for him to know she was safe and resting quietly.

Hawk let his thoughts drift as he watched her sleep, and his mood darkened as he realized the trouble they were going to face when they returned to the ranch. They knew the truth now— Wade was behind the rustling, and he had little doubt anymore that Pete Turner was involved. He still had to find a way to prove it, but he didn't think it would be hard once they returned and told the sheriff what they'd learned.

Hawk knew Randi was worried about Jack, and he was, too. He hoped Jack had reached the ranch safely. Right now he knew Wade had no idea whether he'd caught up with Fred and Randi or not. He figured the foreman would be playing it safe, biding his time at the ranch. The danger was going to come when they did return. He would have to be ready.

For now, though, he was just going to wait and watch over Randi. He was going to make sure no harm ever came to her again.

Randi stirred and came awake. For a moment she felt lost and confused by her darkened surroundings. Then she saw Hawk, stretched out on a blanket across the tepee from her, and she relaxed, knowing everything was all right as long as he was there.

Randi was amazed by how much better she felt already. The potion the medicine man had given her to drink had worked. The throbbing in her head had eased greatly, and she could actually move without any agonizing pain or discomfort.

She turned on her side to watch Hawk as he slept. Her gaze traced over his handsome features, the lean line of his jaw, the firm set of his lips, then moved lower to visually caress the broad, hard-muscled strength of his wide shoulders and chest. Hawk was a strong man in both body and soul. He had had to overcome great odds to make his way in the white world, and he had done it. She had never known anyone like him before.

Randi longed to go to him and kiss him again, but she held herself back. Instead she took the time to enjoy the peace and privacy of the moment.

This was Hawk, and he was the man she loved.

Finally, unable to resist the temptation he offered any longer, Randi moved nearer. With great care she leaned over him and pressed her lips to his.

Hawk awakened with a start at her unexpected kiss, but then immediately relaxed, prepared to thoroughly enjoy himself.

"You're better?" he murmured against the sweetness of her lips.

"Yes, but I thought kissing you might heal me even more," she told him in a soft, seductive voice.

"I'm no medicine man."

"Are you sure?" Randi asked invitingly.

Ever so gently, Hawk took her in his arms and drew her down to him. They lay together, her breasts crushed against his chest, her hips nestled against his. They were totally physically aware of each other. Her soft womanly curves fit perfectly against him, and she reveled in that sensual contact.

Hawk kissed her, softly at first, but when he felt her response, he deepened the exchange.

Randi clung to him, returning his kiss with complete abandon.

When at last they broke apart, Hawk smiled at her.

"Do you feel better now?" His voice was husky with desire.

Randi lifted one hand to caress his cheek.

"A little, I think," she answered, a note of teasing seduction in her voice. "But I think you may need to kiss me again."

Hawk was more than willing to oblige. He had found his heaven in her embrace. His lips sought hers in a hungry exchange that told her all she needed to know about his feelings for her.

Randi was caught up in the pure delight of his embrace. She wanted him. She needed him. When she'd thought he was dead, her torment had been endless. Now he was here with her, and she knew that nothing else mattered but loving him.

Hawk gloried in the pure pleasure of holding Randi close. She was a firebrand upon him, and he was hard-pressed to control himself. He wanted her desperately. He wanted to love her, to be one with her. He never wanted to let her go.

What little semblance of logic there was left in Hawk warned him to move away from her. He knew he should get up and leave the tepee now, while he still could. Randi was an innocent, and he shouldn't take advantage of her. Calling on every bit of inner strength he had, he ended the kiss and moved out of her embrace to sit up. He faced away from her, for she was too much of a temptation to him.

"Hawk?" Randi was devastated that he'd stopped kissing her.

"I need to leave you now," Hawk said, his voice gruff with emotion.

"But why? What's wrong?" Randi was bereft, believing he didn't want her.

She sat up, too, confused and hurt by his seeming rejection.

Hawk heard the confusion in her voice, and her true innocence touched him deeply. He managed a wry half smile as he glanced over at her, struggling to bring his raging emotions under some semblance of control.

"I must leave you now, because if I don't, I will never leave you."

Suddenly empowered by his confession, Randi smiled seductively back at him. "Don't ever leave me, Hawk. I want you with me—always and forever."

She went to him and took his hand to draw him

back down upon the blanket with her. She looked up at him with all that she was feeling for him shining in the depths of her gaze. "I love you."

At her words, the dam of his self-control broke. Hawk kissed her, telling her without words just how much she meant to him, too.

Wrapped in each other's arms, they shared kiss after passionate kiss. The fire of their desire for each other ignited and flamed out of control.

Caught up in the firestorm of their need, Randi moved instinctively against him.

She wanted him.

She needed him.

She gave herself eagerly over to him.

When Hawk began to caress her, Randi surrendered willingly to his touch. Nothing else mattered but showing Hawk just how much she loved him.

Hawk was lost in the glory of his love for Randi. He began to unbutton her blouse, and she quickly moved to help him. They wanted no barrier between them. They stripped away their clothing and came together. With each kiss and caress, the power of their need for each other grew.

Hawk kissed her hungrily, then trailed arousing kisses down her throat to her breasts. A thrill of excitement trembled through Randi, and she arched against him in love's age-old offering.

Hawk could wait no longer to be one with her. With utmost care, he moved over her to make her his own. Randi opened to him like a flower to the sun. He sought the sweet depths of her.

Randi gasped as he breached the proof of her innocence.

Hawk went still, fearful that he'd hurt her. He raised his head to gaze down at her.

"I love you," he told her in a soft voice.

She looked up at him, seeing the man she loved above all others, the man who had rescued her from the horror of her captivity, the man she wanted to be with for all time.

"I love you, too," Randi returned.

At her words Hawk could no longer deny the need to make her his in all ways. He claimed her lips in a passionate kiss as he began to move deep within her.

Randi held him close and began to move with him. She matched his rhythm and was caught up in the ecstasy of his possession, the heaven of loving Hawk.

Together they sought the perfection that was their love. Each gave totally to the other. They surrendered their hearts and their souls to the promise of endless devotion.

When at last the rapture of their need swept over them, they clung together, one in spirit and one in body. Afterward they lay together quietly, savoring the beauty of what had just passed between them in their loving union.

"I didn't know it would be so wonderful," Randi finally whispered to Hawk.

"You're wonderful," he said as he raised himself off her and kissed her again.

When the kiss had ended, she gazed up at Hawk, seeing the warrior who had claimed her heart, the man she would love forever.

They passed the night together, holding each other close, never wanting to be separated.

After Jessie, Hawk had believed he would never love again, but Randi had proved him wrong. He loved Randi, and he would never let her go. They would be together always.

Jack had been lying down, resting in his room, when he heard the sound of riders coming in. He got up eagerly, hoping Randi was back. He made his way to look out the window, only to see Wade, Rob, and the others returning. There was no sign of Randi with them.

Jack grew desperate and furious. Though he was still feeling weak, his anger and his concern for his daughter strengthened him. He hurried downstairs and went outside on the porch to watch the riders approach and to wait for them to reach the house.

"What the hell are you doing back here without Randi?" Jack demanded. "Where is she?"

Wade spoke up, "We were on the trail when a bad storm came up. By the time it had stopped raining, their tracks had been washed away. We looked around, but we couldn't find the trail again."

"You gave up?"

"There was no trace of their tracks anywhere."

"So you quit? You just quit? I told you to find my girl!"

"There was nothing more we could do."

"What about the posse the sheriff sent out?" Jack demanded. "Did you see them? Are they still looking for her?"

"We ran into them on our way back," Wade told him. "Once we told them what had happened, they turned back, too."

Jack was beyond fury as he yelled at his men, "Sheriff Johnson was out to see me. He told me he thinks Fred is the one who pulled off the ambush and kidnapped Randi. Now you're all telling me you aren't good enough to track down Fred? It looks like it's going to be up to me to find her. Go on—get out of my sight." He turned his back on them and started inside.

The men began to ride away, but Rob dismounted and went after Jack.

"Boss, we tried. We really tried," Rob told him as the others stopped and looked back. They couldn't believe Rob was trying to reason with the boss. When Jack was like this, they knew there was no talking to him.

Rob faced him on the porch.

"If you tried, you'd have her back here now!" Jack raged. He was ready to ride out after Randi himself. If he had been able to ride with them in the first place, they would never have abandoned the search for her. They would have kept looking no matter how long it took to find her. There could be no quitting where Randi was concerned.

"Boss, we really did do our best," Rob insisted.

For an instant as Jack glared at him, he saw the look in Rob's eyes and realized what the ranch hand was doing. He was pushing his point in order to get a private word with him.

"Your best wasn't good enough, was it?" he snarled, turning his back on Rob and heading inside.

"Boss," Rob went on, acting as though he was trying to calm Jack as he followed him indoors.

Wade and the other hands were looking on.

"Rob's fighting a losing battle," Wade said with a shake of his head.

The men went on out to the stable, leaving Rob behind and thinking him a fool for even trying to talk to Jack in the mood he was in.

Jack stomped back inside the house. He waited until Rob had closed the front door behind him; then he faced the cowboy.

"Let's go in the study," Jack directed. His anger had impelled him this far, but his physical weakness finally took its toll. What little strength he had was gone. He grew dizzy and swayed a bit. He reached out to prop himself up. Rob was quickly there at his side to help him.

"Are you all right?" Rob worried.

"Hell, no, I'm not all right. Not as long as Randi's in danger!" he swore as Rob helped him to sit down at his desk. Once he was seated, he looked up at Rob. "All right—what really happened? Tell me everything."

Rob quickly described their search.

"What about Wade? Did you keep an eye on him? Did he do anything unusual?"

"Early on, when we first reached Black Canyon, he rode right past the entrance to the secret passageway. I found it easily from your directions, but Wade was leading us, and he just kept riding. I had to call him back and show it to him."

Jack nodded solemnly. "Go on."

"Then after the rainstorm hit, he was ready to turn back right away. He didn't even want to bother to try to look anymore. I argued with him about it and so did some of the other boys. We told him we couldn't just quit. We told him we had to keep on searching for Randi. We finally convinced him to ride farther out and keep looking. Not that it mattered; we really did lose the trail. The storm was that bad."

Everything Rob was telling him convinced Jack that Wade was somehow a part of the ambush and kidnapping.

"Is there anything else you can think of that's gone on lately that seems strange or suspicious?" Jack asked him.

Rob thought for a moment before answering, "The only thing Wade's done a little different lately was to sneak out to go visit the widow Walker."

"He did? When?"

"Why, just the other night before all the trouble

started. He's been sweet on her for quite a while, you know. They spent a lot of time together the weekend of the Stampede."

Jack considered all of what Rob had just told him. He knew Pat. He knew her quite well. She was a lady, and he had serious doubts that she'd be welcoming Wade to her bed any old time he showed up.

"All right, Rob, thanks," Jack said, his mood serious.

"What are you going to do about Randi? Is there anything more I can do? Anything I can help you with?"

Jack appreciated Rob's concern. He knew it was real, but he also knew his own limitations. Physically, he wasn't capable of riding out to search for his daughter yet.

"Just keep the faith that Hawk will find her and bring her home."

"I will."

Wilda had heard all the commotion earlier, and she came to check on Jack when she saw Rob leave. She saw how pale and shaken he looked.

"Are you all right?" she asked.

"Hell, no, I'm not all right!" he snarled. "And I won't be until Randi's back here with me safe and sound!"

Jack quickly told the housekeeper what had happened. Gritting his teeth against his own weakness, he got up from his desk and started up to his bedroom to rest for a while.

"Should I send to town for the doc?"

"No, just leave me alone," he said brusquely.

She knew Jack well enough to take him at his word. She went back to her chores in the kitchen.

Jack made it to his room and lay down. He cursed his situation. He was used to being strong and fit. He was used to taking charge and getting things done. Discovering he wasn't invincible didn't sit well with him.

The only comfort Jack had in all his torment was the knowledge that Hawk was still out there searching for Randi.

Hawk hadn't given up like Wade and the others.

Hawk hadn't come back empty-handed.

Sheriff Spiller had said Hawk was the best tracker around. Jack was counting on Hawk to prove it.

Wade settled in at the bunkhouse. He was acting normal, but, in truth, he was on edge. He'd gotten lucky with the rainstorm during their search for Randi, but that didn't mean Hawk had gotten rained out, too. As far as he knew, the breed was still out there following Randi's trail. Wade just hoped Fred was moving fast enough to avoid getting caught.

Wade knew he was safe at the ranch for now. No one had any idea he'd been involved in the rustling with Pete. He'd outsmarted them all. The only danger he faced was if Hawk caught Fred, and Fred didn't keep his mouth shut. For the time being, though, Wade was convinced that everything was going fine. He'd bide his time and hope for the best—he'd hope Hawk never came back.

Chapter Twenty-three

It was still dark outside when Hawk awoke. Randi was nestled against him, so he remained unmoving, savoring her nearness and the beauty of their love. Those long days on the trail fearing for her safety had been agonizing for him. He had been a driven man, haunted by the memories of another time. Forever he would be thankful that he'd reached Randi in time.

Randi came awake slowly to find herself curled against Hawk. She lifted her gaze to look at him and found that he was awake, too, and that he was staring off into the darkness. His expression was very serious.

"Hawk?" Randi asked softly in a sleep-husky voice. "Is something wrong?"

He was surprised to find she was awake. He smiled down at her.

"No, nothing's wrong." Hawk gathered her even closer, knowing it was time. He had to tell her of his past. It wouldn't be easy, but he wanted Randi to know.

"Good," she replied, drawing him to her for a gentle kiss.

When the kiss ended, Hawk drew back.

"I was just remembering . . . thinking back to another time. . . ."

"When you were young and lived in the village?"

"No, it was after that." He paused for a moment before going on. "Randi, there's a lot you don't know about me."

"I know I love you," she told him.

Her words touched him deeply. "I love you, too. I never thought I would feel this way again."

"Again?" She was confused.

"There was a time," he began slowly, "before I lived in Dry Springs, that I had a different life." He paused to look at Randi. "There was a time, when I lived with my aunt and uncle on their ranch, that I was married."

Randi was stunned. "You were married? But—"

"Her name was Jessie, and I loved her very much." Hawk knew he had to be honest with Randi if they were to have a future together.

She heard the pain in his voice and sensed he was about to tell her something terrible.

"I was gone one day. I was out checking stock with several of the hands when an Apache raiding party attacked the ranch."

She was horrified by his story. She could see the pain etched in his expression as he went on.

"By the time we returned, the house and out-buildings had been burned to the ground. We found everyone dead—everyone except Jessie."

"What happened to her?" Randi had to know.

"They'd taken her captive." Hawk looked at Randi, and their gazes met in understanding.

"Oh, Hawk." She slipped her arms around him to hold him tightly to her and to comfort him.

"We went after the raiding party. We tracked them for days and were just closing in on them when we found Jessie."

"Was she . . . ?" For a moment Randi was hopeful, but Hawk's next words ended her hope.

"Jessie was lying dead on the side of the trail."

Randi could imagine the horror he had faced. "Oh, Hawk—I'm sorry."

He drew a ragged breath. "After losing Jessie, I never thought I would be able to care for anyone again, but then I met you." Hawk paused for a moment before going on. "I love you, Randi. When you were taken captive—"

She quickly spoke up. "Hawk, you saved me."

"Thank God."

"I love you," she whispered, drawing him down to her. She kissed him, a passionate, caring kiss. She wanted to show him without words the depth of her feelings for him.

Hawk responded to her fully. They came together in a glorious sharing of true love and devotion. With each kiss, with each intimate caress, their passion grew untamed until rapture's ecstasy burst upon them. They were lost in the splendor of their desire.

Sated, their passion spent, Hawk cradled Randi in his arms. They treasured the intimacy and peace of the moment.

Randi stared around the interior of the tepee and smiled to herself.

"You're smiling," Hawk noticed.

"I was just remembering the first time I saw you. I thought you were a warrior." She raised herself over him to look down into his face. "Now here we are in a tepee, and I know for sure you are one. You're my love warrior."

Hawk didn't say a word. He just showed her how a love warrior responded to an invitation.

It was some time later when exhaustion claimed them both, and, once again they slept.

Hawk awoke at dawn and moved carefully away from Randi. After dressing, he went out to face the new day. The village was still quiet, so he made his way down to the nearby spring to wash up. He was surprised when a pretty young maiden appeared on the bank a short distance away.

"You are the one they call Hawk," Dove Song stated, moving a little closer to him. She'd just left her own tepee when she'd seen him heading down to the spring. She knew she was being very bold, but she didn't care. He was so handsome and strong. She wanted to let him know of her interest in him. Her gaze went over him hungrily, taking in the broad width of his shoulders and his lean waist. She was tempted to reach out and touch him, but she stayed a slight distance away.

"Yes, I am Hawk," he answered her.

"You are new here in our village. Have you come to stay?"

"No. My woman and I must return to our home."

Dove Song was irritated to learn that the injured white girl was his woman. She had hoped he was unattached and would find her attractive.

"That is too bad," she said, giving him an inviting look. "You could have been happy here—very happy."

Hawk didn't bother to respond. He did not want to encourage her. Randi was the only woman he cared about, the only woman he wanted.

Dove Song left, her disappointment evident.

Hawk took the cloth from his head. The wound was beginning to heal, so he left the wrap off. When he'd finished getting cleaned up, Hawk started back toward the tepee to look in on Randi.

Randi woke up to find Hawk gone. She was sorry he wasn't with her, but as she lay there, remembering all that had happened between them in the long, dark hours of the night just past, she smiled. Hawk had been a thrilling lover. What they'd shared had been beautiful. Even in the light of day, she had no regrets about giving the gift of her innocence to him. She loved him and wanted to be with him always.

It surprised Randi that she'd slept so soundly.

She stretched carefully and was glad to realize she was feeling much better this morning. The potion the medicine man had given her had worked wonders.

Getting up, Randi saw the container of water nearby and was glad. She took the time to bathe as best she could under the circumstances. She longed for clean clothes, but settled for shaking the dirt and dust out her own garments before donning them again. She stepped out of the tepee, feeling a little uneasy going out into the village alone, but she wanted to find Hawk.

Randi was tentative as she made her way through the maze of tepees. She was very aware that the Comanche women and children were staring at her with open interest. She smiled at them, but they didn't smile back. They just watched her pass by. The villagers' cool reaction to her definitely made it clear to Randi that she didn't belong there with them, that she was an outsider. Randi felt isolated, but she continued on, hoping Hawk wasn't too far away.

Dove Song saw the white woman coming in their direction and pointed her out to Moon Flower.

"There is the white woman. Why does Hawk want her? She is ugly," she said snidely.

"He has lived in the white world too long," Moon Flower agreed. "It is too bad."

"I know. I would have enjoyed being married to

the warrior who claimed the phantom stallion for his own."

They turned their backs on her.

Randi noticed the looks the two younger women had given her and the way they'd turned away as she walked by. She continued on a little farther, but when she saw no sign of Hawk, she retraced her steps. Settling down again inside the tepee, she anxiously awaited his return. She hoped he wouldn't be long.

Hawk had been on his way back to Randi when he'd noticed Running Wolf standing near a clearing at the far end of the village. He went to speak with him and found that some of the men from the tribe were there breaking horses.

"How is your woman?" Running Wolf asked.

"Sun Chaser is a fine medicine man. The potion he gave Randi seemed to work well."

"Will you stay with us for a while?"

Hawk would have liked to linger there and visit with his old friend, but he knew how worried Jack must be back at the ranch. "It will depend on Randi. If she's feeling strong enough to ride, then we will have to leave today."

"One of the warriors found her horse and brought it in for you this morning."

"Thanks."

The news was a relief to Hawk. He'd known he could bargain with Running Wolf for one of the tribe's horses for the trip back, but he'd been worried about Randi riding one of them, especially without a saddle. It would have been a difficult trek, even for an accomplished rider like Randi.

Hawk stayed on with Running Wolf for a little while longer, then left him to return to Randi. He was anxious to see how she was feeling this morning. He reached the tepee and went in to find her awake and dressed already. She was sitting on the blanket, her hair loose around her shoulders.

Randi had not heard Hawk's approach, and she tensed when the flap was thrown aside. When she saw it was him, she relaxed and smiled brightly in welcome.

"Good morning."

"Yes, it is," he responded.

"I've been waiting for you," Randi said. Her heartbeat quickened at the sight of him. He was so tall and lean and handsome—and he was hers.

"I like the sound of that," he said, going to Randi and taking her in his arms. "How do you feel?"

"After last night . . ." Her words were softly spoken, and she actually blushed a bit at the memory of the passion they'd shared. "I feel fine."

Hawk couldn't resist any longer. He kissed her, savoring the sweetness of her lips. They clung together for a moment; then Hawk put her from him. If she stayed in his arms, he would be hard-pressed to concentrate on making their plan to return to the ranch.

"Are you strong enough to ride out today, or do you think you need another day's rest?" he asked, ignoring the heated ache that had grown within him at the touch her lips.

"I think I'm strong enough, but how's your head?"

"It's much better."

She was glad to hear that. "Good."

"Running Wolf said one of the warriors found Angel and brought her in for us."

Randi smiled happily at the news. "That's wonderful! I was afraid I'd never see her again."

"She's here and ready to go whenever we are."

"I'm ready. I need to get home. I need to make sure my pa's all right."

"Then I'll let Running Wolf know we'll be riding out today."

"Hawk . . ." She said his name softly and went to him, slipping her arms around him and resting her head against his chest. "Thank you for everything you've done for me."

"I love you, Randi."

He held her close and tried to ignore his concerns about their future in the real world. This tepee had been their haven, but now they were going to have to leave it. Wanting to treasure this last moment of time they had alone, he held Randi to his heart.

Randi looked up at Hawk. He saw the invitation in her eyes and couldn't resist. His lips sought hers, and they stood locked in each other's arms, unaware of anything but the depth of their love.

With great reluctance, Hawk finally put her from him.

"If we don't leave now, we may never make it back to the ranch. In fact, we might never leave this tepee again," he told her with a wry grin.

Randi ached to go back into his embrace, but somehow she managed to control the urge.

"You're right." She smiled up at him. "We'd better go while we still can."

They left the peace and serenity of their haven and went to find Running Wolf. He was eating breakfast near a campfire at the center of the village, and they joined him in that meal.

Hawk told him of their plan to leave that day.

Randi was hungry and glad for the food, but she felt out of place and uncomfortable as she listened to Hawk and Running Wolf speaking in their native tongue. She came to understand then just how difficult it must have been for Hawk as a child to leave the tribe and the only way of life he'd ever known, and go to live with his aunt and uncle in the white world. He would have known no one, and he would not have been easily accepted into white society.

She looked up at him and realized, too, what a hard life he'd had. He had learned the white man's ways and worked to fit in. He had found happiness with Jessie, and then the whole life he'd made for himself had been destroyed. Randi had always known Hawk was a strong man, but now she knew just how strong he really was.

Running Wolf said, "It would be good if you could stay on with us."

"I have missed you, my friend, but I must take Randi home to her father."

"You are taking her to her father?" Running Wolf gave him a curious look. "I thought you said she was your woman. You have not taken her as your wife?"

At his words, Hawk faced the reality of what was to come once they returned to the Lazy S. He loved Randi and wanted to make her his wife. It wouldn't be an easy life for her, being married to him, but he hoped their love was strong enough to overcome any troubles that might come their way.

Hawk looked Running Wolf straight in the eye and smiled. "Not yet."

His friend returned his smile and was about to answer when they heard someone yelling at them.

"Running Wolf! Hawk!"

They looked up to see Black Cloud running toward them.

"Come quickly! Red Eagle is trying to ride the phantom!"

Chapter Twenty-four

"What is it?" Randi asked Hawk, seeing how excited everybody was. "What's he shouting about?"

"One of the young warriors is trying to ride Phantom," Hawk explained quickly.

He got up to follow the warrior, Black Cloud, and Running Wolf went with him. A warrior's horse was his most prized possession. This Red Eagle needed to be taught a lesson. If Phantom didn't do it, then Hawk knew he would.

"I'm coming, too!" Randi said, hurrying after them.

They made their way to the clearing.

It angered Hawk to discover that Red Eagle had two of his friends helping him. Each had managed to get a rope on Phantom, and they were trying to keep him under control as Red Eagle struggled to mount the stallion. Even fettered as he was, Phantom was putting up a good fight. Hawk knew the young warrior was soon going to discover he wasn't the horseman he thought he was.

"What are you going to do?" Randi asked as she stood at Hawk's side, watching.

"Right now, nothing. I'm sure Red Eagle believes he can live the legend and be claimed the finest warrior by riding Phantom, so I'm going to let Phantom take care of him."

Red Eagle looked at his two friends as he gripped Phantom's mane and prepared to swing up on his back. "As soon as I am on him, untie him and turn him loose," he directed.

His friends were nervous. They could tell just how strong and powerful this stallion was. They also knew his owner, Hawk, was standing there watching them, but it was too late to back out on Red Eagle now.

Word of what was happening had quickly spread through the village. Many came running up and stood with Hawk, Randi, and Running Wolf to watch the excitement.

"This stallion belongs to Hawk," Running Wolf called out to Red Eagle.

"This stallion belongs to the gods," the young warrior responded arrogantly. "I will prove myself today! I will ride the phantom stallion."

Red Eagle didn't care that Hawk and the others were there. In fact, he was glad they were, for he wanted them to witness his success. He wanted them to know he was the finest of warriors.

Ready for the ride of his life, Red Eagle vaulted onto the phantom's back in one smooth move.

His two friends immediately did as he'd directed. They unfettered Phantom and set him free.

Phantom was ready. His power unleashed, the stallion bucked violently and twisted in a savage manner that almost threw the warrior from his back.

Many were surprised Red Eagle managed to keep his seat. Their surprise was short-lived. The stallion raced a short distance, then came to an abrupt halt and reared mightily up on his hind legs. The stallion bucked again and tossed Red Eagle from his back.

Red Eagle landed heavily on the ground.

Phantom trotted proudly away from the fallen warrior.

Randi looked up at Hawk. "Only you can ride him. You are the warrior of the legend."

Hawk met her gaze, but said nothing. Instead, he left her there with Running Wolf and the others, and walked forward into the clearing. Phantom was unfettered and free to run off and roam the range again. Hawk watched the stallion where he was standing on a low rise in the distance. He waited to see what he would do.

Phantom remained unmoving for a moment as he looked out over the land; then he reared up on his hind legs again and was silhouetted against the sky.

Hawk had always known Phantom was a magnificent animal, and watching him only proved it.

Hawk was about to go to him when the stallion suddenly raced off down the far side of the rise and out of sight.

Hawk stared after him, devastated that he was gone. The stallion had come into his life at a moment when he'd truly been desperate, and he had helped him rescue Randi. Without Phantom, Hawk realized he would never have reached her in time.

Hawk stood there, hoping against hope that the stallion would return.

But he didn't.

Finally Hawk turned away. He started back to where Randi and the others were waiting.

Red Eagle got slowly to his feet with the help of his friends. He was humiliated at having been thrown so quickly and so violently. He'd always considered himself good at breaking horses. The phantom stallion had just proven otherwise. Uneasiness filled him as he prepared to face Hawk, but as a warrior, he knew he must.

"Hawk," Red Eagle called out. He was ready to give the other man his own horse and anything else he wanted to atone for what he'd done.

Hawk started to turn toward the younger man when suddenly, out of nowhere, Phantom charged back over the rise.

An audible gasp of shock went up from everyone. They watched in awe as the legendary stallion galloped straight to Hawk and stopped directly in front of him.

Hawk forgot all about his anger with Red Eagle. Instead he smiled and reached out to stroke the stallion's neck, praising him in a low voice.

"Ride him," Randi called out.

Hawk continued to speak quietly to Phantom as he smoothly swung up on his back.

Everyone watching expected a repeat of what had just happened to Red Eagle. They were stunned when Phantom moved docilely about the clearing and obeyed Hawk's every command.

"He is truly the legendary warrior!" Running Wolf said, telling the others what he'd already known about his friend.

"Yes, he is," Red Eagle agreed. Though he was still humiliated by his own failure, he watched the way Hawk handled the stallion with amazement and respect.

News of all that had happened traveled quickly through the village. Everyone looked upon Hawk with even more admiration.

It was near noon when most of the villagers gathered together to see Hawk and Randi off.

"Come to the village again, my friend," Running Wolf told him.

"I will try," he answered. "Thank you for all you've done for us."

Running Wolf nodded. He had seen to it that they had food for the return trip. "May your trip back be a safe one."

Hawk raised a hand in farewell. He would forever be grateful for his people's help rescuing Randi from Fred.

"You're sure you feel well enough to do this?" Hawk asked Randi one last time.

"Oh, yes. I want to go home. I need to see my father. I need to make sure he's all right."

Hawk nodded in understanding. He opened his saddlebag and took out her handgun. "Here. I want you to have this on the ride back. Just in case."

Randi took the gun from him, appreciating the weight of the weapon in her hand. She was taking control of her life again, and it felt good. "Thanks."

Randi slipped the gun into her waistband.

They rode from the village. It would take them about four days, but they would return to the Lazy S.

Jack was resting. He didn't want to be, but he had no choice. He had to get his strength back. Only then would he be able to ride out and try to find Randi and Hawk.

"Jack," Wilda called up to him from the foot of the steps. "Someone's coming. I think it might be Pat Walker."

Jack got out of bed and made his way to the window to take a look. He'd been wanting to talk to Pat, and he was glad to see her. He was anxious to let her know what had happened out at Black Canyon. He made his way downstairs.

"Jack! Thank God, you're up and moving!" Pat said when she drew up in front of the house and Jack came out on the porch. She quickly dismounted and went up to him. She noticed how pale he looked and how slowly he was moving. "I only got word about what happened to you late yesterday. One of the hands had ridden into town and heard you'd been shot and Randi had been kidnapped. What happened? This is terrible! What's going on?"

"Come on in. I'm glad you're here. There's a lot I have to tell you."

Jack led the way inside. She was surprised when he went into his study and closed the door behind them. She'd thought they would just sit in the parlor. Now she knew that what he wanted to discuss was serious.

"What is it?" Pat sat down in the chair in front of his desk and watched as Jack painfully lowered himself into his desk chair. "Who did this to you?"

As she listened, Jack related the whole story. He told her of finding the hidden passage in Black Canyon that the rustlers were using. He explained how they'd ridden out there to take a look around, and how they'd planned to come and see her that day, but then they'd been ambushed.

Pat was shocked by the news of the hidden passage and outraged to learn the rustlers had been using her property. She was even more furious to learn about the ambush.

"Do you have any idea who was behind it?"

"I spoke with the sheriff, and the general feeling is that it was Fred Carter."

"He tried to kill you, and he kidnapped Randi just because you fired him?"

"Well, yes, but there may be more to it than that." Jack paused and looked down at his desktop.

"What about Randi?" Pat was desperate to know more. "You said Hawk rode after her. Have you heard anything back from him at all?"

"No, nothing. I sent the boys out to try to track them, but their trail got washed out."

"I'm sorry, Jack. I'm so sorry." She could just imagine how worried he was about his daughter. "At least you know Hawk's still tracking her."

"And Hawk will find her," Jack said, repeating his belief to reassure himself. After drawing a deep breath, Jack looked up at Pat. "I have to ask you something, Pat. It's personal, but I've got to know."

"What is it?"

"Have you been seeing a lot of Wade?"

"You know, he did help me out there for a while with some work around the ranch, and we spent time together during the Stampede. I like Wade."

"But have you seen him since the weekend in town?"

Pat frowned, wondering why Jack was questioning her this way. "No. The last time I saw him was the night of the dance. Why?"

Her simple, straightforward answer stabbed at

Jack. His worst fears were confirmed. Rob had told him that when Wade had sneaked off the night before the ambush, he'd said he was going to see Pat. Pat had just proved Wade was a liar. True, Wade had been on the ranch at the time of the shooting the next morning, but if he hadn't gone to see Pat the night before, who had he gone to see? Fred in town? Or someone else?

Jack still wondered how Wade had known about their trip to the canyon. He thought back to the afternoon when Randi and Hawk had told him about their discovery of the secret passageway in Black Canyon. Had Wade somehow overheard their conversation? He frowned. They'd been here in the study.

"Jack? What are you thinking?" Pat asked, seeing his dark expression and fearing what he was about to reveal to her.

Jack lifted his gaze to hers. "I hate to tell you this, Pat, but I think Wade may be involved in this. He may be working with the rustlers."

"How can you say that? Wade's a good man!" she protested, shocked by his accusation. She cared for Wade.

"That's what we've all believed, all along. Randi said that same thing about him not too long ago, but the night before the ambush Wade told Rob he was sneaking off to see you."

"He said what?"

"He said he was riding over to your place to see you. Did he visit you that night?"

Pat went pale at Jack's revelation.

"No," she finally answered him in a tortured voice as she met his gaze. "No, he didn't. As I said, I haven't seen Wade since we were in town."

"Why would he lie to Rob?"

They fell silent as each considered the terrible truth they'd just discovered.

"I can't prove anything yet," Jack went on seriously, "but I'm keeping an eye on Wade. I'll know what I have to do when Hawk gets back here with Randi."

Pat heard him say "when," and she prayed he was right—that Hawk would rescue Randi and bring her safely home.

"What can I do to help you?" she offered.

"Don't tell anybody what we just talked about, and if you do see Wade, don't let him know I've found out he lied to Rob."

"I plan on riding straight back to the ranch when we're done here, so I won't see him at all."

"Good." He was glad she wasn't so attached to Wade that she would try to find him and tell him what she'd learned. "There is one other thing."

"What?"

"Pray that Hawk finds Randi and brings her back home safe."

"I will," she promised. "You told me Hawk was the best tracker around. He'll find her."

Chapter Twenty-five

Hawk kept their pace smooth and steady as they rode for the Lazy S. He'd been worried that Randi wasn't as strong as she'd claimed to be, so he didn't want to make the trip too arduous. He was glad she was able to keep up without any difficulty.

As sundown neared on their first day of riding, they made camp near a watering hole. They ate their meal, and Hawk got ready to settle in for the night. Randi, however, had been eyeing the watering hole with interest, for she had other ideas.

"Come on," she said, standing up and giving him an inviting grin as she held out her hand to him.

He gave her a curious look. "What are you up to?"

"You'll see," Randi countered.

Hawk didn't hesitate. He got up and took her hand. He walked with her down to the water's edge.

"Want to go for a swim?" she asked him.

The water wasn't very deep, but just the

thought of being in the cool water with Randi aroused Hawk. He didn't bother to answer. He simply reached out and began to unbutton her shirt. She helped him with the buttons, and then they both quickly worked at shedding the rest of their clothing.

Randi finished undressing first. She gave a delighted laugh as she raced ahead of Hawk into the water. He didn't mind one bit that she'd undressed more quickly. He just sat back and watched her go.

"You are one beautiful woman," Hawk told her.

"Thank you." She turned to face him as she sank down up to her shoulders in the water. "What's taking you so long?"

"I was just enjoying the view."

He finished ridding himself of his clothes and followed her in. No more words were necessary as they came together. Wrapped in each other's arms, they delighted in the beauty of their love. They clung to each other as the tidal wave of their passion swept over them, making them one.

"We didn't get much swimming done," Randi murmured when at last she relaxed against Hawk. She caressed his water-slicked broad shoulders and his chest. "I didn't know a man could be beautiful, but you are."

Hawk kissed her as he let his own hands drift erotically over her sleek, silken curves. When at long last they moved out of the spring, they used one of the blankets to dry off.

"We've only got one dry blanket left," Randi remarked.

"I know." Hawk smiled, enjoying the thought of spending the night sharing one blanket with her.

She returned his smile. "I like the way you think."

It was late as Jack sat alone in his study. He had a decanter of whiskey and his half-full glass on the desk before him. His mood was as dark as the night outside, and it was growing darker with every passing minute. The days and nights had seemed endless since Randi had been taken from him. Jack could no longer fight off or ignore the dire feeling of loss that hung over him.

Tipping his glass, he took a deep drink of the potent liquor. Randi had to come back home to him; she had to. He had lost her mother—he couldn't lose her, too.

Jack thought of Hawk and of the way Sheriff Spiller had sung his praises. If anyone was capable of finding her, it was Hawk.

He told himself he needed patience and faith to get through this hard time, but right then he had neither.

Jack told himself he would bide his time for a while longer, but he could not—and would not— wait forever. He would give Hawk another week to ten days to return with Randi. If he hadn't heard from him or Hawk hadn't returned by then, he was going to ride out on his own with any of his men who wanted to go with him. And he would not return to the ranch until he had his daughter.

Set on a course of action, Jack drained the last of the liquor in his glass and slammed it back down on his desktop. He got up and staggered from the room. He made it upstairs to his bed and collapsed there, giving himself over to his drunken stupor. At least this night he would get some rest.

Randi and Hawk were up at dawn and riding out a short time later. They were eager to cover as many miles as they could that day, and they did. Traveling at a ground-eating pace, they rode ever closer to the Lazy S.

Each night they spent together on the trail was a testimony to their love. They spent the long, dark hours making love and enjoying the peace and serenity of being together.

As they made camp on their last night out, Hawk knew they had reached the point when they had to deal with the reality of what their lives would become the next day. Soon, very soon, Randi would be home. She would be back on her ranch with her father.

Hawk loved Randi, and he believed she felt the same way about him. She had given him her greatest treasure: she had given him the gift of her innocence. Now he would offer her the gift of his unending devotion. He wanted to marry her. He wanted to make her his wife and to spend the rest of his days showing her how much she meant to him. If she would have him, he would do just that. Hawk only hoped his heritage wouldn't stand between them. He had to find out what their future was, and he had to find out that very night.

Randi's mood was volatile as she sat before the campfire with Hawk. The thought that the very next day she would be back home and reunited with her father left her jubilant. Her joy was tempered, though, for fear that returning home meant an end to all that she and Hawk had shared.

Randi's heart ached at the thought that Hawk would take her home to her father and then ride away and never look back. She loved him. He was the man she'd waited her whole life for. She never wanted to be parted from him. She wasn't sure what it would take, but she was determined to let him know how she felt. She had given herself over to him in body and soul. She wanted to be with him always and forever.

Randi glanced over at Hawk as he sat before the fire with her. He had hardly spoken a word as they'd eaten the meal. He seemed troubled, and she almost felt as if he were deliberately distancing himself from her.

"Hawk?" she said softly.

He looked up and met her gaze across the low-burning campfire. Still, he did not speak.

"What's wrong?"

"Nothing." He smiled gently at her. "Nothing is

wrong. In fact, everything is right. In just a few more hours you'll be safely home with your father."

"Thanks to you," Randi told him, all the love she had for him shining in the depths of her eyes.

"I love you, Randi. You've shown me how to live—and love—again. Until I met you I didn't know that was possible. And now that I've found you, I don't ever want to let you go."

Heartfelt emotion filled her at his words, and tears burned in her eyes.

"You'd better not let me go, Hawk Morgan. You'd better marry me—the sooner, the better."

Hawk hadn't been sure what to expect, and he was delighted with her open answer.

"I'd been hoping to do just that," he told her with a wry grin, moving to take her in his arms. "But Randi . . ." He hesitated before kissing her. "Are you sure?"

Randi looked up at him, seeing the man who'd put his own life on the line to save her from a fate worse than death. He was the man whose very nearness left her breathless with desire. "Oh, yes, Hawk," she whispered. "I'm sure."

Ever so sweetly she kissed him, telling him in that devoted exchange the truth of all she felt for him. She loved him with all her heart and soul. She would be his forever.

When the kiss ended, they sat close together in silence, cherishing their love and dreaming of the future that stretched endlessly before them.

"I can't wait to see my father tomorrow and to

tell him our news." Randi sighed after a quiet moment. She refused even to consider the possibility that her father might not be there at the Lazy S in good health, waiting for their return.

"I hope he won't have any objections."

"He won't. How could he?" She gazed up at Hawk. "He knows what a fine man you are."

Hawk hoped she was right, but some of his past experiences still left him a bit unsure.

"Just remember, when we ride in tomorrow we'll have to be careful. We don't know exactly what's been going on with Wade while we've been away, so stay close beside me and watch out."

"What do you think could have happened with him?"

"I wish I knew. I was surprised we didn't run into a search party on our ride back in. I expected your father to have every ranch hand from the Lazy S out scouring the countryside for you. The fact that we didn't see anyone troubles me."

"Me, too."

"We'll have to be careful. There's no telling what Wade might try once he sees us." Hawk's expression turned fierce as he thought of facing the foreman down.

Randi saw the strength in Hawk and knew he truly was her warrior. She knew he would do whatever was necessary to protect her.

"Hawk?"

He looked her way questioningly.

"How does a warrior get married in the Comanche village?"

"He goes to the girl's father and usually offers him several horses in exchange for the daughter."

"There's no ceremony or anything?"

"No. Once the father agrees to take the horses, the girl goes with the man to his tepee."

"That's all there is to it?"

"That's as much as I remember. Why?"

"I was just curious. I thought maybe if there was only a vow taken between the man and his wife, we could be married tonight."

Hawk took her in his arms and kissed her deeply. "The only horse I have to offer your father is Phantom. Do you think he'd be happy with him?"

"You'd be willing to give up Phantom for me?"

"Of course. For you, no bride-price would be too great," he said, just before he kissed her again.

"I love you, Hawk."

And then she showed him how much.

Chapter Twenty-six

"Jack!"

It was late, almost dark, when Jack heard one of the hands shouting to him from down by the stable. He hurried out on the porch as quickly as he could to see several of the men crowding around what looked like Hawk's horse, Bruiser.

For a moment Jack's hopes soared.

For a moment he believed Hawk had returned. Jack was sure Randi would be with him.

He started running toward them.

And then he got a look at Bruiser and realized the gelding had returned alone, without his saddle or bridle.

Jack stopped in his tracks, crushed by disappointment. He watched as Rob slipped a halter on the gelding and led the animal to him. Bruiser's gait was uneven, and he favored one leg.

"What happened to him?" Jack asked worriedly.

"It looks like he damaged his hoof when he threw a shoe. Hawk must have removed his tack and the other shoes before he turned him loose, so Bruiser could make his way back here to the ranch."

Jack's expression turned stony. He looked out across the land. Hawk was out there somewhere trying to track down Randi on foot. Jack hadn't thought things could get any worse than they were, but they just had.

Jack knew then that he had only one chance left to try to find Randi. He was just angry that it was so late in the day. It was too dark to do anything until the next morning.

"I'm riding out tomorrow morning, so have my horse saddled up and ready to go," he ordered sharply.

"But, boss, you're in no condition—" Rob began.

Jack cut him off in a commanding tone that brooked no argument. "I said, I'm riding out. The only hope I've got left to find Randi is to follow Bruiser's trail. If I can find out where Hawk freed Bruiser, I may be able to find Hawk's trail."

Rob knew it was a very slim chance, but at least it was a chance.

"I'll go with you," he declared. "And I'll get some of the other boys to ride with us, too."

Jack looked at Rob, appreciating his loyalty. "Tell them I don't know how long we'll be gone."

"It doesn't matter. You won't be riding alone," he assured him.

Jack turned and went back up to the house to tell Wilda to start gathering all the supplies they were going to need for the trek.

This last disappointment with Bruiser had made up his mind. He was going to find Randi and bring her home—or he was going to die trying. He couldn't live this way any longer.

Randi's spirits were high as she rode beside Hawk on the last leg of their journey home. She hadn't slept much all night and had been up long before dawn, eager to be reunited with her father.

"I can't believe we're finally here," she said excitedly. "There were times when I was with Fred when I didn't think I'd ever see the Lazy S again." Randi looked over at Hawk as he rode by her side. "Thank you."

"I'm just glad I found you."

"I'm glad you did, too."

They shared a look of understanding.

Then, as ready as she would ever be for what was to come, Randi drew her gun from her waistband.

"Be careful," Hawk warned.

"You, too."

They urged their horses on to an even faster pace as they rode for the ranch house.

Rob returned from the main house to join Wade and several of the other hands out by the corral, where they were getting their horses saddled up so they would be ready to head out.

"We'll be leaving soon. Jack shouldn't be too much longer," Rob told everyone.

"Any problems?" Wade asked. Since the night before, when he had learned of Bruiser's return, his emotions had been mixed. Obviously Hawk had run into some kind of trouble and was now on foot. Wade liked that idea. It definitely gave Fred the advantage in getting away with Randi. Even so, Wade was still uneasy.

"No, but Jack's not as strong as he thinks he is, and he won't listen to anybody."

The men understood. They all knew how stubborn their boss was.

Rob had just finished saddling his own mount when he glanced up and saw two riders in the distance.

"Someone's coming," he called out. He turned to watch their approach, and in that instant he recognized them. "Good Lord! It's Hawk and Randi!"

Rob ran for the house to let Jack know while the rest of the men left their horses where they were and hurried to welcome them as they rode in.

Wade saw them coming, too, but he chose to hang back. He silently swore to himself. It was Hawk and Randi, all right, and they were back—without Fred.

Where was Fred?

Wade realized Hawk couldn't have gotten to Randi without facing Fred down. Had there been a shoot-out? Had Fred had been killed? And if Fred was dead, what had he revealed to Hawk and Randi before he died?

Wade wasn't a man generally given to panic, but he was feeling jittery now. He forced himself to stay calm as he tried to figure out what to do next. He didn't know whether he should make a run for it right away, or stay around and see what happened.

He looked up toward the house as he heard Jack come running outside, yelling.

"Randi's coming? Randi's here?"

Jack rushed down the steps of the porch with Rob following him. His heart leaped as he spotted his beloved daughter riding in with Hawk. The first time he'd seen Randi with Hawk with his shirt off, he'd been furious. Not this time. He was thrilled to see them both.

Word spread fast. Wilda and all the other hands who'd been working nearby came at a run to witness Randi's return.

"There's your father," Hawk told Randi when he saw Jack come out of the house.

"Thank God," Randi breathed. Her relief was immense now that she knew her father was home and appeared to be in good health.

She was filled with joy.

And then she saw Wade.

Her joy turned to rage in an instant. She was flooded with fury at the sight of him standing apart from the other men, watching them.

Randi gave no thought to her own safety. She gave no thought to anything but getting even with the man who'd betrayed them.

In spite of Hawk's earlier warning to be careful,

Randi decided to take action. She put her heels to Angel's sides and urged the mare to a headlong gallop. Randi charged forward, never letting Wade out of her sight.

"Randi!" Hawk knew instantly what she was up to, and he gave chase.

Phantom had yet to be outrun by any horse, but as close as they were to the crowd hurrying forward to greet them, he couldn't allow the stallion the freedom of full rein. Still, he stayed close behind Randi and Angel. He had no idea what Wade might try when Randi confronted him.

Excitement and joy filled Jack as he watched Randi racing toward them.

"Randi! Randi!" he shouted. He was eager to hug her. He was anxious to have her in his arms so he could really be sure this wasn't a dream.

Rob and the other men cheered as she closed in, but when she kept on riding right on past them at top speed, they became confused.

Wade wasn't confused, though. He'd been biding his time, trying to decide what action to take. When he saw the way Randi galloped right past her father and the ranch hands, Wade knew he was in trouble. He turned and started to run toward the stable.

Randi saw what he was doing and grew even more furious. She charged on until she'd closed the distance between them. She maneuvered Angel in front of Wade and cut off his escape route.

Then she reined Angel in and held her gun straight on him.

"You going somewhere, Wade?" Randi demanded hotly.

Wade tried to run past her. He hoped to reach the stable so he could get his horse, but Randi was too fast for him. She urged Angel forward, blocking his path just as Hawk rode up beside her.

"It's over, Wade," Hawk dictated. He had his gun drawn, too.

"Like hell it is!" Wade swore. In a violent move, he made a grab for Randi. He wanted to pull her off Angel and use her as a shield.

But Randi was having none of it. She was ready for him. She swung out with her gun and hit Wade savagely on the temple. Wade didn't have to worry about pulling her down. Randi launched herself at him and attacked him with all her might.

Hawk understood Randi's fury, but he still knew she was no match for Wade. Hawk was there in an instant, grabbing Randi around the waist and hauling her off of Wade.

"Hold still, Randi!"

"No!" She kept struggling to be free.

Wade started to go for his gun, but Jack had come up with Rob and the other men.

"Don't even think about it, Wade," Jack ordered, his own gun aimed right at his foreman.

Wade froze as he realized there would be no escape.

Jack went on: "I know what you've been doing."

"Know what? There's nothing to know!" Wade protested.

"Liar!" Randi all but spat out the word at him as Hawk finally turned her loose.

"That's right—if there's nothing to know, why are you running?" Jack said tightly.

"I know you paid Fred to shoot Hawk and Pa! Fred told me all about it!" Randi told him.

"You're crazy!" he countered.

"We know you paid Fred to shoot us. We know you're behind all the trouble," Hawk explained.

"That's not true!" Wade asserted. "It wasn't me!"

"Oh, yeah?" Jack sneered.

"Who are you going to believe? The breed? Or me?" Wade argued angrily.

"Who do you think?" Jack pinned him with a deadly glare. "You've got every reason to lie. You're trying to save your sorry ass, but it's too late. You've been lying to me for a long time, Wade. We know everything. Why, Hawk even saw you with Pete in town."

"You what?" Wade looked quickly at Hawk.

"That's right," Hawk said with confidence. "I saw the two of you talking late one night out back behind the saloon."

"That doesn't prove anything!" Wade argued.

"Oh, yeah? Then why did you lie about going to visit Pat that night?" Jack demanded, cornering him.

Wade went pale at his words. "Pete's the one responsible! Pete's behind it all!"

"You can tell the sheriff that when he gets here, Wade," Jack said grimly. He glanced around at Rob. "Rob! Get some rope and tie him up. Then take him over and lock him in the tack room. One of you boys ride to town for the sheriff! I think he's going to be interested in hearing what Wade has to say."

Rob took charge of Wade, while Jack turned to Randi.

At last—she was home. The moment of rejoicing and peace he'd been praying for had come. Once Wade had been hauled off, Jack opened his arms to his daughter. Randi handed her gun to Hawk and went straight into her father's loving embrace.

"I love you, little girl," Jack told her in a gruff, emotional voice. His joy overwhelmed him, and he began to weep. "It's been hell around here without you."

"I love you, too, Pa. If it hadn't been for Hawk . . ." Randi was crying, too, as she looked over at Hawk and offered him a trembling smile.

Jack held her close for a moment; then, regaining some of his composure, he turned to Hawk and held out his hand. "How can I ever thank you?"

"I'm just glad she's home safe," Hawk answered, shaking his hand.

"Let's go inside." Then Jack turned to Rob and directed, "Keep a guard on Wade until the sheriff gets here."

"I'll do that, boss," Rob answered. "I'll watch him myself."

"Good." Jack fixed Wade with one last censoring glare. "I trusted you, and I believed in you, but not anymore. You're a fool, Wade—a damned fool."

With that, Jack turned his back on the man who had been his foreman and his friend, and walked off with Randi.

Hawk followed them.

As they approached the house, Wilda and the other hands crowded around to welcome Randi back. It took a while, but they finally made their way indoors.

Once they'd gone inside and into the study, Jack couldn't help himself. He hugged Randi again.

"Now tell me everything," Jack told Hawk. "When Bruiser showed up here last night, I didn't know what to think. We were just about to ride out and start searching for you again by following Bruiser's trail when you rode in. Rob, Wade, and some of the hands tried to track you right after the ambush, but a storm washed out your trail."

"That's why we didn't run into anyone on the way back," Randi said.

"Yes. The storm was a bad one, according to Rob. So ever since they got back, I've just been sitting here with nothing to do but wait and hope Hawk could find you and bring you back."

"And he did," she finished for him.

"Yes, he did." Jack was smiling. "Now, speaking of Bruiser . . . If you had to turn him loose and go on after Randi on foot, where did you find that stallion? He's a beauty."

Randi didn't wait for Hawk to answer. She told her father, "He's the phantom stallion. Hawk caught him."

Jack looked at Hawk in surprise. "You caught the phantom?"

"I'd been on foot for a while when I found him."

"You found him and you rode him," Jack said in astonishment.

"Without Phantom, I would never have gotten to Randi in time."

Jack had already thought Hawk a good man, and now his respect for him grew even more. "I have to agree with the legend, Hawk. You've proven yourself to be the finest warrior."

"He is. I know," Randi agreed, all the love she felt for Hawk shining in her eyes. "Pa, there is something else."

"What?"

"Something that happened while we were away . . ."

"What?" She sounded so serious that Jack was suddenly on edge. He had no idea what she was talking about.

Randi gave Hawk a slight smile as she faced her father. "Hawk and I fell in love, Pa. We want to get married."

Chapter Twenty-seven

Jack was completely taken aback by Randi's revelation. There had been a time not too long before when he would have opposed such a union. But not now. Now he knew exactly what kind of man Hawk was, and he admired and respected him.

"That's wonderful!" Jack told them.

Randi had been holding her breath in anticipation of her father's response. She'd prayed for the best, but was prepared to deal with the worst. At his words she gave a smile of relief.

"You approve?" she asked in delight, just needing to hear him say it again.

"You couldn't have picked a better man, Randi."

Randi looked over at Hawk, and she was positively glowing. Hawk was gazing back at her with the same intensity.

Jack stifled a grin as he looked at his future son-in-law. He began seriously, "Hawk, there is one thing."

Hawk faced him, ready to do whatever was necessary to make Randi his wife. "What?"

"I know by riding the phantom stallion you proved you were the finest warrior, but are you sure you're up to being married to my daughter?" By the time he finished, he was chuckling.

Hawk was smiling, too, as he answered, "There will never be a dull moment; that's for sure."

"Oh, you two!" Randi laughed at them both and got up to kiss her father on the cheek. "I don't know how I'm going to handle both of you."

"Somehow I think you'll find a way," Jack told her. "You always do."

"Pa, you said Bruiser is here?" Randi asked.

Hawk wondered why she had suddenly changed the subject. Then he saw the impish twinkle in her eye and knew she was up to something.

"Yes, he's out in the stable. Why?"

"Well, Hawk told me that in the village where he grew up the groom has to give the bride's father a gift as a bride-price, and usually that gift is a horse."

Jack knew where she was going now, and he told her, "I've got news for you, little girl. With all the trouble you get into, I should probably be the one giving Hawk a horse for wanting to marry you."

"Oh, Pa."

Again they all laughed together.

Jack sighed deeply when they stopped laughing. "Thank God you're here."

"I know," she agreed.

"Are you all right?" Hawk noticed that Jack suddenly looked pale and exhausted.

"It's been a long morning already," he admitted.

"How's your wound?"

"It still hurts, and as much as I hate to admit it, I'm still weak, too."

"And you were planning to ride out and look for me?" Randi was shocked.

"I'd waited as long as I could. When Bruiser came back . . . well, I knew I had to do something. I couldn't just sit here anymore. I had to go and try to find you." Jack met her gaze. "You're the most important thing in the world to me, Randi."

She went to hug him again.

"I'm going to go up to my room to get cleaned up a bit," she finally told them. "How much time do you think we have until the sheriff shows up?"

"I hope he gets here by noon," Jack answered. "We have to go after Pete today. The faster we act, the better chance we have of catching him off guard."

"All right. I'll be ready to ride whenever you are."

"Wait a minute, young lady," Jack said sharply. "You're not riding there with us. I want you to stay right here, where I know you'll be safe."

"Pa, after what I've been through, there is no way I'm staying behind. I'm going to be right there with you and Hawk when the sheriff takes Pete in."

"But I want you safe," he repeated.

"There's no safer place in the world for me than with you and Hawk."

Jack was exasperated, but he knew that arguing with Randi when she was in this kind of mood was pointless. "Go get cleaned up."

"I'll be back," she said as she left them alone.

"Do you know what you're getting yourself into?" Jack asked Hawk, smiling wryly.

"Yes, and I'm looking forward to it."

The two men looked at each other with respect.

"Good," Jack said, pleased to hear it.

Hawk left him then, so Jack could rest until the sheriff arrived. Going out to the bunkhouse, he washed up and changed his clothes, then went to the stable to keep Rob company while they waited for the lawman to arrive.

Sheriff Johnson had been in his office when the ranch hand from the Lazy S had shown up to tell him what had happened. He called together a group of men to make the trip out to the ranch with him. From the sound of things, he was going to need a posse to go after Pete Turner right away.

Hawk and Rob saw the lawman and his posse coming. They were waiting for them when they drew up in front of the house. Jack and Randi quickly came outside to speak with them. They told the lawman all that had happened.

"I'm glad you're back safe, Randi," Sheriff Johnson said.

"Thanks, Sheriff."

"I'll need to talk to Wade myself," Sheriff Johnson insisted.

"We've got him locked up out in the stable," Hawk told him.

Hawk, Randi, and Jack went with the sheriff to confront Wade. They unlocked the tack room door and remained standing in the open doorway as Sheriff Johnson went in.

"I hear you're in deep trouble, Wade," the sheriff began. "You might as well tell me everything now. It'll go easier on you in the long run."

Wade looked at the lawman skeptically. He knew how the law treated rustlers in these parts, but he figured it was worth a try. He had nothing to lose; that was for sure. "Pete Walker came to me a while back and offered me real good money to help him with some rustling."

"And you said yes?" Sheriff Johnson was amazed by his stupidity.

"It was a lot of money, and it was easy enough to pull off. The way he set it up, I was never really involved in the actual rustling. I was just his middleman. The same way with the shootings—I just delivered Pete's money to Fred Carter, but I didn't have anything to do with the ambush. Fred's the one who did it all. Fred's the one who shot Jack and Hawk."

Jack was filled with anger as he listened to Wade.

"God help you," Jack muttered.

"God's got nothing to do with this," Wade responded defensively.

"You're right about that," Jack countered.

"Why is Pete so determined to cause trouble for the Lazy S?" Sheriff Johnson asked.

"Pete hates Jack. He always has. He figured he could never beat him any other way, so he decided to rustle some of his stock and try to run him out of business."

"And run Pat Walker out of business, too," Jack added in disgust.

"So?" Wade was indifferent.

"I thought you cared about Pat," Jack said.

"Hell, no. The widow never meant anything to me. I was just using her, is all."

"I've heard enough," Jack snarled. He turned and walked away, not stopping until he was out of earshot.

"Me, too," Sheriff Johnson agreed.

The lawman directed several of his deputies to escort Wade back into town and to lock him up in the jail.

"You ready to ride with me to the Turner ranch?" Sheriff Johnson asked Jack and Hawk.

"We're ready," Hawk, Randi, and Jack all answered.

Hawk didn't want Randi to ride along with them either, but he knew there was no way they would be able to convince her to stay behind. Everything that had happened had been so upsetting for her that she wanted to be there to see justice done. She wanted to watch Pete Turner be arrested and taken off to jail, just as Wade had been.

Most of the hands from the Lazy S decided to

accompany them to the Turner ranch. Only a few stayed behind to keep an eye on the ranch.

The plan was made for the best way to corner Pete as they covered the long miles to his ranch. Their hope was to catch Pete at the main house. If they were lucky enough to find him there, they could surround the place and force him out.

When they drew close to the house, but were still out of sight, Sheriff Johnson sent several of his men to take up positions around the building. He wanted every angle covered just in case Pete or any of his men tried to sneak away. That done, those who were riding in girded themselves for what was to come.

"Randi, I want you to ride between me and Hawk. I don't want you anywhere out in the open where you might get hurt," Jack said as the house finally came into sight.

"Yes, Pa. Let's just hope we don't have to worry about that. Let's hope Sheriff Johnson can take care of this and make his arrest without any trouble."

There were close to twenty in the posse as they thundered up the road toward the house. They were all armed. As much as they would have liked for things to go smoothly, Sheriff Johnson and Jack both understood the kind of man Pete Turner was and the very real danger they might be facing this day.

"Pete! It looks like we got some trouble coming!" Stan Lawson, the foreman, called to him.

Pete had been working in the corral out back behind the stable, and he came around front to see what Stan was talking about.

"Ain't that Sheriff Johnson?" Stan asked.

"It sure as hell looks like him," Pete answered, immediately concerned. "Go warn everyone. Tell them to get their guns and keep watch."

Stan hurried off to do as he'd been ordered.

Pete knew the sheriff and his men were too close for him to try to avoid facing them. He stood by the stable entrance with his hand resting on his sidearm as he waited for the confrontation to come.

Stan returned quickly. He'd gotten his own gun and came to stand behind Pete with some of the other hands from the ranch to back him up.

Pete swore under his breath when he saw that Jack, Hawk, and Randi were with the lawman. It only proved to him that Wade had failed miserably. Things couldn't have turned out any worse.

"Afternoon, Jack. What brings you out this way, Sheriff?" Pete asked, trying to sound cordial as he walked forward to speak with them.

"I need to talk to you, Pete," Sheriff Johnson told him in a tone that was deadly serious.

"What's wrong, Sheriff? Is there some kind of trouble?" He pretended innocence.

"Yes, Pete. There's trouble. You know damn well there's trouble," Sheriff Johnson stated with certainty. He recognized the rancher's stalling tactic and slowly drew his gun to emphasize the point he was about to make. "You're under arrest, Pete."

"For what?"

"Rustling."

"What are you talking about?" Pete cast his men a sidelong glance that warned them to be ready.

"Look, Pete, you can talk real nice all you want, but the truth is, I know everything. I know what's been going on out here, and I've come to put a stop to it."

"I don't know what you mean."

"We've already arrested Wade. He told us everything. We're taking you in. You can make this easy for yourself or—"

"You ain't taking me in!" Pete shouted, erupting in fury.

Filled with anger, he drew his gun and started firing as he ran for the cover of the stable. His men joined in, firing wildly as they, too, fled for safety.

The posse was ready. The instant gunfire erupted, they attacked.

"Stay here!" Hawk ordered Randi as he and Jack followed the posse's lead, pursuing the rustlers.

Pete hated Jack. Jack always won. Jack always came out ahead in everything he tried! He despised him! Pete knew that if he were going to hang, he wanted Jack dead along with him. He spun around and took aim at the hated rancher.

As Pete paused to get a shot off at Jack, the sheriff's aim proved true. Pete fell to the ground. Several of his main gunmen were shot, too. The rest of the men made it to the stable and continued to fight, but it didn't take them long to realize there would be no getting away. They were trapped, outnumbered, and running out of ammunition.

Sheriff Johnson had feared the situation might end up in a siege, but the battle ended relatively quickly.

"We're coming out!" one of Pete's men finally yelled.

"Throw your guns out first!" Sheriff Johnson ordered.

They watched anxiously as several guns were tossed out the stable door.

"Now come out with your hands up!" the lawman dictated.

Pete's men did as they were told. The deputies made short work of restraining them and getting them ready for the trip back to town and to the jail.

The fighting over, Hawk rode back to where Randi waited a short distance away.

"It's over?" she asked nervously. She had her own gun in hand, just in case.

"It looks that way."

"Let's ride up and see if Pa needs us."

They rode forward to join her father.

Jack and Sheriff Johnson had dismounted and were going to check on Pete, who lay unmoving on the ground.

Hawk and Randi drew near and were about to dismount when they saw something. There, leaning out of the stable's loft area, was Stan, and he was ready to take a shot at Jack.

Randi and Hawk acted instantly. They both fired their guns at the same time.

Stan screamed as he was hit. He fell from the loft. He was dead when he hit the ground.

Hawk and Randi dismounted and rushed forward to make sure Jack was all right.

"Oh, Pa! When we saw him up there, I didn't know what to think!"

"I sure am glad I taught you how to use a gun, darling," Jack told Randi; then he looked at Hawk. "That was some fine shooting. Thank you."

Randi's relief was overwhelming as she stood with the two men she loved.

"Jack," the sheriff said from where he knelt beside Pete, and turned him over. "It looks like Pete won't be causing any more trouble. His rustling days are over."

Jack nodded slowly. "Thanks, Sheriff."

Jack looked at Hawk and Randi. "Let's go home."

Randi nodded and slipped her arm through her father's as they walked back to where they'd left their horses.

Hawk watched them walk on ahead of him for a moment.

Randi looked back at him, wondering why he hadn't come with them. "Let's go home, Hawk."

Hawk gazed at the woman he loved and knew she was right—he was going home.

Chapter Twenty-eight

Four Weeks Later

Everyone gathered for the wedding reception in the church hall watched happily as Hawk and Randi made their way to the center of the room. The wedding had gone perfectly, and now it was time for their first dance as a married couple. Randi was lovely in her gown, and Hawk handsome in his dark suit. They looked perfect together as he took her in his arms.

"I remember the last time you gave me a dancing lesson," Hawk murmured to Randi.

"And I remember what a fast learner you were," she said, smiling.

The music began, swirling around them as they began to move about the dance floor.

Hawk gazed down at Randi, thinking how beautiful she was and how lucky he was to have her. The days since their return had been filled with excitement, planning the wedding and building the small home that would be theirs a short distance from the main ranch house. Hawk and Rob and the other men had worked long hours to make sure it was finished before the wedding.

"What are you thinking about?" Randi asked. "You look like you might be up to something."

"I was thinking how much I'm looking forward to the rest of the evening," he told her with a devilish grin.

Randi couldn't help herself; she blushed. "I like the way you think."

They both laughed as they continued to dance. In the time since they'd returned to the ranch, they'd had very little time alone together. Her father had seen to that, making sure they'd been chaperoned every minute. Tonight would be different, though. Now, they were man and wife, and they would begin what would be the rest of their lives together.

At the side of the dance floor, Andy and Sherri stood together watching them dance.

"I'm glad everything turned out so well for them," Andy said.

"So am I. If it hadn't been for Hawk saving Randi from that terrible man . . ." Sherri shuddered as she thought about everything her friend had been through. "But she's going to live happily ever after now."

"Yes, she is." Andy paused, gathered his nerve, and then asked, "And what about us?"

"What about us?" Sherri looked up at him, a bit confused.

Since the first time they'd met, Andy had been attracted to her, and the more time he spent with her the more he'd come to realize how special Sherri was. During the time when Randi had been missing, they'd grown closer, and now he knew what he wanted to do.

"Well, do you think we could live happily ever after, too?" he asked.

Sherri blinked in surprise and then broke into a beaming smile as she answered, "Are you proposing to me, Andy?"

"Yes, I am," he stated with certainty now that the hard part was over.

"Then I suppose I'd better give you an answer."

Andy waited anxiously.

"Yes," she told him.

He wanted to kiss her right then and there, but instead took her hand and drew her outside.

"You're sure about this?"

"I've never been more sure of anything in my life."

Andy took her in his arms and kissed her.

"Why wouldn't I want to marry you?" Sherri said teasingly when they broke apart. "You're handsome, and I love you, and being married to you, I'll always have all the candy I want. I don't think marriage gets any better than that. We'd better go tell my parents." She took his hand to lead him back indoors.

"In a minute," he said, drawing her into his arms again for one last delightful kiss.

Jack stood with Wilda watching Hawk and Randi dance.

"I never thought I'd say this, but Randi's got herself a good man," Wilda told him. She had come to admire and respect Hawk.

"Yes, she has," he agreed.

Pat walked up then, and Wilda moved away to chat with other friends.

"She looks so beautiful and so happy," Pat observed.

"That she does," he agreed. He couldn't have been more content this evening. Only weeks before he would never have believed things could have turned out so well. "Things can only get better around here now that the rustling's been stopped."

"I'm hoping I can hold things together at my place till roundup."

"I'm here if you need anything, Pat. You know that."

"Thanks, Jack. You've always been a good friend."

"It's just a shame we both trusted Wade the way we did. I always thought I was a good judge of character, and I believed Wade was a good man at heart for all those years. He sure proved me wrong," Jack admitted.

"Me, too," Pat remarked, feeling saddened at being so used. She'd actually believed Wade had cared for her. She was angry with herself for being so naive.

"The good news is the trial is coming up soon, and Sheriff Johnson believes he'll be locked up for a long time. Once that's over with, we can get back to normal around here." Jack knew that was going to feel real good after all they'd been through.

Randi and Hawk's dance ended, and the musicians began another tune.

"Pat, would you like to dance?" Jack invited, wanting to lighten their spirits. It was time to put thoughts of Wade and his betrayal behind them and enjoy the celebration.

"I'd love to, Jack," she answered.

He guided her out onto the dance floor.

It was much later when Hawk and Randi were finally able to slip away from the reception. They made their way to the hotel and hurried up the staircase to their room. Hawk unlocked the door and then swung Randi up into his arms and carried her inside. With utmost care, he set her on her feet.

Randi didn't move away from him, though. She linked her arms around his neck and pulled him down to her for a passionate kiss.

Her kiss was all the enticement Hawk needed. He worked at the buttons on the back of her gown as she unbuttoned his shirt. The fever of their need grew as they undressed and fell together upon the welcoming softness of the bed.

They came together in a glorious celebration of

their love. With each kiss and caress, their desire grew. Hawk whispered the truth of his devotion to her as he moved over her to make her his own. Randi welcomed him to her, loving him, needing him, wanting him forever.

Rapture swept over them and left them breathless in love's aftermath. They held each other close, thrilling at the joy of being husband and wife.

"I think I'd better give your father both Phantom and Bruiser," Hawk murmured contentedly. "You're worth it."

Randi rolled over him to look down at him. She was smiling. "I love you, Hawk."

"And I love you," he said.

And then he showed her just how much.

AUTHOR'S NOTE

Crown Candy Kitchen is real! I participated in a fundraiser for Annie's Hope, a charity sponsored by KMOX Radio personality John Carney. We auctioned off "Be a Character in a Bobbi Smith Novel," and Andy Karandzieff, one of the owners of Crown's, won the auction. He wanted me to write his fiancée, Sherri Sadowski, into the story. So, I not only wrote Sherri into *Halfbreed Warrior*, I put Andy in the story, too, along with the famous Crown Candy Kitchen, his family's wonderful candy store. It's in Old North St. Louis, where I used to hang out as a teenager. Check out their Web site at www.CrownCandyKitchen.com!